Stylistic Approaches to Nigerian Fiction

Stylistic Approaches to Nigerian Fiction

Daria Tunca

First published 2014 by
PALGRAVE MACMILLAN

Palgrave Macmillan in the UK is an imprint of Macmillan Publishers Limited, registered in England, company number 785998, of Houndmills, Basingstoke, Hampshire RG21 6XS.

Palgrave Macmillan in the US is a division of St Martin's Press LLC, 175 Fifth Avenue, New York, NY 10010.

Palgrave Macmillan is the global academic imprint of the above companies and has companies and representatives throughout the world.

Palgrave® and Macmillan® are registered trademarks in the United States, the United Kingdom, Europe and other countries.

ISBN 978–1–137–26440–4

This book is printed on paper suitable for recycling and made from fully managed and sustained forest sources. Logging, pulping and manufacturing processes are expected to conform to the environmental regulations of the country of origin.

A catalogue record for this book is available from the British Library.

A catalog record for this book is available from the Library of Congress.

Typeset by MPS Limited, Chennai, India.

For my mother

Contents

Acknowledgements

First and foremost, I would like to express my sincere gratitude to Bénédicte Ledent for her invaluable guidance and support, for commenting on countless drafts and, above all, for never giving up on me. Her generosity and scientific rigour have been sources of both admiration and inspiration throughout the years.

I have been fortunate enough during my research to be able to rely on the kindness of scholars and informants who shared with me knowledge that books alone cannot provide. I am particularly grateful to Dagmar Deuber, Izuu Nwankwo, Frances Pritchett, Obiora Udegbunam and Chika Unigwe. Moreover, I wish to extend my appreciation to Archibald Michiels, for offering insightful comments on early versions of Chapters 2 and 4.

Special thanks go to Chimamanda Ngozi Adichie, who kindly allowed me to reproduce copyright material from audio and video interviews, as well as some information shared in a conversation that we had in Brussels, Belgium, in March 2006.

For financial assistance, I thank the University of Liège in Belgium, the Belgian scientific research fund F.R.S.-FNRS, and the Communauté française de Belgique. I am also indebted to the Centre of African Studies at the University of Cambridge, for welcoming me as a visiting scholar while I was working on this project between February and August 2010.

As academic research is not only about access to sources but also about learning from experienced intellectuals, I would like to pay tribute to the late Hena Maes-Jelinek, the pioneering critic who introduced postcolonial literary studies at the University of Liège in the 1960s; and to Chantal Zabus, whose book, *The African Palimpsest*, provided renewed intellectual stimulation during my research. I am indebted to both of these scholars for important words and gestures of encouragement.

For bibliographical references, pointers, coffees and chats, I am grateful to my colleagues, past and present, at the University of Liège – especially Rebecca Ashworth, Yasmine Badir, Lot Brems, Martine

Delavignette, Marie Herbillon, Houda Joubail, Céline Letawe and Delphine Munos.

For their patience and moral support, I thank my family: Marie-Hélène Huys, Önhan Tunca and Natacha Tunca. I am also grateful to my friends: Delphine Etienne and Caroline Larock, who promised to buy this book long before it even existed, and, finally, to Sarah Hansoul – in loving memory, always.

Introduction

Poems, novels, short stories, even the very sentence you are reading would not have come into existence without the medium of language. Words describe, inspire, reveal. But words also conceal – they becloud, daze, manipulate. Words create. They shape literature and, conversely, language finds in literary writing one of its most fascinating sites of innovation. Reading literature, one might say, means witnessing a kind of linguistic alchemy at work – no wonder, then, that the Nigerian poet and novelist Ben Okri calls writing 'an act of magic' (2012a: 105). Or that his compatriot Chimamanda Ngozi Adichie speaks of the 'magic' of realist fiction (2012: 4). And yet: as we all know, every magician has a trick. To discover it, onlookers must not simply allow themselves to be dazzled, but rather observe and analyse – meticulously, systematically, and with appropriate technique. This is the aim of stylistics.

In more scientific terms, stylistics is 'an approach to the analysis of (literary) texts using *linguistic* description' (Short, 1996: 1, italics in original). Formulating this in a slightly broader way, one might say that '[s]tylistics is a method of textual interpretation in which primacy of place is assigned to *language*' (Simpson, 2004: 2, italics in original). But what, exactly, does it mean to study 'language' in Nigerian fiction, as I intend to do in this book? This question finds no single, straightforward answer, for the word 'language' itself has at least three different – yet related – meanings. In its uncountable form, the term has the general sense of 'system of communication' – think, for instance, of a child's 'acquisition of language'. In its countable version, the word can refer to the 'tongue' of 'mother tongue' (taken here to be synonymous with the 'code' of 'codeswitching'). The term also has a third meaning of immediate relevance to this study, namely that of 'style' – one can speak, for example, of 'the elaborate language of a novel'.

The three meanings of 'language' are not always easy to distinguish, since they tend to be spread along a continuum rather than fall into neatly separate categories. Indeed, language in its uncountable form finds expression in codes, while codes make up styles. The distinction between code and style is even more difficult to uphold in the domain of African – and more largely postcolonial – studies, in which the insertion of items from different codes into literary works is often considered a feature of their styles. Symptomatically, while a book such as Ismael S. Talib's *The Language of Postcolonial Literatures* announces that it will be examining the 'use [of English] in contemporary world literatures' (2002: i), that is, the *style(s)* of postcolonial literatures, it cannot but include a chapter subtitled, 'English, dialects and other languages' (p. 137), which deals, among other things, with the alternation between different *codes* in works of fiction. The matter is further complicated by the fact that many postcolonial literatures, including those of the Anglophone African tradition, feature a large number of phrases and sentences that use 'English vocabulary but indigenous structures and rhythms' – a phenomenon that Chantal Zabus, following Loreto Todd, has called 'relexification' (Todd, 1982: 303, n22, cited in Zabus, 2007: 112). These overlapping meanings of 'language' need not put a curb on stylistic enterprises in the domain of Nigerian fiction. Nonetheless, it is crucial to clearly delineate the methodological and ideological consequences that the unruly use of the polysemous term 'language' has had in studies of African literatures over the years. This question can only be clarified by starting with an evocation of the (in)famous debate on the 'language of African literature', a controversial issue that will be taken up in Chapter 1.

Another, no less contentious point concerns the discipline of stylistics itself, in its 'mainstream' (Western) incarnation. Even if stylistics has been a well-established academic area of research for several decades now, non-specialists seem particularly prone to question its methods and relevance. To many literary critics, the phrase 'linguistic description' used by Short in the definition quoted above more often than not evokes pointless grammatical dissection and equally meaningless statistical tables. Such a stereotype, it must be said, is as appropriate to describing the skilled practice of the discipline today as the ungenerous labelling of literary critics as academics who have a 'habit of using terms in a semi-technical, pseudo-descriptive fashion' (Simpson, 1993: 4). Rather than join this ruthless war of disciplinary clichés, I will call upon Chimamanda Ngozi Adichie as the somewhat unexpected arbiter of this joust: 'the problem with stereotypes is not that they are untrue, but that they are incomplete' (Adichie, 2009a). Hence, the second part of Chapter 1 will both address the 'not-entirely-untrue' reasons behind the clichés that have become attached to stylistics, and attempt to complete the picture by outlining the discipline's potential benefits.

As the rationale behind the organization of Chapters 2–6 is largely methodological, details of their content are best left until the end of Chapter 1, when all readers will have acquired the necessary knowledge to appraise the relevance of the book's general structure. What may already be briefly discussed at this stage, however, is the motivation behind my selection of texts by Chimamanda Ngozi Adichie, Chris Abani, Ben Okri and Uzodinma Iweala – writers whom I would call 'post-Achebean', an admittedly unusual category that invites a few words of explanation.

I simply use the adjective 'post-Achebean' as a shorthand to refer to post-first-generation Nigerian authors, including those of the diaspora. It is far more common for scholars in the field of Nigerian literature to separate 'second-' and 'third-generation' writers. The former category usually includes figures such as Ben Okri and Ken Saro-Wiwa, who were 'born into the colonial event but [whose] formative years were mostly shaped by independence and its aftermath of disillusionment and stasis' (Adesanmi and Dunton, 2005: 14). The latter group generally comprises authors like Chimamanda Ngozi Adichie and Uzodinma Iweala, 'born mostly after 1960' (Adesanmi and Dunton, 2005: 14). My wish is not to challenge the usefulness of such divisions but, as cognitive linguists (especially Lakoff, 1987) have amply shown, all categories are partial reflections of reality – both in the sense of 'subjective' and 'incomplete'. Consequently, if a grouping such as 'third generation' can be helpful in giving a unifying shape to the movement of twenty-first-century Nigerian writing, it must also be recognized as an artificial construct. For instance, Chris Abani is routinely considered a member of the 'third generation' and, on the basis of his thematic boldness and formal inventiveness, he is even regarded by many as the quintessential embodiment of this group of writers' innovative qualities. But Abani himself, who was born in the 1960s and published his first novel only four years after Ben Okri did, does not claim any strict generational allegiance, and even states that he is 'multigenerational because [he] published early enough to be part of Ben [Okri]'s generation but didn't really achieve success and notoriety until the arrival of the younger generation' (2006d: 24). The existence of such grey zones does not mean that the label 'third generation' lacks legitimacy, or that it should be discarded altogether, but simply that it is not the *only* possible entry into recent Nigerian fiction. I believe that there is something to be gained in considering Abani alongside Okri, without trying to determine at all costs who belongs to which generation and why. Ultimately, beyond all criteria of differentiation, second- and third-generation writers have at least one major thing in common: everyone, from Nigerian academics to American radio hosts, obsessively compares them to their illustrious compatriot, Chinua Achebe.

This is barely an exaggeration. In Elleke Boehmer's words, Achebe 'has become a dominant point of origin, a *hyper-precursor* ... in whose aftermath virtually every African author self-consciously writes' (2009: 142, italics in original). I would suggest that Boehmer's statement applies with equal force to critics of African literatures, many of whom have consistently measured up the work of the younger African – especially Nigerian – authors against Achebe's earlier achievements. Considering the decisive role played by the Igbo writer in the 'language debate' that I will discuss shortly, and the distinctive style of his literary works, his 'hyper-precursor' status in the context of a linguistically-oriented study needs no further justification.

Although Achebe's reputation overshadows that of even the most prestigious of his contemporaries, the influence of other writers' formal originality should not be underestimated either. Whether it be Wole Soyinka's creative use of Nigerian Pidgin, Gabriel Okara's experimental prose (which used his native Ijaw as a syntactic basis), or Amos Tutuola's Yoruba-tinted English, all have left more or less visible traces on the generations of writers to come. Other, less spectacular markers of linguistic creativity in the rich tradition of Nigerian writing have gone virtually unnoticed. This book mainly sets out to examine such features in the work of the younger generations.

Ultimately, my aim is to show how stylistics can enrich, supplement, even challenge, existing literary interpretations of Nigerian fiction. In this context, my intention is to use linguistic methods and terminology with the purpose of enlightening – not confusing – readers. As Obioma Nnaemeka once put it, 'theory should be used to elucidate, not to obfuscate and intimidate' (2003: 363). I will attempt to put these words into practice.

1
Towards an 'African Stylistics'?
Historiographical and Methodological Considerations

Whether at public readings or academic conferences, the mention of the words 'language' and 'African literature' in the same breath usually elicits one of three responses: a sigh of boredom, an irritated mumble or, if there is an eloquent person in the room, an exasperated question akin to the one formulated by the late Nigerian writer, Ken Saro-Wiwa: '[W]hy do we insist on having an "African literature" and debating what language it should be written in?' (1992: 155).

Saro-Wiwa had a point. Ever since the Nigerian scholar Obiajunwa Wali famously declared, in a 1963 article published in the journal *Transition*, that 'any true African literature must be written in African languages' (p. 14), overzealous critics have insistently asked African authors writing in English, French or Portuguese to justify their decision not to use their mother tongues instead. The question, with its veiled accusations of un-Africanness and neo-colonialism, has grated on many writers' nerves – and one would be tempted, if only on these grounds, to dismiss the matter of language altogether. Yet in the context of this study, it is impossible to do so for two reasons at least: first, the so-called 'language debate' sparked off by Wali has had far-reaching effects on the stylistic study of African literatures, as I argue below; and second, the Nigerian critic's incendiary piece, despite its prescriptive rhetoric, underscored at least one disturbing, undisputable fact: that African literatures written in European languages were, and continue to be, inaccessible to '[t]he ordinary local audience, with little or no education in the conventional European manner' (p. 14). The language issue is, in short, an intricate and unavoidable one, with valid arguments on both sides of the divide.

Predictably, Wali's indictment of Europhone African writing attracted more hostility than sympathy. Shortly after its publication, it elicited a string of responses from both creative writers and literary critics in *Transition* itself;[1] two years later, it was notoriously countered by Wali's compatriot Chinua Achebe, in his seminal essay, 'English and the African Writer'.[2] Achebe, defending a pragmatic position adopted by many Anglophone African writers since, maintained that English should not be rejected on the sole basis of its being 'part of a package deal which included many other items of doubtful value and the positive atrocity of racial arrogance and prejudice' (1965: 28). In an often quoted passage, Achebe further expressed the conviction that, even though his mother tongue was Igbo, 'a new English, still in full communion with its ancestral home but altered to suit its new African surroundings' (p. 30) would 'be able to carry the weight of [his] African experience' (p. 30).

Not everyone was won over by Achebe's arguments. Ngũgĩ wa Thiong'o, the Kenyan writer, is the most famous case in point. Recasting some of Wali's statements, but with a more distinctively Marxist twist, Ngũgĩ deplored 'the petty-bourgeoisie readership automatically assumed by the [Europhone African writer's] very choice of language' (1986: 22). More explicitly than Wali, the Kenyan novelist and playwright also claimed that, since '[l]anguage carrie[d] culture' (p. 16), the imposition of English on African children who had hitherto been raised in their mother tongues led to a sense of 'colonial alienation' (p. 17). Therefore, according to Ngũgĩ, English was a 'means of ... spiritual subjugation' in Africa (p. 9), and writing in this language inevitably reinforced the 'neo-colonial slavish and cringing spirit' (p. 26) that had succeeded independence. For all these reasons, Ngũgĩ announced that the book containing these forceful declarations, *Decolonising the Mind*, would be his 'farewell to English as a vehicle for any of [his] writings. From now on it is Gĩkũyũ and Kiswahili all the way' (p. xiv).

But neither Ngũgĩ's resolve nor his passionate arguments have stood the test of time. Several people pointed out the gaps in the Kenyan writer's reasoning: for example, African languages were no less prone to yielding unequal power relations than English, as the cases of 'minority' ethnic groups in Africa demonstrated (Saro-Wiwa, 1992); others remarked that the 'authentic' Africanness to which Ngũgĩ aspired simply did not exist (Adejunmobi, 1999). However, what eventually gave the 'Achebe side' of the language debate the upper hand was not so much ideology as feasibility: as the Nigerian writer himself had already remarked in the essay mentioned above, Africans of different ethnicities needed 'a manageable number of languages to talk in' (Achebe, 1965: 28). Even Ngũgĩ had to recognize the untenability of his uncompromising proposition for, while he kept his promise of writing novels in his native Gĩkũyũ, he could not but continue to publish essays and deliver lectures in English.

Clearly, since the 1960s, the language debate has caused a lot of ink to flow.[3] Contemporary discussions, while still occasionally heated, seem to have lost the virulence of the early years, as most writers and critics broadly agree with Achebe's initial suggestion that both Europhone and African-language literatures have a vital role to play in the continent's cultural development. Importantly, however, the controversy has had a lasting impact, not so much on African literatures themselves as on their study in academic contexts. Indeed, Wali's provocative assertion that Africans writing in the former colonial languages were 'merely pursuing a dead end, which c[ould] only lead to sterility, uncreativity, and frustration' (1963: 14), brought to the fore considerations about the linguistic specificities of African literatures in European languages. In the sphere of Anglophone literary criticism at least, this increased emphasis on form translated into a growing interest in linguistically-oriented studies of African works, as many commentators attempted to identify the stylistic qualities of novels, poems and plays written in the former colonial language. Most of these linguistic studies set out to examine the specifically 'African' elements present in such literary pieces, and thereby implicitly denied Wali's claim that Europhone African literatures (and their critics) mindlessly enforced standards dictated by the Western academy. Despite this upsurge in scholarship, however, African studies has not witnessed the advent of a distinctive 'school' of stylistics. In the Anglophone domain, the area covered by the present study, hardly any sustained efforts have been made to approach the stylistic make-up of African works in any systematic way. Why, one may wonder, is this so?

In my opinion, the reasons for this relative lack of development are chiefly epistemological. Put differently, the current shortcomings in the elusive field of 'African stylistics' originate in scholars' disagreement, or even indecisiveness, over the sources and methods of knowledge that should be used to carry out linguistic analyses of African literatures. These epistemological hurdles have presented themselves on at least two levels: that of the *origin* of the object of investigation, and that of the *discipline* of stylistics itself. While the difficulties faced on these two planes have been chronologically coterminous, they will be considered separately here – not only for the sake of clarity, but also because the obstacles have been encountered in two distinct lines of research into the language of African literatures: one focusing on the culturally-specific aspects of texts, and the other attempting a less context-dependent examination of literary pieces.

The former is undoubtedly the more developed of these two branches. Within this culturally-oriented body of research, a further distinction needs to be drawn between two types of analyses: on the one hand, some studies, undertaken by literary scholars, have rather successfully assessed the narrative significance of tropes such as proverbs or folktales, but without conducting in-depth linguistic examinations of the texts containing them (e.g. Griffiths, 1971; Obiechina, 1993). On the other hand, different kinds of investigations, more accomplished on the technical level, have focused on the influences of local African languages on the prose or verse of writers from the Sub-Saharan region of the continent. Because the thorough analysis of specific semantic and syntactic features requires the mastery of sophisticated linguistic tools, these enquiries have mostly been conducted by linguists (e.g. Igboanusi, 2001; Bamiro, 2006). No doubt as a consequence of their authors' area of expertise, these works have mostly privileged the minute linguistic description of selected passages from novels over their narrative interpretation, leaving some literary critics with the feeling that the formal analysis of African literatures did not provide a decisive contribution to the *aesthetic* understanding of these texts. More disturbingly perhaps, some of these linguistic examinations have tended to consider literary extracts as samples of African varieties of English, thereby bestowing on fictional excerpts an aura of authenticity that ignores the crucial input of writers' creativity. In some cases, representatives of this approach, which tends to conflate literature with reality, have only narrowly avoided succumbing to the linguistic equivalent of what Henry Louis Gates Jr has called the 'anthropology fallacy' (1984: 5), which consists in disregarding the aesthetic value of literary texts and considering them as sociological documentaries or anthropological treatises.

However, among the studies that have concentrated on the culturally-specific features of literary texts, at least one work has managed to perform precise linguistic analyses without ever losing sight of how a text's formal traits could bear relevance to its poetic strategies. The book in question, Chantal Zabus' *The African Palimpsest: Indigenization of Language in the West African Europhone Novel* (1991), was groundbreaking at the time of its first publication, and has remained highly relevant since, as suggested by the 2007 release of a second expanded edition. The study's long-lasting pertinence can be ascribed to its impressive scope – it tackles a range of linguistic characteristics of West African literatures in both French and English – but also to its methodological incisiveness. To give but one example, Zabus did not take at face value that the passages in Pidgin found in Anglophone Nigerian novels perfectly mirrored the language as it was spoken in reality, and she proceeded to analyse such extracts in detail. She convincingly claimed that most of the literary occurrences of the linguistic code only qualified as 'pseudo-pidgin', since many of these renderings displayed numerous influences of English not typically associated with 'real-life' Pidgin. Importantly, Zabus went beyond these strictly formal conclusions and, rather than dismiss the fabricated language for essentialist reasons, she attempted to account for its presence and examine its functions within Nigerian fiction.

Zabus covered so much methodological ground that few of those doing language-oriented research in African literatures in her wake have succeeded in improving on her findings. Admittedly, some scholars writing during the 1990s managed to gain insight into specific literary texts (see, for instance, some of the essays contained in Epstein and Kole's collection, *The Language of African Literature*, 1998). However, even as the literary value of cross-cultural Europhone African literatures had been convincingly established – and thereby the 'dead end' scenario predicted by Wali once and for all disproved – critics were, ironically enough, heading towards another cul-de-sac. Indeed, research into the culturally-specific features of African writing focused, almost by definition, on language as a cultural (or, in some cases, social) signifier in given contexts, completely disregarding in the process the linguistic traits that the literatures might have in common with traditions from other continents. As African literary texts began to be consistently considered in terms of their linguistic 'otherness', language-oriented enquiries ran the risk of losing their critical potency.

The scant attention given to the literatures' possibly universal qualities can partly be explained by the pervasive influence of the language debate. Nevertheless, one might suggest – perhaps a little provocatively – that it also finds its origin in another series of incidents that defined the critical climate in the last three or four decades of the twentieth century. While Wali had indicted both Europhone African writers 'and their western midwives' (1963: 14), others had denounced some Western critics' inclination to make sweeping statements about African literatures in the name of universality. There was undoubtedly some validity to this accusation, since certain European and American commentators claimed to uncover '"universal truths"' which, in Kadiatu Kanneh's felicitous words, 'act[ed] merely as euphemisms for *European* [or, more broadly, *Western*] truths' (1997: 81, italics in original). This tendency was forcefully condemned in the 1970s by the Ghanaian writer Ayi Kwei Armah, who even gave it a name, 'larsony' (1976), after the literary critic Charles Larson who, in his eyes, was guilty of peremptorily perpetuating cliché-ridden representations of Africa. The term coined by Armah was later used by Chinweizu, Jemie and Madubuike in their controversial *Toward the Decolonization of African Literature* (1983), in which they rebuked Larson's and others' wholesale universalism, and explicitly pleaded in favour of a system of aesthetic evaluation based on what they perceived as 'authentic' African paradigms.

Chinweizu *et al.*'s Afrocentrist views did not meet with unanimous approval. The 1975 article in which they first articulated their position was vehemently countered by Wole Soyinka (1975), who exposed the critics' limited knowledge of traditional and contemporary Africa, and debunked the misguided, or even inaccurate, readings that resulted from their simplistic, one-dimensional approach to African cultural practices. Chinweizu *et al.*'s stance also co-existed, more peacefully this time, with other positions in the area of Black and African studies, such as that of Henry Louis Gates Jr, who emphasized the 'complexity' of Europhone Black and African texts, a result of their 'double heritage' (1984: 4). In the field of traditional literary criticism, many scholars discreetly sided with Gates, in that they continued to analyse African literatures using a mixture of theories originally arising out of Western contexts (the works of post-structuralist thinkers come to mind) and more distinctly postcolonial approaches that had been developed to address the specificities of formerly colonized territories.

In the contention-prone domain of language-related studies of African literatures, on the other hand, many Europeans and Americans seemed intent on *not* becoming the next Charles Larson. Thus, while the warnings by Armah and Chinweizu *et al.* had the positive effect of urging Western academics to carry out contextualized stylistic research into African literatures, they might also have been among the factors that discouraged many postcolonial scholars from undertaking linguistic examinations based on Western theoretical models, whose application may have risked aligning African works with canonical European texts. As a result, the linguistic criticism of African literatures remained largely – though not entirely – impervious to methods of systemic-functional and cognitive inspiration privileged by 'mainstream' Western stylisticians over the same decades. A few scholars *did* nevertheless make brave attempts to apply Western stylistic models to African objects of inquiry.[4] It is interesting to note, though this may only be incidental, that most of these studies were conducted by African scholars – who, one may assume, ran a lower risk of being labelled paternalistic for applying 'white' models to works written by black authors.[5] Ultimately, most of these experimental ventures had a limited impact on the field of African studies, not only because of their modest circulation, but also because of some of their weaknesses – starting with a leaning towards descriptiveness, inherited from some brands of Western stylistics.

Today, descriptiveness is considered a major shortcoming in any type of stylistic analysis, but it was not always perceived as such in the Western world. As contemporary stylisticians point out, it was acceptable practice for early linguistic studies of literary texts to be primarily concerned with establishing the 'literariness' of a specific piece, without attempting to show the impact of the text's formal traits on its possible meaning. Despite the sea change witnessed in the 1970s, when formalism and structuralism were largely superseded by functionalism and cognitivism as dominant theoretical paradigms, the discipline has never quite lost its reputation as a pointless 'clause counting' exercise (Mills, 1995: 7). This negative image seems to have persisted even more strongly in African and postcolonial studies, where the interpretation of writers' social and political positions has traditionally taken precedence over formal considerations of any kind – unless linguistic specificities could actually be shown to reflect the social and political stances under scrutiny.

Understandably, then, when Emmanuel Ngara published his Marxist-oriented *Stylistic Criticism and the African Novel* in 1982, he attempted to distance himself from those who endlessly listed the linguistic features of literary works but did little else. To this effect, he introduced a distinction between the 'stylistician' and the 'stylistic critic':

> [T]he stylistician ... uses the principles of general linguistics to single out the distinctive features of a variety of [*sic*] the idiosyncracies of an author. He uses the principles of general linguistics to identity the features of language which are restricted to particular social contexts, and to account for the reasons why such features are used and when and where they are used ... The stylistic critic ... certainly must use the analytic tools of the linguist and stylistician ... But more than that he must relate his analysis of linguistic features to considerations of content value and aesthetic quality in art.
>
> (1982: 11–12)

The contrast proposed by Ngara is helpful (if somewhat prescriptive, as indicated by the author's repeated use of the modal 'must'), but it did not gain wide currency. Even so, this distinction embodied the scholar's desire to develop a rigorous critical framework for the linguistic study of African writing, a challenge to which he attempted to respond in the stimulating introduction to his study. Aware of the complex historical heritage of African literatures, Ngara advised that 'the African critic should search for African solutions in criticism, or should search for those solutions which, though not specifically African, will do justice to African works of art' (p. 6).[6] As is made clear in the book, Ngara was above all claiming his allegiance to Marxism when writing these lines, but he also argued in favour of using terminology developed in Western systemic-functional models, for example.

Unfortunately, once put into practice, Ngara's ideas fell short of fulfilling their promise. Although the author skilfully avoided the pitfall of descriptiveness, his study did not offer the expected methodological breakthrough. His analyses, while often insightful, rested on techniques more akin to close reading than modern stylistic analysis. Yet, the importance of Ngara's contribution to 'African stylistics' should not be underestimated. First of all, even though the language-related examinations that he proposed did not provide the technical basis for a literary-linguistic model, such close readings offered an invaluable prelude to potentially more thorough stylistic analyses. Second, the value of Ngara's attempt can only be fully appreciated when resituating his study in its historical context. One should remember that, at the time the author was publishing his book, some of the most influential works in stylistics and linguistics had only just been released – the first edition of Geoffrey Leech and Mick Short's *Style in Fiction* (1981), and George Lakoff and Mark Johnson's *Metaphors We Live By* (1980), had come out respectively one and two years prior to the publication of Ngara's study and, unsurprisingly, they do not feature in his bibliography. Other major works, such as Roger Fowler's *Linguistic Criticism* (first published in 1986), were still several years away.

Despite its shortcomings, then, *Stylistic Criticism and the African Novel* remains a landmark in the stylistics of African literatures. Not only did the author emphasize the centrality of linking the linguistic features of a literary work to its content – as indicated in the subtitle of the book, *A Study of the Language, Art and Content of African Fiction* – but he also insisted on the importance of creating a model that might help one examine African literatures from different formal angles, using critical perspectives that had emerged on the African continent and elsewhere. It may be regretted that Ngara's pioneering efforts were not emulated – in the words of Charles E. Nnolim, 'Ngara ... dangled an apple, but there were no takers' (2000: 14).

Nevertheless, one should not be too quick to judge those scholars who let that dangling apple hang: the fruit proffered in their direction was, in fact, riddled with worms. Indeed, if the field of African literary criticism had had to contend with its practitioners' disagreement over criteria of aesthetic evaluation, 'mainstream' stylistics – represented predominantly by Western scholars working on European and American texts – had long faced its own epistemological battles too. Here, the discordance among researchers did not concern the cultural origin of the analytical models to be applied, but the very relevance of the discipline's methodological foundations. This challenge to the scientific nature of stylistics was led by the American literary theorist Stanley Fish. In the wryly entitled piece 'What Is

Stylistics and Why Are They Saying Such Terrible Things about It?'
(first published in 1973), Fish condemned what he perceived as the
circularity and/or arbitrariness of stylistic methods, be they used
in computer-based corpus analyses, in experiments performed by
transformational-generative grammarians, or in examinations based
on systemic-functional theory. Fish provocatively asserted that,
despite the supposedly 'rigorous' and 'scientific' nature of their work
(1980: 70), stylisticians either manipulated their data until they
found an interpretation that 'fit[ted] [their] preconceptions' (p. 73),
or they 'interpose[d] a formidable apparatus between [their] descriptive and interpretative acts, thus obscuring the absence of any connection between them' (p. 73).

Although Fish's criticism was aimed at a stylistic movement still
largely in its formalist phase, the 'demolition job' he performed
(Leech, 2008: 9) retained its momentum through the decades, surviv-
ing several rejoinders and significantly affecting the reputation and
development of the discipline (Adamson, 2003, cited in Leech, 2008:
9). The influence of Fish's biting critique was still clearly perceptible
in Ray Mackay's effort to undermine stylistics based on what he identified as its practitioners' belief in the 'myth of objectivity' (1996:
82). Even though Mackay misrepresented these scholars' claims for
the benefit of his argument,[7] it is abundantly clear that he reacted,
much like Fish did before him, to some stylisticians' tendency to
pitch their chosen speciality against the 'subjectivity' of literary
studies – a discipline regularly dismissed in stylistic circles, and
sometimes derisively so, as arbitrary and impressionistic. The attentive reader will, of course, not have missed the irony here, which
is perhaps best captured in Shakespearean terms: 'hoist with [their]
own petard', as Hamlet once said.

The endless disputes over the scientific relevance of stylistics have
tended to obscure the fact that all academic disciplines – stylistics,
theoretical linguistics and literary criticism included – can be used in
support of interpretative aberrations when they fall into incompetent
hands. Arbitrariness, in other words, cuts across disciplines. And so
does subjectivity, some measure of which is inevitably found in any
critical endeavour, in the humanities and beyond. As Michael Toolan
has rightly stated, 'there are no absolute context-free models or theories. Interpretation and persuasion are always at work' (1990: 12). Thus,
regardless of what hard-line representatives of either stylistics or literary

criticism may claim, the difference between the two disciplines is not a matter of *quality*, but of *focus*. Stylistics is undoubtedly better equipped than non-linguistic literary criticism to explore the correlation between the formal features of a text and the aesthetic judgements that may be derived from its reading, but traditional literary studies tends to fare better in the critical evaluation of larger corpora. For example, tracing the evolution of a writer's approach to a particular theme over the course of his or her career is, more often than not, more successfully done without recourse to a sophisticated linguistic apparatus. Provided one is ready to accept such division of disciplinary labour, it is possible to regard stylistics and traditional literary criticism as complementary rather than competing interpretative approaches. This is the viewpoint adopted in the present volume.

Yet, any recourse to stylistic methodology in the context of African literatures, a domain traditionally dominated by more conventional hermeneutics, demands that the charge of circularity levelled against stylistics be at least briefly addressed. Unlike Fish, I do not believe that linguistic 'description performed at the direction of a preformulated literary hunch' (1980: 95) necessarily entails that one 'pre-decides [meaning] arbitrarily' (p. 95), and that one provides a circular non-demonstration of an unfounded personal response to a literary piece. Being 'guided by [a] hunch', as Fowler puts it (1996: 9), does not mean that one eventually establishes what one had in mind at the onset of the procedure. In this regard, Leo Spitzer's 'philological circle' provides an interesting conceptualization of the process of stylistic analysis. The notion is here explained by Leech and Short:

> Spitzer argued that the task of linguistic-literary explanation proceeded by the movement to and fro from linguistic details to the literary 'centre' of a work or a writer's art. There is a cyclic motion whereby linguistic observation stimulates or modifies literary insight, and whereby literary insight in its turn stimulates further linguistic observation. This motion is something like the cycle of theory formulation and theory testing which underlies scientific method.
>
> (2007: 12)

The movement described here, although cyclic, is very different from the circularity observed by Fish. One of the most important ideas put forward by Spitzer is that literary assessments and choices of linguistic features to examine evolve, in dialectical fashion, as the critic proceeds. Such recalibration – or, in some cases, drastic revision – is part and parcel of the analytical process but, for obvious reasons of clarity, it is usually not reproduced in the published research results. This is an important fact to keep in mind, for a piece of stylistic criticism should not be considered circular by virtue of its providing evidence in support of a hypothesis formulated in its opening paragraphs. To bring the point closer to home: when, for instance, I declare in Chapter 2 on *Purple Hibiscus* that I intend to show that the narrator's statements are ideologically biased, and I end up doing precisely that, it does not mean that I set out to analyse Adichie's novel with this particular idea in mind, and that I organized my entire study around this preconceived judgement. Quite the contrary, actually. In announcing my final objective, I deliberately leave unstated the unhelpful fact that my initial hypothesis – the 'hunch' described by Fowler – was as embarrassingly vague as 'page 102 looks slightly odd'. Instead, I opt to save readers some painstaking philological circling and provide them with what is hopefully a more constructive sense of structure and direction.

It is the general climate of suspicion surrounding stylistics in the post-Fish era that has made such – at first sight, largely unnecessary – clarifications indispensable. Nevertheless, not all of the discipline's woes can be laid at the door of Stanley Fish, for rejection has come from other corners too. Because stylistics is technically speaking an 'interdiscipline' (Leech, 2008: 1), it does not 'count as real linguistics' in the eyes of the vast majority of theoretical linguists, and it is deemed 'too analytical, ... too full of linguistic jargon' (Short, 1996: 1), and therefore superfluous, by many literary scholars. To make matters worse, a type of stylistic analysis that focuses on the examination of African literary texts – rather than on European or American texts, or on the theoretical advancement of the discipline – tends to be viewed with mild condescension even by some of the much maligned Western stylisticians. Hence, the literary critic interested in African fiction is entitled to wonder: is it worth bothering with stylistics at all?

The best way of tackling this vast question is perhaps to 'think small' first. Let us, for a few paragraphs, trade the broad strokes of the brush for the fine lines of the pencil, and try to establish whether the tools provided by stylistics can enhance the critical appreciation of a short passage of fictional prose. *The Street* (1999), the third novel by the Nigerian writer Biyi Bandele, seems a good place to start. The book opens with an epigraph by the American essayist Ralph Waldo Emerson ('We fly to beauty as an asylum from the terrors of finite nature') and displays structural divisions that, in the Nigerian literary context, unmistakably evoke the writings of Ben Okri. Judging by Bandele's previous work, this combination is more readily suggestive of mock-solemnity than seriousness, but one cannot be entirely sure at this stage. The novel proper then begins:

> On the morning of the day Nehushta finally phoned Dada, several months after Dada had temporarily disappeared into his own mind and re-emerged feeling like a landmine, or an oath of vengeance whose time may come, two things happened: Dada had a strange dream and his neighbour Haifa Kampana failed to achieve an orgasm.
>
> (1999: 5)

Readers, depending on their disposition, may find this passage funny or not, but few would dispute that this opening aims for some kind of humorous effect. My own reaction when first reading Bandele's incipit over ten years ago was a chuckle, accompanied by a slight sense of puzzlement, as I usually tend to respond poorly to 'jokes' involving any type of bodily function – Bandele's scatological humour in *The Sympathetic Undertaker and Other Dreams* (1991), for instance, had left me rather sceptical. Moreover, I thought, there is nothing inherently funny about 'fail[ing] to achieve an orgasm' – one could easily imagine a counterexample where such an incident would be used to indicate estrangement between sexual partners. So, why is this passage comical at all? Or, for those who do not find it particularly funny, why does the joke fall flat, according to them? In academic discussions, such questions need to find an answer, for, despite what some may think, it is simply not enough to praise or dismiss a novel, or a writer, on the sole basis of taste. At least *some* justification is needed.

The first step of appreciation does not require any specifically linguistic skills. Simply looking at the passage a little more closely reveals that the final clause, 'his neighbour Haifa Kampana failed to achieve an orgasm', seems hardly relevant, thematically speaking, to the rest of the sentence. Theories of humour predict that laughter can be induced by incongruity, and this indeed partly explains the impression left by the extract. However, a shortened version of the opening sentence, such as 'On the day Nehushta phoned Dada, Dada had a strange dream and his neighbour Haifa Kampana failed to achieve an orgasm' contains the same incongruity, but does not *quite* have the same effect. Enter stylistics to explain why.

The most salient feature of Bandele's opening sentence is probably its length. The sentence is not only long, but it is also difficult to process. This is due to the fact that the subject and verb of the main clause, 'two things happened', are preceded by a long list of anticipatory constituents, themselves containing several levels of syntactic embedding (for example, prepositional phrases within prepositional phrases), appositions, and coordinated clauses. This kind of sentence structure, in which the main part of the main clause is saved for the very end, is called 'periodic' (see Leech and Short, 2007: 181). This sentence type is stylistically interesting because (still following Leech and Short, 2007: 182) anticipatory constituents such as those used in overabundance here introduce an element of suspense. Since these constituents cannot be fully interpreted in isolation, readers have to make an effort to keep them in mind until reaching the main part of the sentence. In Bandele's case, the subject and verb, 'two things happened', do not even relieve the suspense, but further heighten it. Readers then eagerly move on to the explanation on the other side of the colon, expecting a climax and a resolution. Instead, they are told that 'Dada had a strange dream' (a rather vague statement still very much shrouded in mystery, keeping the suspense almost intact) and that 'his neighbour Haifa Kampana', a character who has not been previously introduced, 'failed to achieve an orgasm'. As this final clause appears to be entirely irrelevant to the rest, readers feel massively let down: they are not given the expected 'reward' after their cognitive effort. They are, in other words, forced to realize that they have been tricked by the writer, whose build-up of tension is revealed to have been a sham all along.

Another element adding to Bandele's humour is his use of register. His opening sentence at times edges towards formal or literary discourse (e.g. 'an oath of vengeance whose time may come'), and at other times towards colloquial spoken discourse (e.g. 'feeling like a landmine', 'two things happened'). The final clause, 'his neighbour Haifa Kampana failed to achieve an orgasm', leans towards the first type. More precisely, the high register borrowed in the verb phrase 'failed to achieve' smacks of officialese, the type of formal, sometimes overly pedantic language used in official or academic discourses. So, while the propositional content of the final clause – that is, its meaning, here the event represented – is private, domestic, and seemingly trivial, its form sends the opposite signal, a clash which increases the incongruity of the statement. Adding to the general sense of absurdity is the fact that the final clause contains the negative form 'fail to': the major revelation expected after the mention that 'two things happened' turns out to be a non-event. The pragmatic relevance of such a negation is not obvious at all: why is it important to let readers know that Haifa Kampana has *not* 'achieve[d] an orgasm'?[8] In short, readers are left with yet another question mark where a resolution would have been expected; they are, as a consequence, prompted to read on.

This rather detailed stylistic analysis of the opening sentence of *The Street* will, of course, not change the fact that I may find Bandele's passage amusing, while others may not share my enthusiasm. Some may well argue that the long periodic sentence would only have been truly funny if it had contained a more radically irrelevant final clause – for example, one without the syntactic cohesion contained in the phrase 'his neighbour'. Others may claim that the Nigerian writer's use of mock-suspense trivializes his character's sexual dysfunction, or the matter of sex altogether. Crucially, however, the discussion of Bandele's use of humour has shifted from the mention of unsubstantiated opinions to a critical appreciation based on the evaluation of the novelist's craft. At the very least, the analysis has established 'a systematic basis ... for agreement and disagreement' (Carter and Simpson, 1989: 5), which could be broadened if one were to undertake a more substantial study of Biyi Bandele's work.

In humour as in research, there is no accounting for taste: some readers may find this type of linguistic dissection overly painstaking, and therefore a little too tedious for their own liking. But they would be mistaken in underestimating the significance of stylistic micro-effects such as those observed above. As Leech and Short remind us, '[i]f a reader feels that such minutiae are unimportant, writers, at least, do not' (2007: 107). And indeed, most authors are known for repeatedly editing and rewriting their work, sometimes compulsively so – Chimamanda Ngozi Adichie has published most of her stories in two or three different versions; Chris Abani often adjusts the wording, line breaks and punctuation of his poems between their first appearance in literary journals and their final publication in his book-length collections; and Ben Okri has gone as far as rewriting an entire novel. This punctiliousness shows that these artists have at least one belief in common with stylisticians, namely that *form*, and not just subject matter, determines meaning and, ultimately, the way in which a work of art is received and interpreted. As Okri once put it, 'People think it is content which endures; but it is form which enables content to endure' (2011b: 125). The significance of an analytical method 'as much focused on *how* texts mean, as on *what* they mean' (Wales, 2006: 213, italics in original) is slowly starting to emerge.

By providing an 'interface between linguistic description and interpretation' (Leech, 2008: 3), stylistics also allows for a greater sense of systematicity than traditional literary criticism. Again, I do not mean to suggest that stylistics has an inherent superiority over non-linguistic methods – it is just as easy to get bogged down in the accumulation of linguistic details as it is to devise fanciful interpretations by half-ignoring the text on which these insights are supposed to be based. Rather, my point is that stylistics more readily favours what its practitioners call a 'tool-kit' approach, which encourages readers to pay systematic attention to specific aspects of texts; some critics even provide checklists of questions that might be asked at the onset of stylistic investigations (e.g. Short, 1996; Leech and Short, 2007: 60–6). The 'tool-kit' strategy of stylistics does not ensure analytical success (the scholar's judgement is just as vital as the theoretical guidelines, if not more), but it has at least three advantages over the less formalized approaches often favoured by traditional literary criticism. First, working with a checklist or a particular linguistic model encourages methodological awareness, and therefore reflexivity; second, the precision of the methods used may favour structure and clarity in pedagogical situations; and, finally, stylistic tools are more readily transferable from one text to another than most highly abstract literary theories.

These are some of the widely recognized potential benefits of stylistics, but the above should not give the mistaken impression that there is such a thing as a single, unified practice of the discipline. A recent reference work lists no fewer than 14 'key branches' in the field, such as cognitive stylistics, stylistic approaches to emotion, functionalist stylistics and reader response criticism (Nørgaard *et al.*, 2010: 7–48). Needless to say, the preparation of the present volume has involved a rather drastic selection among the many linguistic approaches available to stylisticians. Another choice that I have made has been that of situating my analyses on the side of '*literary* stylistics', which 'is concerned with using linguistic techniques to assist in the interpretation of texts', rather than of that of '*linguistic* stylistics', which 'is about doing stylistic analysis in order to test or refine a linguistic model ... – in effect, to contribute to linguistic theory' (Jeffries and McIntyre, 2010: 2, italics in original, see also Wales, 2011: 400–1). In short, this study is designed neither as a stylistics handbook nor as a work of theoretical linguistics, and my main concern always remains with the individual text under examination. My motivation for doing so is to show the scholar who specializes in African literatures that a language-based approach has a decisive contribution to make to the understanding and appreciation of African fiction. Stylistics does not end where I left my analysis of Biyi Bandele's sentence above – the metalanguage provided by the discipline is but the foundation of a methodology that becomes truly engaging only when it helps one gain a clearer view of the bigger picture, that is, when linguistic descriptions can be coupled with broader interpretative conclusions.

Keeping in mind the shortcomings of the disparate strands of 'African stylistics' catalogued above, I will attempt in this volume to outline methodological guidelines that implicitly acknowledge, but do not solely focus on, the social and cultural specificities of literary works from Africa, and I will aim to provide analyses that escape the descriptiveness that has tended to undermine stylistic examinations of African novels. My use of the hypernym 'Africa(n)' in this context evidences my belief that such a framework has the potential, if suitably adapted and expanded, to be fruitfully applied to the analysis of Anglophone fiction from all over the continent. The realization of such a long-term project, however, first requires a focused approach to a smaller selection of texts – here, seven works of 'post-Achebean' Nigerian fiction.

Chapter 2, on Chimamanda Ngozi Adichie's *Purple Hibiscus* (2003), lays the foundations of the book's stylistic enterprise. It starts with what is most likely to be familiar territory for the reader

of African literatures interested in language, namely the use of proverbs in novels. The aim behind the inclusion of this short examination is at least twofold. First, as the analysis finds theoretical
inspiration in work that specifically addresses language in African
fiction, this opening section underlines the richness of the existing
research into culturally-related linguistic aspects of the continent's
literatures. It is hoped that readers will allow this acknowledgement
of past critical accomplishments to stand metonymically for all the
valuable culturally-oriented approaches that have not found their
way into the final version of this book.[9] Second, since the origins of
proverb analysis in Nigerian fiction are largely literary and ethnolinguistic, this section does not rely on complex grammatical models,
a fact that may help to progressively ease the non-specialist into
the book's stylistically-based methodology. The chapter then moves
away from methods conventionally applied to African literatures,
and goes on to focus on the ways in which the teenage narrator's
use of language reflects the development of her ideological stance,
especially as it relates to the Catholic doctrine whose principles are
fiercely upheld by her overbearing father. To examine this aspect
of the novel, I rely on a series of well-known stylistic or narrative
models, including M. A. K. Halliday's famous theory of transitivity
(see Halliday and Matthiessen, 2014: 211-358). This requires the
introduction of some linguistic terminology, which will help me to
show how a systematic analysis of specific features in a literary text
can help to uncover its workings. In sum, the second part of this
chapter focuses on how a writer can produce the 'magic' that I spoke
of in my Introduction.

Chapter 3, on Adichie's *Half of a Yellow Sun* (2006b), pursues a
somewhat similar aim, but it more thoroughly explores the relationship between the aesthetic and the political in the author's widely-
acclaimed civil war novel. Two concepts lightly touched upon in
Chapter 2 on *Purple Hibiscus*, namely ideology and polyphony, are
here combined and used as the basis for a broader interpretative
framework. The claim underlying the analysis is that *Half of a Yellow
Sun*, while ostensibly told from the alternating perspectives of three
different characters, is in fact an orchestration of voices commanded
by the third-person narrator, who deftly puts across political and
social ideologies most likely aligned with the author's own. With
attention devoted to elements such as underlexicalization, schemas,

vocatives, exemplification and deictics (all of which will be explained in due course), this chapter perhaps offers the most explicit demonstration of how the 'tool-kit' approach mentioned above can be put into the service of a central argument.

Chapter 4 deals with Ben Okri's second novel, *The Landscapes Within* (1981), and the author's rewriting of this early *Künstlerroman* under the title *Dangerous Love* (1996). After a short survey of the main changes implemented by the writer between the two versions of the narrative, the analysis focuses on the linguistic expressions of metaphor in the books. Using conceptual metaphor theory, I examine the linguistic representation of the artistic process in the novels, and argue that metaphor is used more creatively and consistently in the revised version. My approach is a little less overtly anchored in traditional 'postcolonial' thinking than in the preceding chapters, a deliberate change in emphasis that mirrors the multiplicity of Okri's own cultural allegiances in the artistic domain. The point is certainly not to disregard the Nigerian specificities of *The Landscapes Within* and *Dangerous Love*, but rather to suggest that the novels offer reflections on the Nigerian situation through meta-artistic considerations that are not always culturally bound. This chapter on Okri's work also proposes a broadening of scope on the disciplinary level, by devoting its final section to the ways in which stylistic findings can be built upon to reassess the role played by certain characters or narrative incidents. Behind this temporary methodological shift lies the idea that, while one must learn to walk the tightrope between linguistics and literary criticism when attention is required to the stylistic features of a text, one might as well occasionally come down to assess one's progress from the ground. Such an emphasis on literary appreciation recurs to different extents throughout the study, but is developed in a more significant measure here.

Chapter 5, on Chris Abani's *Becoming Abigail* (2006b), zooms in again on micro-stylistic patterns by investigating what critics have repeatedly called the 'poetic' features of the novella. In the field of stylistics, the adjective 'poetic' is defined as a text's propensity to display 'deviation' from linguistic norms. Such unexpected irregularities may, for instance, be semantic or syntactic. Isolating some 'deviant' passages in the book, this chapter establishes that Abani's poetic technique contributes to the creation of the narrative's idiosyncratic conceptual framework, which challenges some of the most fundamental binary distinctions of Western thought, such as the opposition between absence and presence, death and life. In addition to providing insights into the liminal existence of the novella's protagonist, this subversion of traditional opposites, I will argue, suggests a close relationship between form and content that is also evidenced in what might be termed the book's 'incantatory' function.

The final chapter, on Uzodinma Iweala's *Beasts of No Nation* (2005a) and Chris Abani's *Song for Night* (2007a), may be considered a methodological synthesis of my experiment in 'African stylistics', in the sense that it confronts two novels with similar themes but with distinctive styles, each of which calls for its particular set of linguistic tools. Iweala's narrative is written in an invented idiom mostly inspired by Nigerian English (and, to a lesser extent, Nigerian Pidgin), but which does not display any regularity in its use of non-standard grammatical patterns. This gives rise to localized stylistic effects, which significantly impact upon the book's more general representational strategy. Abani's novella, on the other hand, does not experiment with language overtly, but exploits the linguistic medium in such a way as to give readers the mistaken impression that the dead hero of the narrative is alive. Using semantic and pragmatic concepts, I explain how the novella first creates this illusion, and how it then pokes fun at its readers' and its own narrator's cluelessness by introducing multiple instances of irony. As in the case of *Beasts of No Nation*, the linguistic strategy deployed in *Song for Night* gains particular relevance in light of the contemporary debates around the literary representation of the child soldier experience, making an examination of these two works' stylistic features a necessary addition to the rich scholarly material already available on the subject.

To literary critics, the stylistic exercise proposed in this study may appear a little arduous at first, involving as it does terminological stretching and a search for methodological balance, but the effort, I believe, is worth it. As Chris Abani once said, 'The art is never about what you write about. The art is about *how* you write about what you write about' (2005, my italics). What follows is an attempt to find out exactly what Abani meant.

2
Of Palm Oil and Wafers
Characterization in Chimamanda Ngozi Adichie's *Purple Hibiscus*

What's in a name? Or, perhaps more to the point here: what's in an Igbo name? I remember asking myself these questions as I was trying to understand why the narrator of Chimamanda Ngozi Adichie's *Purple Hibiscus* (2003), Kambili Achike, had an Igbo first name even though her staunchly Catholic, authoritarian, Anglophile father, Eugene, despised his native culture and his mother tongue. I quickly realized that finding an explanation would involve some 'cheating', for the solution was not to be found between the covers of the book. So, when curiosity got the better of me, I asked the author herself to put an end to my speculations. Adichie's informal answer, non-verbatim, went as follows: in the back story that she had imagined for her characters before they stepped into the pages of the novel, Kambili's mother had suffered several miscarriages and had thus insisted on giving her daughter an Igbo name that evocatively meant 'let me live'.

Intriguingly, this answer taught me more about my approach to literary criticism than it did about *Purple Hibiscus*. I became aware, almost instantly, that my initial curiosity had been symptomatic of an impulse shared by many readers: that of systematically transporting characters and fictional situations to the 'real' world to try and assess their degree of authenticity. This practice is not entirely irrelevant, for realist fiction can be expected to have a reasonable level of plausibility, but the strict insistence on such conformity tends to induce normative judgements about literary texts – a critical stance that is, more often than not, misguided. For instance, several reviewers and academics have dismissed the ending of *Purple Hibiscus* as improbable, and therefore flawed and unconvincing, on the basis that a subdued Igbo wife like Beatrice Achike, Kambili's mother, was not possibly capable of plotting to kill her husband. The conclusion to the book is indeed surprising, and it was no doubt intended by its author to be perceived as such, but it is certainly not artistically inconsistent. So, rather than expressing premature criticism, frustrated readers should perhaps first try and find out if apparent 'inconsistencies' are not due to their own skewed perceptions.[1] If no immediate explanation can be found, a further challenge consists in assessing whether puzzling elements 'work' for a text, that is, whether they have a convincing artistic function, regardless of what the author's original intention might have been.

These considerations bear relevance to my discussion of language in Nigerian fiction because critics interested in the linguistic features of African literatures seem especially prone to offering evaluative judgements based on rigid, normative principles. For example, in a largely laudatory appraisal of Adichie's use of Igbo features in *Purple Hibiscus*, Christopher Anyokwu declares that 'Adichie does not quite succeed in her characterization of Papa-Nnukwu', Eugene Achike's traditionalist father, and the scholar goes on to express his surprise at the author's stylistic choices:

> It is hard to believe that throughout the entire novel, Adichie hardly uses Igbo proverbs, apart from one or two instances ... it is a marvel that the author does not allow Papa-Nnukwu to utter a single proverb as an Igbo elder. A patriarchal figure who ordinarily should be *the* custodian of culture, Papa-Nnukwu remains to all intents and purposes an *effect* while his son, Eugene, towers in comparison as the *cause*.
>
> (2011: 88, italics in original)

Anyokwu's evaluation of Papa-Nnukwu as an 'effect' (of what?) would deserve clarification, but what interests me here is that the critic derives a qualitative judgement from a disappointed expectation about Adichie's use of language. The expectation itself does not strike me as unreasonable; the final verdict, on the other hand, leaves me more doubtful. What Anyokwu is advocating, even if indirectly, is that Adichie's writing should conform to what he had earlier called the 'Achebe model', a type of literature replete with 'folklore, proverbs, wise sayings, folksongs and other allied forms of language games' (p. 81). As Susan Arndt has rightly observed, the use of oral devices in African literatures did not originate with Achebe (1998: 20), but his success has meant that all those writing in his wake were invariably judged on their capacity to 'imitate' his style (p. 20). Anyokwu's remark indicates that this critical trend is still very much alive. In the past few years, endless parallels have been drawn between Achebe and Adichie, sometimes legitimately, but these comparisons should not eclipse the fact that the authors' works display at least as many differences as they do similarities. This is undoubtedly true in respect to the writers' use of language. In fact, Adichie's own evaluation in this regard is far more categorical than mine: contrasting her prose with Achebe's, she boldly declares, 'I don't think that our styles are similar in any way' ('Out of Nigeria', 2009).

Strictly speaking, Adichie's provocative comment is not entirely accurate, for both writers abundantly draw on their mother tongue in their fiction, either by inserting Igbo words and phrases into their texts, or by applying techniques of relexification whereby, as already mentioned in the Introduction to this book, English vocabulary is combined with indigenous structures and rhythms (see Zabus, 2007: 111–20). To take but one example, an expression such as 'I do not know if my head is correct', used by Kambili's mother in *Purple Hibiscus* when she wonders if she is entirely lucid (Adichie, 2003: 248), is a literal translation of an Igbo turn of phrase. Proverbs also fall into the category of relexified items, and Adichie's limited use of traditional sayings is worth noting indeed. However, scarcity need not mean deficiency: even if the Igbo believe that 'proverbs are the palm oil with which words are eaten', the same people also warn us that 'if one puts excess oil in the soup, it is not good-tasting'.

Adichie has demonstrated her ability to put proverbs to creative use in her short story 'Half of a Yellow Sun' (2002, not to be confused with the 2006 novel of the same name), but there is little doubt that she resorts to this rhetorical strategy far less often than Achebe does in his fiction, essays and interviews. This difference can easily be read as a sign of the younger writer's contemporaneity, considering that the urbanization of Africa and the committing of traditional lore to writing have led to a gradual decline in the transmission of proverbs (Zabus, 2007: 159–65). Added to the generational gap between Achebe and Adichie is the authors' difference in gender, which is relevant inasmuch as proverb use is largely considered a 'male art' in Igbo society (Oha, 1998: 94; Unigwe, 2004: 129). Transposing these arguments to the fictional sphere, the sparse use of traditional lore in *Purple Hibiscus* can be explained by factors as diverse as the temporal setting of the novel (the late twentieth century), the narrator's gender (female), her age (15), and her limited exposure to traditional Igbo culture.

Most of these facts do not apply to the character of Papa-Nnukwu, with whose proverbless speech Christopher Anyokwu takes issue. Nevertheless, as the critic himself remarks, Papa-Nnukwu tells his grandchildren a folktale in the novel. Such traditional stories, known as *ifo* in Igbo, have also been called 'narrative proverbs' because they perform the same 'organic and structural functions' (Obiechina, 1993: 124) as shorter sayings, which are called *ílú*. It is significant that the grandfather in *Purple Hibiscus* delivers the sole story of this kind in the entire book, and that he does so in the village-like atmosphere recreated when a power failure leaves Kambili, her brother Jaja and their three cousins unable to watch television. Moreover, the *ifo* is over three pages long (Adichie, 2003: 157–61), and it is one of the few passages in the novel where Kambili's narrative interventions are kept to a minimum. Even though the story is still filtered through the young heroine's gaze, her limited intrusions allow readers to become acquainted with one of the many facets of Igbo culture, without having to constantly distance themselves from the narrator's parroting of her father's intolerant Catholic views. As such, the tale is the novel's first extended reversal of epistemological perspective, a change of outlook which intimates that traditional Igbo culture possesses a repertoire of knowledge as valid as that of Christianity. The *ifo* also positions Papa-Nnukwu as a symbolic repository of the Igbo cultural heritage, which means that the folktale effectively performs the same function as that which might have been assigned to a string of shorter proverbs. This interpretation makes Adichie's portrayal of the old man appear less inconsistent than Anyokwu made it out to be. In my view, whether this coherent depiction is an entirely faithful reflection of what is most likely to occur in reality is irrelevant; as Austin Shelton reminds us, Achebe too opted for an 'unrealistic' strategy when choosing to use proverbs far *more* frequently than is customary in Igbo society (1969: 110).

Because such appreciations heavily rest on individual critics' opinions of what literature can or should be, it is unlikely that a consensus will ever be reached on the acceptability of poetic licence. A more constructive approach therefore consists in temporarily leaving issues of mimesis aside, and trying to determine if the formal features of a text, regardless of their supposed 'authenticity', lend themselves to literary interpretations of any kind. This principle will guide my analysis of *Purple Hibiscus*, which will start by evaluating whether an examination of some of the proverbs contained in the novel may contribute to shedding light on the book's characters and the relationships between them. Following this, the discussion will more specifically focus on the narrator, and particularly on the way in which her use of language reflects her evolving personality.

One of the leitmotifs in this investigation will be that the formal features of *Purple Hibiscus*, from culturally-related items to recurrent grammatical patterns, perform specific functions in the narrative. For instance, the folktale told by Papa-Nnukwu, already mentioned above, is certainly instrumental in relation to character development – not so much in terms of its content, but because it enables the recording of Kambili's response to the traditional practice of audience participation. The teenager's cousins, who are used to being told stories by Papa-Nnukwu, are well acquainted with this custom and punctuate the old man's tale with a response signifying attention and interest: '*Njemanze!*' Kambili, on the other hand, has never attended any of her grandfather's storytelling sessions and remains mute throughout. Listening to her cousins' banter at the end of the tale, she silently comments: 'I watched them [Papa Nnukwu, her cousins and Jaja] and wished that I had joined in chanting the *Njemanze!* response' (Adichie, 2003: 161, italics in original). Kambili's failure to participate in the ritual mirrors her inhibitions and introverted personality, but it no longer reflects the categorical rejection of 'heathen' traditions that characterized her at the chronological beginning of the novel. Her unspoken response to Papa-Nnukwu's story signals her tentative emancipation from her father's authoritarian grip. In short, the *ifo* acts as a catalyst for Kambili's personal development – according to one critic, this function of the folktale is even 'the moral of th[e] story, for Adichie's purposes' (Cooper, 2008: 124).

Like the folktale told by Papa-Nnukwu, the few *ílú* contained in *Purple Hibiscus* are tell-tale elements in many respects. Their significance is not to be measured exclusively in terms of their influence on the progression of the plot, but neither do they serve solely ornamental purposes. Rather, their importance lies in their double status as culture- and context-bound figures of speech or, as Donatus Ibe Nwoga has put it, in their function as 'philosophical statement[s]' and in their 'contextual relevance' (1975: 188). The attribution of certain proverbs to particular characters in specific circumstances gives readers further insight into the beliefs espoused by the imaginary individuals who utter the *ílú*. In this sense, proverbs act as strategic devices of characterization – a key aesthetic function identified decades ago by such critics as Austin Shelton (1969: 87) and Bernth Lindfors (1973: 77).

Performing an analysis of the proverbs featured in a work of fiction inevitably requires some familiarization with existing ethnographical research, but this type of stylistic exploration has the advantage of providing a relatively stable methodological foothold for those with minimal knowledge of linguistics. It is now widely accepted that the formal analyses of proverbs once conducted by structuralists failed to account for the context-bound effects of traditional sayings (Adeeko, 1998: 35–7). Therefore, an investigation centred on the use of proverbs in fiction – a study in which the context of the sayings' occurrence is necessarily central – can largely dispense with linguistic theory, and may instead take as a point of departure a series of simple questions: who utters the proverb under examination? To whom is it addressed? In what circumstances? What is the meaning usually assigned to the proverb by ethnolinguists or native informants? Is the expected meaning also the one conveyed in the text? If so – or if not – to what effect?

To illustrate that the systematic application of these guidelines can enhance the understanding of a literary text and its characters, I would now like to examine three proverbs that occur independently from each other in *Purple Hibiscus*: the addressers, as well as the circumstances in which the sayings appear, differ in all three situations. The first proverb, or more accurately proverb-like statement, is shouted by an elderly man as Eugene chases him from his compound, calling him a 'worshipper of idols': '*Ifukwa gi!* You are like a fly blindly following a corpse into the grave!' (Adichie,

2003: 70, italics in original). The introductory exclamatory sentence *"Ifukwa gi!'* means 'Look at you!' and is commonly used in Igbo to give a bite of emphasis to a rebuke or admonishment; it can, for example, be addressed to someone who has delusions of grandeur. The longer sentence in the old man's rejoinder is based on the saying 'the fly that has no one to advise it follows the corpse into the grave', a slightly different version of which can be found in Achebe's novel *Arrow of God*: 'The fly that has no one to advise him follows the corpse into the ground' (1974 [1964]: 226). Commenting on Achebe's novel, Emmanuel Ngara has remarked that this metaphor can be considered a criticism of the main character's stubbornness, since the protagonist's refusal to take other people's advice leads him to his own destruction (1982: 76). This explanation may also be applied to the modified version of the saying in *Purple Hibiscus*. By comparing Eugene to the fly in the proverb, the elderly man is warning him that his strong-headed refusal to compromise with, and be advised by, non-Christians will lead him on the road to ruin. The expression does not occur in its complete form but is formulated indirectly, as a reproach which presupposes the interlocutor's familiarity with the original version of the proverb. This shows that the old man not only expects the figure of speech to be known and understood by the Christianized Igbo of Eugene's age, but also that he has the ability to speak fluently in proverbs and is therefore most probably regarded with great reverence in traditional society. By insulting and driving the man away, Eugene fails to acknowledge this crucial social factor. Furthermore, he ignores another traditional Igbo convention in refusing to show the deference owed to the elders. This short incident epitomizes the self-righteousness with which Eugene looks down upon his ancestral culture; to the reader initiated into the customs of Igbo society, the linguistic features of the passage subtly add another layer of signification to the more visual qualities of the scene being described.

Unsurprisingly, Eugene never uses *ílú* himself, unlike his moderately Christian sister Ifeoma. She addresses one such saying to her sister-in-law Beatrice, referred to as 'Mama' by the narrator, when the two women are at Kambili's bedside at the hospital, after the girl has suffered a severe beating at the hands of her father: 'This cannot go on, *nwunye m* ... When a house is on fire, you run out before the roof collapses on your head' (Adichie, 2003: 213, italics in original). Already the vocative '*nwunye m*' is indicative of Ifeoma's attitude towards traditional Igbo culture. This kinship term, which means 'my wife', covers a wider semantic area than its British English equivalent, and draws on the idea that an Igbo wife is married not only to her husband, but to his entire family (Adichie, 2003: 73; Bamiro, 2006: 320). Ifeoma appropriates this form, considered by some an item of patriarchal discourse since it views the wife as the 'property' of her in-laws (Bamiro, 2006: 320), to battle another form of patriarchy: the authority of the father embodied in the head of the Achike household. Indeed, while Eugene himself dismisses the term of address as 'the remnants of ungodly traditions' (Adichie, 2003: 73), Kambili's mother welcomes this metaphorical baptism, and tells her daughter that the phrase is to be viewed as a sign of Ifeoma's acceptance of her (p. 73). Beatrice never objects to the vocative of which her husband disapproves – it is thus through an absence of protest, in passive, small but significant ways, that she defies Eugene's authority.

Ifeoma, for her part, actively proclaims her Igbo identity by exploiting traditional lore. Making a basic philosophical interpretation of the proverb cited above is not a demanding task: the metaphor is an exhortation to act before a dramatic situation becomes irrevocable. In the novel, Ifeoma urges Beatrice to protect her children and herself from Eugene's repeated acts of violence, in the hope of preventing a fatal outcome. Since Ifeoma's admonishment raises the highly sensitive issue of domestic violence, her use of an indirect statement to warn her interlocutor may be regarded as a politeness strategy (Nwoye, 1991). As it turns out, Beatrice applies her sister-in-law's proverbial advice in a most drastic way. After Eugene's death, she admits that she 'started putting the poison in his tea before [she] came to Nsukka' (Adichie, 2003: 290), a journey chronologically situated shortly after this episode at the hospital (p. 247).

In addition to the role that Ifeoma's intervention may have played in Beatrice's decision to murder her husband, the status of this cautionary advice as a proverb also invites a few comments. Considering that, as mentioned above, the use of *ílú* is mostly viewed as a 'male art' in Igbo society, it may not be coincidental that Adichie has assigned the only full proverb spoken by a female character in the novel to Ifeoma, whom the author has identified as 'the embodiment of [her] African feminism' (Adichie, 2004a). Kambili's aunt displays man-like authority on many occasions, and unashamedly asserts her status as a single mother:

> '*Umunna* [the extended family] will always say hurtful things,' Mama said. 'Did our own *umunna* not tell Eugene to take another wife because a man of his stature cannot have just two children? If people like you had not been on my side then …'
>
> [Ifeoma:] 'Stop it, stop being grateful. If Eugene had done that, he would have been the loser, not you.'
>
> 'So you say. A woman with children and no husband, what is that?'
>
> 'Me.'
>
> (Adichie, 2003: 75, italics in original)

Beatrice's question summons up the stereotypical image of the unmarried mother as a marginalized member of West African society. The ideological implication behind her remark is that women are subordinated to their husbands and the latter's extended family, and that it is in their best interest to remain so. In retrospect, this statement gets tinged with irony, since Beatrice eventually acquires such a husbandless status by her own doing. Ifeoma, on the other hand, openly refuses to be confined to the submissive role of wife and procreator from the beginning. While being a positive maternal figure, she challenges male authority on a number of fronts – she raises her children single-handedly, is her family's only source of income, and works in academia, a field traditionally dominated by men. It is therefore not surprising that she should make use of a figure of speech more typically associated with masculinity. If this strategy of characterization works subversively in *Purple Hibiscus*, it is because the novel features a small number of proverbs, but from a historical perspective the insertion of this *ílú* situates Adichie in the tradition of female Nigerian writers such as Flora Nwapa and Buchi Emecheta, who attributed many sayings to female characters in their works (Arndt, 1998).

Since proverbs emphasize the speaker's deference to ancestral Igbo wisdom, it may at first seem surprising that Father Amadi, a Catholic priest, should comment on the catching of *aku*, edible flying termites, with a proverb: 'Our people say that after *aku* flies, it will still fall to the toad' (Adichie, 2003: 221, italics in original). Father Amadi's use of what Nwoga has termed an 'illuminative proverb' – that is, a proverb that appeals to traditional wisdom to support a given statement (1975: 198–9) – positions the priest as a teacher to his addressees, most of whom are younger than him. The typical introduction 'Our people say', with its initial first-person plural possessive determiner, appeals to the listeners' community spirit and presents the Catholic clergyman as a guardian of the Igbo oral tradition, just like Papa-Nnukwu. This suggests that, contrary to Eugene's assumption, Catholicism and an active identification with Igbo culture are not mutually exclusive. Father Amadi may be considered an incarnation of this potential reconciliation, as also suggested by the metaphorical interpretation of the proverb selected by the priest. The saying is indeed 'used to show that no one can escape a certain end' (Pachocinski, 1996: 313), an idea which is not incompatible with the Christian doctrine of divine judgement following man's death. To a certain extent, the Catholic priest takes on the role of moral guide in the contemporary urban context, a function traditionally assigned to the elders in rural communities, but he only does so in the absence of Papa-Nnukwu. The two men's authority can thus be seen as complementary, for while the young clergyman strives to counsel his parishioners so that they can come to terms with contemporary society, Kambili's grandfather familiarizes his younger relatives with their cultural heritage but is baffled by the modern world.

As the examination of these *ílú* shows, proverbs do more than simply encode 'Igboness' into the narrative, even if cultural specificity is their most obvious attribute. A similar comment could be made in relation to the characters' use of the English language. Even though the colonial tongue is cherished by Eugene, as it supposedly makes his children 'sound civilized in public' (Adichie, 2003: 13), this language can also be instrumental in subverting his extreme convictions. Thus, when Jaja, Kambili's brother, openly defies his father by refusing to take communion, he says, in English, that 'the wafer gives [him] bad breath' (p. 6). The adolescent deliberately fails to use the Latin word 'host', a term which, according to Eugene, 'c[omes] close to capturing the essence, the sacredness, of Christ's body' (p. 6). Instead, the young man opts for its Anglo-Saxon secular substitute 'wafer', which evokes, as Kambili notices, the 'chocolate wafer[s], banana wafer[s]' made in one of Eugene's factories (p. 6).

Jaja challenges his father's authority not only by refusing to obey him and passing unfavourable comments on the sacred host, but also by purposefully using an informal Germanic word where the more formal Latin one would have been expected. He intentionally dissociates himself from his father by producing speech which departs from the register sanctioned by the man – a sociolinguistic strategy known as 'speech divergence' (Myers-Scotton, 1993: 66), which stands at the opposite pole of the 'speech convergence' favoured by Eugene when he adopts a British accent to address white ecclesiastics (Adichie, 2003: 46). Kambili's remark concerning the biscuits produced in her father's factories indicates that the word 'wafer' does not meet with his approval because it is highly suggestive of commercial exchange in the Achikes' eyes. In this respect, Jaja's comment also indirectly criticizes the commodification of Eugene's sacrosanct religion, and ultimately its hypocrisy. If anything, this incident illustrates that the novel relies heavily on the connotative, non-referential value of language.

Jaja's defiance when refusing to go to Mass stands in sharp contrast to Kambili's silent witnessing of the incident. The narrator's introversion is one of her most prominent personality traits and, at the chronological beginning of the novel, it is accompanied by a sense of boundless admiration for her father. Eugene, a philanthropist and successful businessman, has much to be admired for, as he fights the yoke of military dictatorship in Nigeria by publishing a pro-democracy newspaper. At the same time, however, he is a domestic tyrant whose religious fanaticism leads him to beat his wife and children on a regular basis. Kambili progressively learns to question her father's extremist values, a fact that has led numerous commentators to label *Purple Hibiscus* a *Bildungsroman*. This designation seems appropriate, for the narrator indeed develops from an introverted, acquiescent girl into a more self-assured young woman. For instance, she initially keeps Eugene's physical abuse shrouded in silence, but later admits to the extent of his maltreatment of her during a conversation with her cousin Amaka. The changes in Kambili's attitude have been noted by many critics, and they are highly relevant to the analysis of the character's evolution. Nevertheless, a simple description of the protagonist's actions in the story – such as the act of speaking in which she eventually engages – does little to convey the complexity of her intellectual maturation. It is not only the heroine's behaviour, but also the way in which she perceives her environment and encodes her impressions into her account, that determine the development of her personality and eventually fashion the entire narrative architecture of the novel. So far, the formal features of Kambili's journey into adulthood have been given scant attention, and the distinctiveness of her narrative voice has been assessed only in passing. Interestingly, the appraisals that do exist have been fairly consistent in their use of terms such as 'emotionless' (Okorafor-Mbachu, 2004), 'dispassionate' (Ekwe-Ekwe, 2005), and 'realistic and matter-of-fact' (Ogwude, 2011: 17); Kambili has further been deemed to have a 'flat, unreflective voice' that recounts traumatic events 'without judgment' (Washburn, 2004). These evaluations seem to be based on the apparent straightforwardness of Kambili's account, as she generally privileges the description of her environment, and the reporting of the events she witnesses, over long introspective musings. However, I would like to suggest that there is more to the narrator's fairly accessible style than initially meets the eye. To be more precise, what I will attempt to demonstrate is that Kambili's rendering of events, although it may *appear* to be free of judgement, actually carries ideological undertones that are fuelled by her emotions and that undergo subtle transformation as the novel progresses. That this precise interpretation can be reached only by conducting an in-depth stylistic analysis of the book suggests that purely 'instinctive' perceptions, though often useful, are not always the most reliable guides to aesthetic appreciation. Put more directly, some stylistic devices do not lend themselves to systematic identification without the help of linguistic tools. Just as an archaeologist cannot perform an excavation with a simple shovel, so the stylistician can at times not uncover the hidden patterns of a text without recourse to a particular technical apparatus. In *Purple Hibiscus*, even the examination of an ethnolinguistic phenomenon such as the use of proverbs, which brings a valuable sense of systematicity to the interpretative process and is helpful in mapping out the relationship between the characters, must be regarded as a mere *basis* on which a more meticulous linguistic analysis can be built. In line with this consideration, I propose to take as a point of departure Papa-Nnukwu's storytelling session, whose narrative significance I outlined above.

In this particular scene, there is still a marked discrepancy between the words that Kambili utters (or rather, those she does not) and the feelings that she expresses in narrative passages. This conflict between the narrator's thoughts and her actions is paradigmatic of her attitude in the novel. She repeatedly remains silent or finds herself saying words she did not intend to, often out of fear of displeasing those around her or because she is unable to articulate her response. Thus, she is initially misjudged by Amaka, who interprets her cousin's laconic comment as a sign of world-weariness:

> 'We don't watch a lot of TV,' I [Kambili] said.
> [Amaka:] 'Why? ... Because you're bored with it? If only we all had satellite so everybody could be bored with it.'
> I wanted to say I was sorry, that I did not want her to dislike us for not watching satellite. I wanted to tell her that although huge satellite dishes lounged on top of the houses in Enugu and here, we did not watch TV. Papa did not pencil in TV time in our schedules.
>
> (Adichie, 2003: 79)

Kambili never watches television because her father strictly organizes his children's time, but she never voices aloud the explanations that she so desperately wants to add. It is nonetheless significant that, despite her shyness, 'there's a lot going on in [her] head' (p. 220), as Father Amadi astutely observes. Kambili's thoughts and feelings, and how they sometimes clash with her attitude towards others, are minutely rendered in her narrative account and follow consistent linguistic patterns. For example, formulas such as 'I wanted' (found in the passage above) or 'I wished', iterated by Kambili when evoking actions she would like to perform or wishes she had (not) carried out, are linguistic mannerisms used throughout the novel. Similarly, the teenager's inability to speak or act is expressed through structures such as 'my lips held stubbornly together' (p. 141) and 'my legs ... did not do what I wanted them to' (p. 165). The fact that these clauses identify her body parts as grammatical actors (a phenomenon known as 'meronymic agency') perhaps suggests that, in spite of Kambili's efforts, her mind is unable to take control of her body. While the latter linguistic arrangements do not seem particularly significant in isolation, they nonetheless highlight the centrality of agency in the narrator's discourse – a concept that will feature prominently in my analysis. Taken together, the characteristics mentioned above contribute to the individualization of the narrator's style: they are among the components of an idiolect – that is, a personal dialect – which, following Roger Fowler (1977: 75–8; 1996: 210–32), I will refer to as 'mind-style'.

The concept of 'mind-style' rests on the assumption that language has an ideational – that is, a representational – function. The idea is inspired by the linguist M. A. K. Halliday, according to whom

> [Any] speaker or writer embodies in language his experience of the phenomena of the real world; and this includes his experience of the internal world of his own consciousness: his reactions, cognitions, and perceptions, and also his linguistic acts of speaking and understanding.
>
> (Halliday, 1971: 332, cited in Fowler, 1996: 211)

Experience is thus partly 'cod[ed] in language' (Fowler, 1996: 211), but the way in which this occurs varies according to at least two factors: the complex network of socio-economic relations that have shaped an individual's background, and his or her personal trajectory (p. 211). This linguistic variation not only distinguishes one individual from the next, but also one text from another, since even a single speaker has 'a repertoire of ideational perspectives' (p. 212). In other words, a person may, for example, adopt different registers depending on the context of language use. Despite these situational variations, however, it is crucial to note that the 'regular and consistent linguistic choices' made in a text 'build up a continuous, pervasive, representation of the world' (p. 212). Applying these findings to fiction, one may argue that 'the world-view of an author, or a narrator, or a character' is 'constituted by the ideational structure of the text' (p. 212).

In short, the analysis of mind-style rests on the evaluation of the impact of semantic nuances and syntactic arrangements on the interpretation of the discourses that contain them. Consequently, examinations of idiolects – whether fictional or not – are most efficiently performed using linguistic models that foreground the stylistic importance of particular features of vocabulary and syntax. Thus, it is no coincidence that mind-style has most often been explored using functional grammar, an approach that seeks to ascertain '*why* ... particular linguistic patterns' (Fowler, 1996: 11, italics in original) occur in individual texts. More recently, cognitive models have also been used with similar purposes (e.g. Semino, 2002). Such theories tend to provide more fertile ground for analyses of mind-style than, for example, transformational-generative models, which focus on language universals and offer a more mechanistic view of linguistic variation.

Existing examinations of literary idiolects, whether functional or cognitive in orientation, have predominantly dissected the linguistic particularities present in the speech of mentally disabled, cognitively deviant or psychologically unbalanced characters. But this need not always be the case (see, for example, Leech and Short, 2007: 154–8). In what follows, a functional framework will be used as a basis for linguistic analysis, in an attempt to demonstrate that the concept of mind-style can help assemble some of the linguistic structures frequently used by Adichie's narrator into a coherent interpretative whole. Because, as suggested above, a character's idiolect reflects his or her worldview, I will also try to show that the linguistic changes in Kambili's description of her experiences follow her psychological development.

An examination of the narrator's mind-style in *Purple Hibiscus* requires that attention be directed as much to what the character says, be it in dialogue or narration, as to what she does not express. The theme of silence, in its broader sense encompassing all that is left unsaid, was obliquely broached above when evoking Mama's silent acceptance of the vocative '*nwunye m*', and the divergence between Kambili's thoughts as they are rendered in narrative passages and the words she utters. Even if the heroine's muteness during most of the novel has left some reviewers frustrated, it seems to me that, as Karen Bruce has extensively demonstrated, silence is not merely a 'form of oppression' in *Purple Hibiscus* – in the sense that Kambili's speechlessness can be attributed to 'her father's abuse' – but it also becomes 'a mode of resistance' (Bruce, n.d.). The crux of the matter probably lies in the simultaneous presence of these opposite functions in single instances where words are left unspoken. For example, Kambili and her brother Jaja dare not say some things aloud, but their 'asusu anya', or 'language of the eyes' (Adichie, 2003: 305), allows them to 'speak about subjects [of] which [their] father might disapprove' (Bruce, n.d.). Bruce foregrounds another passage revealing this double quality: after Eugene, furious at Jaja's disobedience, has thrown his missal across the room and broken

Beatrice's ballet-dancing figurines, the narrator attempts to comfort her mother. The girl reports: 'I meant to say I am sorry Papa broke your figurines, but the words that came out were, "I'm sorry your figurines broke, Mama"' (Adichie, 2003: 10). Bruce, echoing Hilary Mantel (2004) and Heather Hewett (2005), observes that Kambili 'avoids implicating her father' in his own act of violence. At the same time, however, the critic notices that 'through this indirect and veiled manner of speech, [Kambili] is able to broach the subject of Eugene's abusive behaviour' and 'acknowledge her mother's status as innocent victim'. Kambili's refusal to overtly recognize Eugene's responsibility in the words of sympathy that she addresses to her mother is even more outright than Bruce suggests. The differences between the clause that Kambili considers saying but does not ('Papa broke your figurines') and the one that she actually articulates ('your figurines broke') cannot be precisely pinned down in lay terms, but they can be clearly highlighted using functional grammar, and more specifically the theory of transitivity first developed by M. A. K. Halliday (see e.g. 1985: 101–57), and published in its most recent version in *Halliday's Introduction to Functional Grammar* (Halliday and Matthiessen, 2014: 211–358).[2]

In a nutshell, Halliday and Matthiessen posit that different states, actions and events find expression in various types of 'processes' that involve distinct 'participants', conventionally spelt with an initial capital letter. There are three main types of processes. 'Material' processes reflect 'our experience of the material world' (2014: 247) – broadly speaking, they include 'events, activities, and actions' (p. 228). They involve an Actor (a participant that may be animate or inanimate) and, if applicable, a Goal that is acted upon. Next are 'mental' processes, usually expressed by verbs such as 'think', 'remember' or 'feel', which are 'concerned with our experience of the world of our own consciousness' (p. 245). They involve a Senser and, in some cases, a Phenomenon being sensed. In the third category are relational processes, most typically headed by the verbs 'be' and 'have'. They 'serve to characterize and identify' (p. 259), and involve a Carrier and an Attribute being carried.

In addition to these three main types of processes, Halliday and Matthiessen identify three other 'subsidiary process types', characterized as such because they are 'located at each of the boundaries' of the principal types (p. 300). The details of their exact location need not concern us here. Suffice it to say that the first of these subsidiary categories comprises 'behavioural' processes, which are 'processes of (typically human) physiological and psychological behaviour, like breathing, coughing, smiling, dreaming and staring' (p. 301). The participant who is 'behaving' is called the Behaver. The second subsidiary process, covering verbs of 'saying', is called 'verbal'. 'Verbal' clauses typically involve a Sayer and, in some cases, a Receiver 'to whom the saying is directed' and a Verbiage 'that corresponds to what is said' (p. 306). Finally, there are also processes called 'existential', which 'represent that something exists or happens' (p. 307) and are typically introduced by 'There is/are'.

The clauses from *Purple Hibiscus* that I wish to contrast here, 'Papa broke your figurines' and 'your figurines broke', both feature material processes. Even though the Actor is animate in one case ('Papa') and inanimate in the other ('your figurines'), the so-called 'transitive model of transitivity' presented above is of relatively little help in contrasting the sentences – the relevance of this theory will become clear only later in the analysis. However, Halliday and Matthiessen complement this transitive model with an 'ergative model' (pp. 336–45), which generalizes across process types, and focuses on the idea that every process features a key participant 'through which the process is actualized' (p. 336). This element is known as the 'Medium'. To provide a brief example, in the sentences 'the tourist woke' and 'the lion woke the tourist' (p. 340), the Medium is, in both cases, 'the tourist' who performs the process of waking, and without whom there would be no process at all. Now let us apply this ergative theory to the sentences from *Purple Hibiscus*. The clause patterns are perhaps best represented schematically, so as to provide visual support for the more detailed explanations to come:

	Agent	Process	Medium	
Doing	Papa	broke	your figurines	
Happening			your figurines	broke
			Medium	**Process**

In both clauses, the verb phrase 'broke' realizes the function of Process, and the noun phrase 'your figurines' that of Medium.[3] However, the clauses display a crucial difference in pattern. While

'Papa broke your figurines' is a clause of 'doing', which is to say that 'the actualization of the process is represented as being caused by a participant [the Agent – not to be confused with the Actor of the transitive model] that is external to the combination of Process + Medium' (Halliday and Matthiessen, 2014: 336), 'your figurines broke' is a clause of 'happening', meaning that 'the process is represented as being self-engendered' (p. 336). The latter structure corresponds to a particular way of representing 'reality': 'In the real world, there may well have been some external agency involved in [the process]; but in the semantics of English it is represented as having been *self-caused*' (pp. 342–3, my italics). In other words, Kambili's formulation 'the figurines broke' not only avoids implicating her father, but also refrains from including any form of agency – this type of clause, including no feature of agency, is neither active nor passive; it is said to be 'middle' in voice (p. 349). Crucially, by presenting the process as self-engendered, the narrator even staves off the question 'by whom or by what?' that might have been raised had she used the passive 'the figurines got broken' (see Halliday and Matthiessen, 2014: 343).

Kambili masks the brutality of Eugene's abuse with her words (see also Cooper, 2008: 116), and her mother initially engages in a similar act. When a pregnant Mama is beaten so heavily by her husband that she suffers a miscarriage, she reports to her children, on her return from hospital: 'There was an accident, the baby is gone' (Adichie, 2003: 34). Still using the terminology of functional grammar (this time that of the first, transitive model outlined earlier), one can say that the clause introduced by 'there is' is an existential one. Recall that these clauses simply indicate that 'something exists or happens' (Halliday and Matthiessen, 2014: 307) – here, the use of a material clause, a type of structure that could, in its 'doing' form, integrate an Agent, is avoided altogether. In addition to this, the noun 'accident' denotes an absence of deliberate agency. The second part of the sentence, 'the baby is gone', follows the same pattern as 'the figurines broke' in Halliday and Matthiessen's model, and does not leave any room for an Agent in the 'Medium + Process' structure either. As Debra Beilke has observed, the silence around Eugene's implication in these traumatic events suggests that his abuse 'not only maims [his family members'] bodies but it also serves to control their tongues' (2006: 2).

Kambili repeatedly deploys indirect, euphemistic tactics to describe her father's acts of violence in the course of the novel. The thrashings Eugene gives his wife are either described as 'sounds' which the narrator attempts to ignore (Adichie, 2003: 10, 32), or the beatings can be inferred from their consequences – Beatrice's swollen eye or face (pp. 10, 190, 193), her blood on the floor (p. 33), or her ritual of polishing the figurines on the étagère (pp. 10, 192). Similarly, the act of abuse that has left Kambili's brother with a deformed little finger is recounted by means of a narrative ellipsis: 'Papa took him upstairs and locked the door. Jaja, in tears, came out supporting his left hand with his right, and Papa drove him to St. Agnes hospital' (p. 145).

More benign incidents are described in far less evasive terms. Kambili, for instance, reports in straightforward material, active clauses that 'Papa slapped my left and right cheeks at the same time' (p. 51) and that 'Papa yanked my ear in the car' (p. 94). In Halliday and Matthiessen's transitive model, 'Papa' can unambiguously be identified as a volitional Actor, while Kambili's body parts ('my left and right cheeks', 'my ear') are the unequivocal Goals. Contrast these structures with those employed by the narrator in her first extensive description of one of Eugene's furious outbursts of violence:

> He unbuckled his belt slowly. It was a heavy belt made of layers of brown leather with a sedate leather-covered buckle. It landed on Jaja first, across his shoulder. Then Mama raised her hands as it landed on her upper arm, which was covered by the puffy sequined sleeve of her church blouse. I put the bowl down just as the belt landed on my back. Sometimes I watched the Fulani nomads, white jellabas flapping against their legs in the wind, making clucking sounds as they herded their cows across the roads in Enugu with a switch, each smack of the switch swift and precise. Papa was like a Fulani nomad – although he did not have their spare, tall body – as he swung his belt at Mama, Jaja and me, muttering that the devil would not win. We did not move more than two steps away from the leather belt that swished through the air.
>
> Then the belt stopped, and Papa stared at the leather in his hand.
>
> (p. 102)

The striking, almost romantic comparison between Eugene and a Fulani nomad, whipping cattle with a rod, illustrates the different interpretations which the passage may invite. In Hewett's opinion:

> The juxtaposition of peaceful, rural nomads with Eugene's violent rage startles, but the image does more. By slowing down the moment, it increases the tension, enabling us to see through the eyes of a young narrator who possesses acute powers of observation.
>
> (2005: 82)

While I agree with this comment, I also believe that the image patently relates Papa's violent treatment of his own family to the way Fulani nomads handle animals. The evocation of a switch and the ruthlessness of Eugene's actions further summon associations with the scene witnessed by Kambili while at the market with her mother and Jaja:

> As we hurried past, I saw a woman spit at a soldier. I saw the soldier raise a whip in the air. The whip was long. It curled in the air before it landed on the woman's shoulder. Another soldier was kicking down trays of fruits, squashing papayas with his boots and laughing.
>
> (p. 44)

The descriptions of the soldiers' thoughtless brutality and Eugene's assaults on his family suggest a parallel between national and domestic violence that is made explicit in several other passages in the novel. In addition to the similarity in the bullies' acts and the likeness between their weapons, the comparison is amplified by the use of identical wording: 'it landed' followed by a prepositional phrase functioning as a circumstantial Adjunct of location.

This structure is foregrounded through repetition in the passage describing Eugene's flogging of Mama, Jaja and Kambili. Examining this clause from an ideational perspective (that is, focusing on the way experiences are construed through language) will reveal that this construction and those around it carry significant undertones. One may indeed be struck by the fact that Eugene, the perpetrator of the aggression, is assigned the role of grammatical Subject on only five occasions during the beating: he is the Subject of 'unbuckled', 'was', 'swung', 'muttering' and 'stared'. Even more surprisingly, Papa is the Actor of a material process in only two cases, 'unbuckled' and 'swung', since he is the Carrier of the Attribute in the relational clause 'Papa was like a Fulani nomad', the Sayer in the non-finite verbal clause headed by 'muttering' and the Behaver in the behavioural clause 'Papa stared at the leather in his hand'. Of the two material processes of which he functions as Actor – 'unbuckled' and 'swung' – the former is merely suggestive of the act of brutality that he is about to engage in, and the latter, while it evokes a movement of aggression, does not necessarily denote physical contact with his victims. Significantly, Eugene is the Actor in a clause headed by a verb denotative of destruction only after the beating has ended:

> Papa crushed Jaja and me to his body. 'Did the belt hurt you? Did it break your skin?' he asked, examining our faces. I felt a throbbing on my back, but I said no, that I was not hurt. It was the way Papa shook his head when he talked about liking sin, as if something weighed him down, something he could not throw off.
> (p. 102)

The only action performed by Eugene in which violence is semantically rendered – 'crushed' – is, paradoxically, a gesture of love. This confirms that his conception of affection is inseparable from pain, like when he offers Kambili 'love sip[s]' (p. 8) from his hot tea that burn her tongue, or when he hugs Jaja so tight that the boy thinks that 'his back ha[s] snapped' (p. 22). As Bruce argues, love translates into pain just as violence is justified by love:

> Eugene has made it clear that he views his actions as an unpleasant duty that he undertakes out of love. He tells Kambili: 'Everything I do for you, I do for your own good' (196). His choice of preposition is significant, as it reveals how he conceives of his abuse as something he does *for* his family, not *to* them.
> (n.d., italics in original)

This passing remark takes on a whole new meaning when confronted with the stylistic make-up of the text, as the brief functional analysis

I have conducted demonstrates that Papa does nothing 'to' his family in one of the novel's most brutal passages. Instead, the linguistic arrangement of Kambili's report identifies an object, namely Eugene's belt, as the true culprit. In the structure 'it [the belt] landed', which appears three times in the extract describing the beating, the pronoun 'it' has the function of Actor in a material clause according to the transitive model – meaning that the belt, not Eugene, is repeatedly presented as 'the one that does the deed', the source of energy 'that brings about the change' (Halliday and Matthiessen, 2014: 225). In similar fashion, 'the leather belt swished' and 'the belt stopped' present the object as a potent Actor rather than an instrument with which Eugene inflicts injuries upon his family. Kambili's construal of the situation reflects her father's own hypocritical evasion of responsibility, illustrated in his questions following the assault: 'Did the belt hurt you? Did it break your skin?' (p. 102). Eugene characteristically prefers these formulations to the more accurate 'Did *I* hurt you (with the belt)?'.

The arresting features contained in the description of the beating extend to the so-called 'textual' metafunction, that is, to the organization of the discourse at and beyond the level of the clause. According to Halliday and Matthiessen (here borrowing terminology from the Prague School of linguists), clauses and combinations of clauses (known as 'clause nexuses') are divided into Theme and Rheme (2014: 88–92). The Theme, placed in initial position in the clause or nexus, is 'the element which serves as the point of departure of the message' (p. 88). As such, it is the 'prominent element' (p. 133), the one that 'provides the environment for the remainder of the message, the Rheme' (p. 133). Since the narrator's attention is directed towards her father when he unbuckles his belt, it comes as no surprise that 'He' is placed in thematic position in the opening sentence of the paragraph. When Kambili turns her gaze to the ominous belt, the object becomes the Theme in the next sentence. The belt keeps this initial place in the following sentence, which is consistent with its central role in the passage, as the discussion of the structure 'it landed' revealed. But in the next two sentences, a major shift occurs: not only does the belt move away from the thematic position – both in the clause and in the clause nexus – but the clauses describing its movements, 'it landed on her upper arm' and 'the belt landed on my back', are relegated to hypotactic, that is, syntactically dependent, status. Meanwhile, two of the victims of the assault, Mama and Kambili, are assigned the functions of Actors in the material processes 'raised' and 'put' in dominant thematic clauses. In other words, the belt's violent strokes, despite their fundamental contribution to the action, are assigned rhematic and hypotactic statuses, none of which are dominant in the clause nexus. They are thereby twice removed from the prominent syntactic position that they would have been most likely to occupy. A somewhat similar pattern is repeated in the last two sentences of the paragraph, once with Eugene ('he') as Actor and once with 'the leather belt' in this function: 'Papa was like a Fulani nomad ... as he swung his belt at Mama, Jaja and me', and 'We did not move more than two steps away from the leather belt that swished through the air' (Adichie, 2003: 102). Since the hypotactic clauses describing the belt's movements hardly contain any new information (the last two clauses quoted, I would argue, do not contain any at all), the grammatical principle of 'end-focus', according to which new items are placed at the end of a sentence to achieve communicative saliency (Leech and Short, 2007: 172), is skilfully bypassed. As the reader's expectation of encountering new, semantically significant items is not met, the anti-climactic character of the scene is emphasized, and the assault is stripped of its full narrative force.

In sum, syntactic arrangements inside clauses seem to shift the blame away from Eugene and onto his weapon, while those above the level of the clause appear to minimize the impact of the aggression. These stylistic choices can give rise to a dual interpretation. Since Kambili almost systematically avoids assigning her father the function of Actor in her description of the beating, she portrays him as a passive victim instead of an aggressor. In the aftermath of his outburst of rage, she appears to excuse his behaviour by attributing it to 'something [that] weighed him down, something he could not throw off' (Adichie, 2003: 102). The notion of inability captured in the negative modal 'could not' relieves him of any accountability for his actions. At the same time, Papa is presented as not needing to make any direct intervention to endow his belt with an amount of kinetic energy so forceful that the object seems to come to life. Paradoxically, he thereby comes across as a god-like figure in control of the physical elements around him.

This seeming contradiction admirably captures the complexity of Eugene's personality, in addition to giving a glimpse of his daughter's confused perception of it. On the one hand, he is presented as an omnipotent god, one who believes that everything can be controlled and who projects this conviction onto his family. For example, he tells his daughter, who has come in second position in her class at the end of the school term, that she '*let* other children come first' (p. 39, my italics) and that she 'came second because [she] *chose* to' (p. 42, my italics). Both of these formulations denote volition, whereas Kambili has in this case not deliberately tried to come 'only' second and displease her father as a result. Similarly, Eugene refuses to admit that Mama's nausea may prevent her from visiting Father Benedict, and he accuses her of not '*want[ing]* to visit His servant after Mass' (p. 32, my italics). By anointing himself as moral judge of his family, Papa effectively 'do[es] God's job' (p. 95), as Aunty Ifeoma remarks. On the other hand, however, Eugene falls prey to his own obsession with righteousness. He is so fixated on his family's compliance with his religious ideals that he loses control of his emotions and inflicts torture upon his wife and children at the slightest sign of disobedience.

These two divergent images – Eugene as a god-like judge and Eugene as a victim of his feelings – are reunited in a single passage, in which he pours boiling water onto Kambili's feet for staying in the same house as her 'heathen' grandfather, Papa-Nnukwu:

> 'Kambili, you are precious.' His [Eugene's] voice quavered now, ... choked with emotion. 'You should strive for perfection. You should not see sin and walk right into it.' He lowered the kettle into the tub, tilted it toward my feet. He poured the hot water on my feet, slowly ... He was crying now, tears streaming down his face. I saw the moist steam before I saw the water. I watched the water leave the kettle ... I felt nothing for a second. And then I screamed.
>
> 'That is what you do to yourself when you walk into sin. You burn your feet,' he said.
>
> I wanted to say 'Yes, Papa', because he was right, but the burning on my feet was climbing up, in swift courses of excruciating pain, to my head and lips and eyes.
>
> (pp. 194–5)

Eugene maintains that 'modesty [i]s very important' (p. 5), but he assigns himself priestly authority by performing this perverse re-enactment of the Christian ritual of baptism, synonymous with purification, the cleansing of sins, and ultimately salvation. Unlike the previous passage in which Eugene attacked his family with a belt, Kambili's father is here presented as the Actor in several material clauses. While this may signal a progressive evolution in the narrator's construal of the situation, traces of her earlier state of mind are still present in clauses such as 'the water stopped' (p. 195), which may be viewed as an echo of 'the belt stopped' (p. 102). Moreover, the material processes of which Eugene is the Actor ('lowered', 'tilted', 'poured') evoke the precision of his gestures rather than the cruelty of the corporal punishment he is administering. Finally, passages such as 'His voice quavered', 'choked with emotion', 'He was crying' and 'tears streaming down his face' are all linked to the physiological expression of emotion – reactions typical of victims rather than torturers. In this passage, Eugene passes a moral judgement on God's behalf, yet his emotional fragility does not suggest the power and control that come with this function.

At this stage in the novel, the elusiveness of Eugene's personality is matched by the ambivalence of his daughter's response. While she is still a stunned onlooker ('I saw', 'I watched') and espouses the belief that walking into sin means burning one's feet (as suggested by the line 'I wanted to say "Yes, Papa", because he was right': p. 194), Kambili concurrently overlooks her father's commands by concealing her cousin Amaka's painting of Papa-Nnukwu, although she is fully aware that Eugene will disapprove of her doing so because the old man is not a Catholic. This act of resistance is probably her most overt challenge to her father in the entire novel. Even its climax is mostly conducted in silence on Kambili's part, interrupted only by two monosyllabic, yet powerful, words of protest:

> [Eugene:] 'Who brought that painting into this house?'
> 'Me', I said.
> 'Me', Jaja said.
> Papa snatched the painting from Jaja. His hands moved swiftly, working together. The painting was gone. It already represented

something lost, something I had never had, would never have. Now even that reminder was gone ...

'No!' I shrieked. I dashed to the pieces on the floor as if to save them, as if saving them would mean saving Papa-Nnukwu. I sank to the floor, lay on the pieces of paper.

'What has gotten into you?' Papa asked. 'What is wrong with you?'

I lay on the floor curled tight like the picture of a child in the uterus in my *Integrated Science for Junior Secondary Schools*.

'Get up! Get away from that painting!'

I lay there, did nothing.

'Get up!' Papa said again. I still did not move.

(p. 210)

Kambili's defiance, unprecedented in its intensity, is as much a product of her actions as of her immobility and silence, as indicated by the succession of 'dashed' and 'sank' on the one hand, and 'lay' (which occurs three times), 'did nothing' and 'still did not move' on the other. The verb phrase 'did not move' alone encapsulates the different functions that stillness performs in the narrative, as it can be found in the descriptions of Eugene's first and third outbursts of rage (pp. 102, 210) but with very different implications: a sign of fearful paralysis in the former case, it metamorphoses into an act of confrontation in the latter. In line with this change in attitude, Kambili's account of the beating which her father then inflicts upon her is initiated by a sentence rid of grammatical artifice:

He started to kick me. The metal buckles on his slippers stung like bites from giant mosquitoes. He talked non-stop, out of control, in a mix of Igbo and English, like soft meat and thorny bones. Godlessness. Heathen worship. Hellfire. The kicking increased in tempo, and I thought of Amaka's music, her culturally conscious music that sometimes started off with a calm saxophone and then whirled into lusty singing. I curled around myself tighter, around the pieces of the painting ... The stinging was raw now, even more like bites, because the metal landed on open skin on my side, my back, my legs. Kicking. Kicking. Kicking. Perhaps it was a belt now because the metal buckle seemed too heavy. Because I could hear a swoosh in the air. A low voice was saying, 'Please, *biko*, please'. More stings. More slaps. A salty wetness warmed my mouth. I closed my eyes and slipped away into quiet.

(pp. 210–11, italics in original)

This extract depicts the culmination of Eugene's brutality towards his daughter. Even Mama admits that Papa 'has never punished her like this before' (p. 214) – even if, once again, the more direct 'beaten' would have been more appropriate than the morally justifiable 'punished'. As already suggested above, Eugene's responsibility as the initiator of the attack is no longer dissimulated by syntactic façades: the participants in the action and the act of aggression itself are unmistakably identified in the 'Actor + Process + Goal' structure 'He started to kick me.' If Kambili has torn off the mask of innocence with which she had previously covered her father's face, Eugene still possesses the God-like power to bring objects to life. The buckles on his slippers are said to 'st[i]ng like bites from giant mosquitoes' (p. 210), with the metal 'land[ing] on open skin' (p. 211), just as the dynamic belt did. Eugene, in turn, seems to attribute such elusive supernatural powers to Amaka's drawing, for he orders Kambili to '[g]et away from that painting' even in its shredded state, as if the representation of Papa-Nnukwu were the indestructible incarnation of evil.

Retreating into her mind, Kambili thinks of Amaka's 'culturally conscious music' (p. 211) – 'itself a symbol of resistance', as Hewett rightly observes (2005: 83) – and she relates the increasing force of the blows to the music's intensifying beat. As the experiences amalgamate in Kambili's head, so they mimetically do in the text, which acquires the rhythmical qualities of a song (see also Cooper, 2008: 118). The three elliptical sentences 'Godlessness. Heathen worship. Hellfire' (Adichie, 2003: 211), snatches of Eugene's speech that render Kambili's immediate consciousness of the experience, set the initial pace, before 'The kicking increase[s] in tempo.' The gerund 'kicking' provides the song's main motif. It is first presented in variation under the assonantal, alliterative, and grammatically equivalent 'singing' and 'stinging', a phonological proximity and morphological correspondence perhaps suggestive of their semantic association in the narrator's mind.[4] 'Kicking' is then reiterated thrice in the rhythmic progression 'my side, my back, my legs. Kicking.

Kicking. Kicking' (p. 211). While the accumulation of nouns referring to body parts and the replication of 'kicking' suggest an iconic representation of the beating's repetitive and intensifying quality, the rhythmic chiasmus created by the stress patterns in this sequence may be evocative of Eugene's erratic behaviour. The coda to the song is then provided by the elliptical 'More stings. More slaps' (p. 211). In these sentences, accumulation is again suggested by the determinant 'more' (denotative of an increase in level or amount) and its repetition.

If this paragraph of *Purple Hibiscus* indeed bears resemblance to a musical piece, then it takes the form of a 'freedom song' (p. 299). Kambili does not physically escape her father's blows, but she nevertheless manages a metaphorical flight. She first excludes him by 'curl[ing] around [her]self tighter' (p. 210), a position she associates with that of 'a child in the uterus' (p. 210) found in one of her science books. Her retreat to the maternal womb may be perceived as a break away from patriarchal authority, even perhaps as an act of identification with the foetus that her mother has recently lost at the hands of Eugene (p. 34). This position also acquires high symbolic significance because Kambili's temporary withdrawal may prefigure her own rebirth, a plea for life contained in the semantics of her first name.[5] While Kambili's silent protest 'increases her vulnerability', as the image of the unborn child suggests, it also 'becomes a source of strength' (Hewett, 2005: 83). Significantly, the last sentence of the paragraph features her as an Actor deliberately leaving the scene: 'I closed my eyes and slipped away into quiet' (Adichie, 2003: 211). That her loss of consciousness is rendered with a material clause evoking movement ('slipped away into quiet'), rather than a behavioural process such as 'fainted', seems to emphasize Kambili's voluntary, albeit inconspicuous, retreat to a space where her father cannot reach her.

The above analysis has demonstrated that, if the gradual evolution in Kambili's language reflects a change in her attitude, the shifting linguistic structures which the heroine employs are also symptomatic of a crucial transformation in the apprehension of her environment. I would like to pursue this idea a little further by focusing more specifically on the link between Kambili's relationship with her father and her approach towards religion. My aim in doing so is to show that the narrator does more than excuse her father's violent behaviour in the initial stages of the novel, but that she also inadvertently ventriloquizes his narrow-minded religious principles. Indeed, one of Kambili's most visible personality traits is that she constantly yearns for Eugene's approval and that, as a result, she dismisses the thought that any standards that are not her father's may be equally, or even more, valid than his. In this respect, I concur with Karen Bruce's opinion that 'Kambili has internalised her father's authority to such an extent that it has become an unquestioned part of the way she experiences and interacts with the world' (Bruce, n.d.). Since the narrator at first applies Eugene's principles on all planes (whether religious, cultural or moral), 'authority' in Bruce's sentence might equally read 'values', giving the analysis an ideological slant. I would like to suggest that, stylistically speaking, the author represents Kambili's intense devotion to her father – an admiration that leads to her unwitting 'internalization' of his moral standards – by employing mechanisms of speech and thought presentation. More precisely, I wish to demonstrate how Adichie exploits the two points of view inherent in both indirect and free indirect speech (Leech and Short, 2007: 256–7, 270) to delineate her narrator's ideological stance.[6]

Indirect speech and free indirect speech are often used to subtle effect in *Purple Hibiscus*, particularly when Kambili reports the convictions and judgements that Eugene imparts to his family:

> [Papa] looked sad; his rectangular lips seemed to sag. Coups begat coups, he said, telling us about the bloody coups of the sixties, which ended up in civil war just after he left Nigeria to study in England. A coup always began a vicious cycle. Military men would always overthrow one another, because they could, because they were all power drunk. Of course, Papa told us, the politicians were corrupt, and the *Standard* [Eugene's newspaper] had written many stories about the cabinet ministers who stashed money in foreign bank accounts, money meant for paying teachers' salaries and building roads.
>
> (Adichie, 2003: 24)

As the autodiegetic narrator of the book (that is, the first-person narrator who is also the protagonist), Kambili is the internal focalizer throughout, which means that it is only from her point of view that situations and events are rendered. All three major types of speech presentation (direct speech, indirect speech and free indirect speech) occur in the novel, while thought presentation can be found in the forms of indirect thought, free indirect thought (including represented perceptions) and free direct thought in the last section of the novel.

The opening sentence of the quotation may be considered an instance of represented perception: Kambili guesses that her father is sad based on his appearance, while he may in fact be experiencing other emotions. Because this sentence is a physical description in free indirect thought, the first clause of the following one, 'Coups begat coups', might also be perceived as such until this mistaken impression is corrected by the reporting clause 'he said', indicating that the sentence is an instance of indirect speech in which the reporting and reported clauses have been inverted. This retrospective rectification may be regarded as a pragmatic case of the 'garden path' effect, a psycholinguistic phenomenon whereby the beginning of a sentence misleads readers into making an interpretation that turns out to be incorrect (see e.g. Fowler, 1996: 65–7).[7] Importantly, while the erroneous view that one had initially encountered a case of free indirect thought is rectified, 'the original effect is not entirely subsumed' (Leech and Short, 2007: 267). Put differently, the impression that the clause 'Coups begat coups' represented Kambili's thoughts rather than her father's speech never entirely disappears from readers' minds.

This syntactic construction in indirect speech is followed by two sentences that cannot be attributed to either Kambili or her father with any definiteness: 'A coup always began a vicious cycle. Military men would always overthrow one another, because they could, because they were all power drunk' (Adichie, 2003: 24). On formal linguistic criteria alone, it is impossible to decide whether these sentences are instances of free indirect thought, in which case they mirror Kambili's considerations, or if they exemplify a 'slip' into the free indirect speech mode (Leech and Short, 2007: 272) and are a rendering of Eugene's discourse. The elaborateness of the subject matter and the vocabulary give Eugene an edge over his daughter but, formally speaking, free indirect thought is blended into free indirect speech, resulting in a form of Bakhtinian polyphony.

The beginning of the next paragraph, the adverb 'of course' followed by the reporting clause 'Papa told us', is another example of an inversion of the reporting and reported clause. As in the first case, one has the fleeting impression that the adverb reflects Kambili's convictions, while the phrase is in fact part of an indirect speech construction and therefore most likely uttered by Eugene. Once the 'authorship' of the reported clause has been established, one is inclined to reinterpret the last two sentences of the preceding paragraph as free indirect speech.

The manipulation of speech presentation, illustrated in various garden path effects and in the blending of the spheres of free indirect thought and free indirect speech, blurs the boundaries between Kambili's and her father's words. Provided that the ambiguous passages discussed above are all in (free) indirect speech, undoubtedly the most likely interpretation, this stylistic technique makes the narrator appear as though she has interiorized Eugene's views to such an extent that they come across as being hers. She 'forg[ets] [her]self' (Adichie, 2003: 25), has no critical distance vis-à-vis her father's teachings and weaves his speech into hers. In other words, she has literally internalized his values and blended them into the text.[8]

The impression that Eugene's shadow looms over the narrative is not restricted to passages in which Kambili reports her father's speech. His influence works more insidiously, as shown by her use of the word 'mushroom' in her description of a Catholic mass: 'The congregation said "Yes" or "God bless him" or "Amen", but not too loudly so they would not sound like the mushroom Pentecostal churches' (p. 5). It matters little whether the modifying noun 'mushroom' reflects Kambili's opinion alone or whether it is a view she shares with the entire congregation. Since the passage bears no trace of ironic distance, it is clear in both cases that Kambili espouses the belief that Pentecostal churches are spreading like parasites. In a subsequent passage that nevertheless occurs chronologically before the first, Eugene is attributed the following words in direct speech: 'That young priest, singing in the sermon like a Godless leader of one of these Pentecostal churches that spring up everywhere like mushrooms' (p. 29). Eugene's remark on the buildings erected by the Pentecostal movement sheds light on Kambili's source for the pejorative 'mushroom'. Her father's use of the word 'Godless' to characterize Evangelistic leaders shows that, in his view, anyone who does not follow the precepts of Catholicism qualifies as irreligious. If Eugene is intolerant of Pentecostalism, he is also uncompromising towards traditional Igbo spiritual influences. He calls them not only 'Godless' – a term he also applies to Nigeria's military rulers – and 'ungodly', but also 'heathen' and 'pagan', as if components of Igbo culture were tainted by their African origins; he further depicts the practices of Igbo religion as 'sinful' and followers of this spiritual tradition as 'idol worshipers'.

Any reasonable person would disagree with Eugene's contemptuous attitude towards traditional Igbo religion, a movement embodied in his own father Papa-Nnukwu, but at the same time sympathize with his condemnation of Nigeria's military rulers. The character's indiscriminate use of derogatory religious vocabulary to criticize both forms of what he regards as 'Godlessness' emphasizes the complexity of his convictions. Blinded by her veneration of Eugene, Kambili is unable to discriminate between her father's political stances, which are no doubt worthy of admiration, and his less commendable religious prejudices. At first, because she embraces every position he takes without questioning his motivations, she reproduces his value-laden linguistic choices. Her narrative contains emphatic assertions evocative of her father's rhetoric, among which 'it was sinful for a woman to wear trousers' (p. 80), and pronouncements such as 'Papa-Nnukwu is a pagan' (p. 81) or 'How can Our Lady intercede on behalf of a heathen, Aunty?' (p. 166). However, even in the early stages of the narrative, Kambili finds herself unable to bridge the chasm between the ideology her father has instilled into her and her own visual experiences. Reminiscing about her first visit to her grandfather, she reports: 'I examined him [Papa-Nnukwu] that day, too, for signs of difference, of Godlessness. I didn't see any, but I was sure they were somewhere. They had to be' (p. 63). Even though Kambili is unable to support her beliefs with concrete evidence, her convictions are still unshaken at this stage, as her use of 'had to' to indicate certainty shows. Despite her biases, when the heroine is in her grandfather's compound, she cannot help being attracted to the location, a place which she is unaccustomed to but which nevertheless bears strange resemblance to more familiar surroundings:

> The bench held me back, sucked me in. I watched a gray rooster walk into the shrine at the corner of the yard, where Papa-Nnukwu's god was, where Papa said Jaja and I were never to go near. The shrine was a low, open shed, its mud roof and walls covered with dried palm fronts. It looked like the grotto behind St. Agnes, the one dedicated to Our Lady of Lourdes.
>
> (p. 66)

This description does not present Kambili as being in control of her own movements. Using the terminology of functional grammar, one might describe the inanimate 'bench' as the unusual Actor of material clauses headed by 'held back' and 'sucked in', while the narrator is the Goal, that is, the one being acted upon, in both cases. This means that Kambili does not describe her immobility as a posture dictated by her own will, but rather as an action performed on her by the environment. This stylistic choice renders the irresistible fascination Papa-Nnukwu's shrine exerts on her, and underscores the manner in which this emotion deprives her of agency. Remarkably, the narrator also innocently likens her grandfather's shed to the cave located behind the Catholic church in Enugu. Despite her indoctrination, she already shows intuitive knowledge of what her tolerant Aunty Ifeoma teaches her later on, namely 'that sometimes what [i]s different [i]s just as good as what [i]s familiar, that when Papa-Nnukwu d[oes] his itu-nzu, his declaration of innocence, in the morning, it [i]s the same as our saying the rosary' (p. 166). While Kambili does not comprehend her aunt's views straight away and continues to refer to her grandfather as a 'heathen' and a 'pagan' for much of the narrative, her curiosity about traditional Igbo culture rapidly gets the better of her. After looking at a *mmuo* (a masquerade) and averting her gaze from it because her grandfather tells her that women are not allowed to watch it, she tries to excuse her enjoyment of what Eugene considers 'devilish folklore' (p. 85) by making weak compromises with her conscience: 'It was sinful, deferring to a heathen masquerade. But at least I had looked at it very briefly, so maybe it would technically not be deferring to a heathen masquerade' (p. 86). The rather detailed description of the *mmuo* preceding this passage suggests that Kambili has, despite her claims, carefully observed the masked figure. When her grandfather dies in her aunt and cousins' house during one of her stays in Nsukka, she attempts a similar linguistic subterfuge, though her priorities have perceptibly changed by then:

> Jaja bent down and covered Papa-Nnukwu's body with the wrapper ... I wanted to go over and touch Papa-Nnukwu, touch the white tufts of hair that Amaka oiled, smooth the wrinkled skin of his chest. But I would not. Papa would be outraged. I closed my eyes then so that if Papa asked if I had seen Jaja touch the body of a heathen – it seemed more grievous, touching Papa-Nnukwu in death – I could truthfully say no, because I had not seen everything that Jaja did.
>
> (p. 184)

Kambili is intent on exploiting the minor semantic difference between seeing Jaja 'touch' Papa-Nnukwu's body and seeing him 'touch*ing*' it: while the verb of perception 'see' followed by a bare infinitive means that she has witnessed the entire action, the same verb followed by an '-ing' form suggests just a glimpse. Unlike her reflections on the incident involving the *mmuo*, her linguistic negotiations in this passage no longer concern her actions' moral acceptability, but the relation they bear to what the father she fears finds permissible. Taken in isolation, this development might perhaps not be interpreted as signalling a change in Kambili's attitude. Nonetheless, this line of analysis finds a decisive complement in the sentence 'Papa would be outraged', preferred to the alternative 'it was outrageous'. While both options take the form of what functional grammar identifies as relational clause, that is, a clause in which a Carrier is ascribed an Attribute, Kambili would have assigned a reprehensible quality to an experience if she had used 'it was outrageous', but instead she merely speculates on her father's reaction by reporting that 'Papa would be outraged'. Put differently, 'it was outrageous', modelled on 'it was sinful' (p. 86), would have signalled the narrator's own indignation at the situation, but 'Papa would be outraged' is a comment on her *father's* potential wrath. Similarly, the word 'heathen' occurs in indirect discourse and not free indirect thought, and may be perceived as Kambili's projection of Eugene's words, not the rendering of her own opinion. The accumulation of such textual indications leads to the emergence of a clear pattern in this extract. Indeed, while the 'unacceptability' of traditional religion is still at the centre of her discourse, words signalling disapproval are no longer inserted in free indirect thought as the reflection of her judgements and beliefs; rather, they are attributed to her father, the person who sets the standards of propriety. This linguistic shift can be interpreted as marking an early ideological change.

Kambili's contact with her grandfather and elements of traditional culture allows her to gradually modify her judgement on certain issues, yet the decisive impulse is provided only when Father Amadi exposes the irrationality of her arguments:

> I was always a penitent when I was close to a priest at confession. But it was hard to feel penitent now, with Father Amadi's cologne deep in my lungs. I felt guilty instead because I could not focus on my sins, could not think of anything except how near he was. 'I slept in the same room as my grandfather. He is a heathen', I blurted out.
>
> He turned to me briefly, and before he looked away, I wondered if the light in his eyes was amusement. 'Why do you say that?'
>
> 'It is a sin.'
>
> 'Why is it a sin?'
>
> I stared at him. I felt that he had missed a line in his script. 'I don't know.'
>
> 'Your father told you that.'
>
> I looked away, out the window. I would not implicate Papa, since Father Amadi obviously disagreed.
>
> (p. 175)

Kambili refuses to acknowledge the relevance of Father Amadi's remark, but the changes brought about by this conversation are clearly perceptible in the subsequent pages. After this discussion, Kambili's development is completed: ideas of sinfulness and the related concept of guilt, both of which had visibly or latently preoccupied the narrator for much of the novel, disappear from free indirect thought, and certitudes once and for all vanish to leave room for questioning.[9] From this point on, Kambili no longer refers to her grandfather or to traditional Igbo culture as 'heathen' and 'pagan', except in one striking case which I believe to indicate a decisive turning point. When Eugene discovers that Papa-Nnukwu has been staying with Ifeoma while his children were also residing in the Nsukka flat, he insists on driving them back home: '"I could not let them stay an extra day," Papa said, looking around the living room, toward the kitchen and then the hallway, as if waiting for Papa-Nnukwu to appear in a puff of heathen smoke' (p. 188). Kambili's description of Eugene's expectations is indisputably – and, I would say, deliberately – inappropriate to reality. By virtue of its hyperbolic nature, the projection of her father's beliefs is an example of ironic 'speech allusion', the imitation of a style of speech (Leech and Short, 2007: 280). This mock exaggeration signals the critical distance the narrator has developed towards Eugene's demonization of the harmless Papa-Nnukwu.

Kambili indisputably learns to question her father's principles, but she is never able to completely remove the aureole that she has put around Eugene's head. The ambiguity of her emotions is manifest when, following her return to her aunt's house after another of her father's outbursts of violence, she refuses to speak to him on the phone but cannot rid herself of her desire to please him:

> I did want to talk to Papa, to hear his voice, to tell him what I had eaten and what I had prayed about so that he would approve, so that he would smile so much his eyes would crinkle at the edges. And yet, I did not want to talk to him; I wanted to leave with Father Amadi, or with Aunty Ifeoma, and never come back.
>
> (p. 268)

The narrator's unresolved feelings persist beyond the moment of her father's death, as shown in the closing pages of the novel, set 31 months after her mother has poisoned her husband. Kambili expresses a sense of liberation when she reports that 'a different kind of silence, one that lets [her] breathe' (p. 305) has replaced 'the silence of when Papa was alive' (p. 305), about which she still has nightmares. Yet, despite her disturbing visions, in a paradox that perfectly captures the contradictory sentiments she has developed towards her father, she 'want[s] to see him in [her] dreams', to the point that she 'sometimes make[s] [her] own dreams, when [she]

[is] neither asleep nor awake' (p. 306). While Kambili has distanced herself from her father's inflexible views, many of the responses surrounding his memory are the same as those which his presence produced when he was alive – a mixture of love, silence and fear.

Adichie's skilful handling of style undoubtedly accounts for the way some critics have described her narrator's rendering of events. If one considers again the positions mentioned earlier in this chapter, Kambili may indeed appear to be 'emotionless' (Okorafor-Mbachu, 2004) or to have a 'flat, unreflective voice' that recounts facts 'without judgement' (Washburn, 2004) if one takes her seeming lack of involvement in certain passages at face value. For example, the repeated attention given to the inanimate belt's movements – rather than the protagonists' emotional states – in her first extensive description of the beatings inflicted by her father might be viewed, without further investigation, as being 'objective' by virtue of its factuality. I have suggested that, on the contrary, these structures reflect the narrator's bias, and more specifically mirror her justification of Eugene's behaviour. Thus, the 'mind-style' Adichie creates for her character is a deceptively simple one, since the accessible vocabulary and plain syntactic structures it contains inconspicuously conceal Kambili's prejudices. The subsequent maturation of this idiolect into a far more straightforward type of language shows that the narrator's questioning of her father's narrow-minded principles eventually translates into discursive freedom, as reflected by her eventual rejection of ideologically loaded terms such as 'sinful' or 'heathen'. Nevertheless, while Kambili develops into her own voice by denouncing Eugene's behaviour in her account, her eagerness to please and be loved by him never completely vanishes. The presence of such a rift in the narrator's mind serves to highlight the intricacy of her negotiation of freedom and love; it also suggests that Kambili's intellectual development and her affection for her father, despite their close interaction, are two aspects of her personality that can be theoretically distinguished.

In light of the parallels repeatedly drawn by critics between the domestic world of *Purple Hibiscus* and the condition of Nigeria at large, it may be interesting to note that Kambili's psychological conflict finds echoes in Adichie's non-fictional prose. Indeed, just as her character rejects her father's fundamentalism but cannot help adoring him, so the writer directs scathing criticism against her country but professes her deep attachment to it: 'Buildings fall down, pensions aren't paid, politicians are murdered, riots are in the air... and yet I love Nigeria' (Adichie, 2006a). Ultimately, the split between the narrator's intellectual and emotional allegiances in *Purple Hibiscus* may well mirror the author's awareness of the complexities of her own relationship to postcolonial Nigeria – a bond whose intricacies need to be explored, probed into, examined from different angles, but which cannot, at present, be simplistically resolved.

3
'The Other Half of the Sun'
Ideology in Chimamanda Ngozi Adichie's
Half of a Yellow Sun

When Chimamanda Ngozi Adichie's second novel, *Half of a Yellow Sun* (2006b), was featured on the British television show, *Richard and Judy*, in 2007, co-host Richard Madeley offered the following enthusiastic, but not altogether inspired thought about the book: 'It's a sort of Nigerian version of *Gone with the Wind*.' The presenter's observation was the first in a series of comments visibly meant to underline the 'universal' appeal of the African author's novel about the Biafran War: 'Within three pages', Madeley continued, 'I felt as if I was reading about something that happened here in Britain – the parallels between all of our lives are just so identical' (*Richard and Judy*, 2007). After several references to major world conflicts (all supposedly reminiscent of the civil war between Nigeria and Biafra at the heart of *Half of a Yellow Sun*), the comparison with *Gone with the Wind* was reiterated thrice more in the course of the 13-minute televised sequence. The analogy, rather infelicitous in view of its contrived universalist underpinnings and its unwitting branding of Adichie's novel as a melodrama, even verged on the comical for those recalling the dubious racial politics of Margaret Mitchell's 1936 novel and its 1939 film adaptation. As is commonly known, the sweeping tale of Scarlett O'Hara, whether on the page or on the screen, has often been accused of endorsing the institution of slavery in the Deep South at the time of the American Civil War.

In spite of this, *Gone with the Wind* and *Half of a Yellow Sun* can be said to share one noteworthy feature: both works weave together an absorbing story with an unmistakably political subtext. Yet in Adichie's case, even this seemingly straightforward remark must be

approached with circumspection, as the author has repeatedly discouraged narrowly political readings of her books: 'Sometimes I get
very upset when people talk about my work' and its '"political importance",' she comments. 'It's really about love' (Adichie and Wainaina,
2011). Needless to say, Adichie's provocative statement should not be
taken entirely at face value, but it can easily be viewed as an attempt
to resist interpretative pigeonholing of the kind practised by those
who read African fiction through an exclusively political lens, often
at the expense of the literature's more broadly humanistic or emotional appeal. To an extent, this analytical trend bears resemblance to
the 'anthropological fallacy' discussed in Chapter 1, in the sense that
both practices tend to overlook the artistic essence of literary works
to consider them as social treatises of sorts. However, it would be
just as absurd to regard as apolitical a novel whose title refers to the
rising sun depicted on the Biafran flag (itself a political symbol) as it
would be to read the book as a pro-Igbo or anti-colonial pamphlet.
Upon closer inspection, then, the main issue potentially plaguing
any political reading of Adichie's work is not related to the legitimacy
of such an attempt, but to its methodology. Appraising the ideological purport of the Nigerian writer's production is an entirely valid
undertaking, inasmuch as the examination takes into consideration
the ways in which the *aesthetic* actually shapes the political. As will
be shown in this chapter, the use of distinctive stylistic techniques in
Half of a Yellow Sun encourages readers to privilege certain interpretations over others; these retrieved meanings, I will argue, aggregate to
elicit allegiances with specific points of view, and guide sympathies
towards, or away from, particular characters.

This affective potential of the novelistic text is what Adichie herself
has recognized as being the distinguishing feature of realist literature. Because, she says, 'we are emotional beings' (2012: 5), 'a book
of reportage, an accumulation of facts' (p. 8) will not leave the same
mark on its readers as a well-crafted literary work: 'Logic can con-
vince', she states, 'but it is in fact emotion that leads us to act' (p. 5).
The recognition that fiction is more than a simple lining-up of facts
carries with it the important implication that the literary writer, in
devising his or her fictional tale, consciously relinquishes any attempt
at 'objectivity' that might, for instance, constitute a journalist's ideal.[1]
Instead, '[r]ealist fiction', Adichie explains, 'seeks to infuse the real
with meaning'; it is 'the process of turning fact into truth' (p. 3).

Building on these reflections, this chapter will explore how *Half of a Yellow Sun* constructs its own 'truths' – that is, how it deploys stylistic techniques to enact a particular worldview. Central to the idea of worldview is the notion of 'ideology', which will be adopted as a guiding principle in what follows. The concept of 'ideology' as it is used here should not be understood as systematically having the negative connotations of hegemony and manipulation that it has in Marxist criticism, and which have also seeped into popular uses of the term. Rather, I propose to work with the broader linguistic definition of the word, which simply characterizes 'ideologies' as 'ideas, and in particular those ideas that are shared by a community or society' (Jeffries, 2010a: 5). This description does not preclude negative interpretations of the word, but neither does it necessarily resist positive evaluation – the value of the term thus defined resides precisely in its flexibility. To give an example that will be familiar to readers, the idea of 'Africa' itself is an ideology, largely resulting from the lumping together of disparate cultures by colonial forces. Yet the recognition of this historical fact does not necessarily condition one's response to the notion of 'Africa', which has, for instance, been reinvested with empowering connotations by movements such as pan-Africanism. Therefore, 'Africa' may be viewed either as an unwelcome colonial relic or as a potentially constructive basis for solidarity-based resistance – opinions on the matter remain divided, even among the characters of *Half of a Yellow Sun* (Adichie, 2006b: 20).

From this broad definition of ideology can be derived one basic fact: '*all* texts are ideological' (Jeffries, 2010a: 6, italics in original) and they may, therefore, be examined in this light. Nonetheless, any would-be textual investigator should bear in mind a few basic principles. First, as critical discourse analyst Norman Fairclough reminds us, 'it is not possible to "read off" ideologies from texts' (cited in Jeffries, 2010a: 8), since the views held by the scholar him- or herself will necessarily influence the final analysis. However, I concur with Lesley Jeffries that it is, to an extent, 'possible to separate out some of the ideologies that a text *constructs* (or reinforces) and the assimilation of those ideologies (or their rebuttal) by readers' (2010a: 8, italics in original). Jeffries gives the useful example of far-right political texts, which promote ideas that are retrievable both by their opponents and by their supporters, but which will eventually generate different responses. Another important characteristic of texts, irrespective of their genre, is that they may contain features that are 'unconscious on the part of the text producer', a fact that 'does not necessarily detract from their potency and may even enhance it' (p. 9). In the case of fiction, this observation offers more than a convenient way out of the old conundrum of authorial intention; more generally, it lends support to the idea of a text-based interpretation of the literary piece that is not restricted by the writer's declarations about his or her project or, for that matter, by critical assessments based on what appear to be some of the work's most evident and consciously devised stylistic attributes.

In *Half of a Yellow Sun*, one such obvious feature relates to the points of view adopted in the story. A common 'descriptive' comment made about the novel is that, with the exception of eight vignettes describing a book written by one of the protagonists, it is a third-person narrative alternatively told from the perspectives of three of its main characters: Ugwu, a young villager who, as the tale begins, arrives in the university town of Nsukka to work as a houseboy for a mathematics lecturer called Odenigbo; Odenigbo's girlfriend (and later wife) Olanna, a sociologist from a wealthy family; and Richard, a white Englishman who has a relationship with Olanna's non-identical twin sister, Kainene. In view of this narrative construction, it has often been said that the novel revolves around three 'character-focalizers' (Krishnan, 2012: 26) or three 'central consciousnesses' (Arana, 2010: 286) – in other words, that the book makes use of 'limited omniscient narration' and 'tells only those experiences and thoughts that pass through the mind of a particular character' at a time (Arana, 2010: 324, n8). This description indeed reflects a broad trend in the novel and is useful to familiarize audiences with the structure of the book – after all, the author herself has presented *Half of a Yellow Sun* as a tale told 'through the points of view of characters' (Adichie, 2006c). However, like most generalizations, this account has its limitations. Consider, for instance, the following, apparently unremarkable sentence contained in one of the sections focusing on the Englishman Richard: 'He stretched and ran a quick hand through his hair, as if to shrug off the foreboding (Adichie, 2006b: 307). The 'foreboding' refers to the prediction that Port Harcourt, the town where Richard lives in the newly independent state of Biafra, might fall to the Nigerian army. Of particular interest in this sentence is the phrasal conjunction 'as if', which indicates that, at this precise moment in the novel, Richard is seen from *without* rather than *within*: the narrator is interpreting the motivations of the character based on the latter's behaviour and does not have unrestricted access to his thoughts, contrary to what critics have assumed until now. Technically, the conjunction 'as if' is known as a '[word] of estrangement' – a term that, when used in narrative accounts, signals the presence of an external observer (Uspensky, 1973: 85). This comment, which might seem relatively trivial at first sight, rather crucially suggests that the narrator does not simply render the characters' thoughts but also interprets and, to some extent, judges their actions. Whereas Richard might simply have been attempting to remove hair from his eyes, the narrator encourages us to consider this gesture as a sign of anxiety, or possibly of repression of the fact that the Biafran troops are losing the war.

The control exerted by the narratorial voice in *Half of a Yellow Sun* extends well beyond such microscopic interventions. Its presence is conspicuous even to the naked eye at the larger level of structural organization, since key information is sometimes temporarily withheld from the reader to introduce a sense of suspense. This is for instance the case when, in the first cluster of chapters set in the late 1960s, it is twice stated that Olanna and her sister Kainene are no longer on speaking terms, though any mention of the reason behind the rift is carefully avoided (Adichie, 2006b: 129, 131). Similarly, Richard is said to be unsure Kainene 'had forgiven him for the incident with Olanna' (p. 151), but no details of the original event are provided. The cause of the argument – a brief sexual encounter between Richard and Olanna – is only fully disclosed in the next section, which is set in the early 1960s again.

Of course, the fact that the implied author, via the narrator, arranges the novel in such a way as to serve her artistic agenda is hardly a controversial claim – the old Russian formalist distinction between 'fabula' (the story in chronological order) and 'sjužet' (the sequence in which narrated events are presented) rests on the very existence of this type of structural organization. Still, in *Half of a Yellow Sun*, the effects of the narrator's control over the text have been largely underestimated. For example, when Susan Strehle observes that the novel 'rejects the omniscience common to historical narratives in favor of observations limited to three characters' (2011: 653), she tends to disregard the many ways in which the overarching narrative voice filters the protagonists' thoughts and perceptions, and ultimately attempts to transmit a particular set of ideologies to the reader. Admittedly, such ideologies do not always work overtly, which only emphasizes the need to examine their workings more closely – or, to use an apt metaphor used by Adichie in another context, to 'search for the other half of the sun' (2006b, 'Author's Note': 436). This quest, I will argue, can most fruitfully be pursued by intermittently complementing the image used by the writer with another metaphor: that which depicts novels as orchestrations of discourses (Bakhtin, 1981: 415–16). Bakhtin's well-known theory of the novel, which perceives this literary genre as inherently polyphonic, will be combined with more recent models of stylistic analysis in an attempt to shed some light on the ideological make-up of Adichie's book.

That polyphony is at work within the pages of the novel becomes clear less than two sentences into the narrative. The model of speech and thought presentation used in the analysis of *Purple Hibiscus* in Chapter 2 can help to establish this fact. Thus begins *Half of a Yellow Sun*:

> Master was a little crazy; he had spent too many years reading books overseas, talked to himself in his office, did not always return greetings, and had too much hair. Ugwu's aunty said this in a low voice as they walked on the path.
>
> (Adichie, 2006b: 3)

The first sentence of the book initially reads as a straightforward case of NRA, an acronym that stands for 'Narrator's Representation of Action' (Short, 1996: 296) or 'narrative report of action' (Leech and Short, 2007: 260). This category is not one of speech and thought presentation as such, but encompasses the narrator's recording of actions, states and events (Short, 1996: 296). The impression, typical of NRA, that the narrator is 'apparently in total control of [the] report' (Leech and Short, 2007: 260) rapidly dissipates when reading the second sentence of Adichie's novel, which establishes that the opening of the book was, in fact, a rendering of the words spoken by Ugwu's aunt to her nephew. Just as in *Purple Hibiscus*, readers are faced with a pragmatic 'garden path' effect, for they are forced to reinterpret what they believed to be NRA as free indirect speech (FIS). With this reinterpretation, the authority of the opening statement is reassessed but, also in a manner analogous to the recategorization of speech types that occurs in Adichie's first novel, the original impression of being faced with a reliable narratorial statement never entirely disappears. Importantly, the identification of FIS as opposed to NRA entails recognition of the text's double-voicedness, since the initial statement now appears to be a mixture of the narrator's *and* the character's voices. As the remainder of Adichie's first chapter makes clear, the narrator's intervention lies in the very linguistic code used to report the opinion expressed by Ugwu's aunt, as the words uttered by the woman are actually spoken in Igbo. The English rendering, for its part, offers as much information about the worldview held by the boy's relative as it does about the character it describes, the lecturer Odenigbo: the aunt's mention of '*too many* years reading books overseas' and '*too much* hair' (my italics) testifies to her belief that the academic has certain attributes in excess compared to the particular social standards she deems appropriate. From her short appraisal of the man's reading habits, one can infer her mistrust of Western education; her verdict about Odenigbo's hair, which is more puzzling at first sight, is later revealed to be a reference to his Afro hairstyle. While the peculiar phrase used by the woman signals her unfamiliarity with, and perhaps disapproval of, this typically African-American form of cultural expression, her incongruous description also lends her comment a lightly humorous tinge. This is presumably unintentional on the part of the character, but surely not on the part of the implied author – in this way too, the statement may said to be double-voiced, as it is simultaneously an expression of the 'intention of the character' and of the 'refracted intention of the author' (Bakhtin, 1981: 324).

The opening statement briefly analysed above sets the tone for the entire first chapter, which presents Odenigbo as a benevolent eccentric and adopts a largely comical approach to the differences in class that separate the lecturer from his new houseboy, Ugwu. Already at this early stage, *Half of a Yellow Sun* slips in a large number of social and political statements, but these overshadow neither plot nor characterization, making Adichie's opening chapter something of a stylistic tour-de-force. Of the many techniques used to blend aesthetics with politics here, I will isolate four: the recurrence of underlexicalization, the reliance on schemas, the handling of vocatives, and the use of exemplification.

The first chapter of the novel, which follows 13-year-old Ugwu as he arrives in Odenigbo's house on the campus of the University of Nigeria in Nsukka, achieves the noteworthy feat of, on the one hand, allowing the reader to share in the character's sense of excitement and puzzlement and, on the other, poking gentle fun at the boy's unfamiliarity with the rules that operate in this newly discovered world. For instance, when Odenigbo gives Ugwu initial instructions on how to look after objects in the household, he shows the boy a 'metal box studded with dangerous-looking knobs' (Adichie, 2006b: 7) that even the most perceptive reader would do well to identify. The item is rapidly given a name – it is a 'radiogram' (p. 7) – but in the brief textual interval the reader is invited to experience Ugwu's cluelessness and suspicion first hand. The technique used to achieve this effect is called 'underlexicalization', and consists in 'withholding the usual term for something that is being described' (Fowler, 1996: 58), instead 'render[ing] by a circumlocution' 'the concept or object which is presumably unfamiliar to the perceiving subject' (1996: 217). In this particular case, underlexicalization not only promotes a sense of identification between focalizer and reader, but it also defa-miliarizes for the reader the object being described (p. 59). This is even more clearly illustrated a few pages later, when Ugwu observes that Odenigbo is 'wearing something that looked like a woman's coat' in the morning (Adichie, 2006b: 9). This phrase prompts the recognition that the garment the man is wearing – a dressing gown – is a category of clothing whose function and gender attribution rest on a form of social encoding that is far from evident to the outsider. Besides mildly ridiculing Odenigbo's 'foreign' attire, this instance of defamiliarization also encourages an unobtrusive interrogation of culture-specific norms of gender acceptability.

It is debatable whether the latter case of underlexicalization promotes as strong a type of focalizer-reader identification as the example involving the radio, for the fact that the dressing gown incident is set in the morning may suffice for the attentive reader to correctly identify the garment even before being informed that its owner 'was absently twirling the rope tied round his waist' (p. 9). If this particular occurrence of underlexicalization can be considered a borderline case, there are instances in which the technique more clearly tends to establish distance rather than proximity between focalizer and reader. For instance, when Odenigbo, having asked

Ugwu if he knows where the Congo is, briefly leaves the room and '[comes] back with a wide piece of paper that he unfold[s] and [lays] out on the dining table' (p. 10), the artefact is immediately identifiable by the reader as a map. In this passage where Odenigbo teaches Ugwu about geography and history, the boy's inexperience therefore seems to serve functions other than those already pointed out. First, the lecturer's use of a map on which he also shows the town of Nsukka gives the implied author an opportunity to situate the location of the action, presumably for the non-Nigerian reader; second, Ugwu's limited knowledge provides the occasion for an exposé on the 'rubbish' colonial narrative about Africa (p. 11). The interlude advances characterization by offering a condensed introduction to Odenigbo's progressive political views, but it also serves the novel's larger creative agenda by presenting an unambiguous alternative to the Eurocentric version of African history. Even more eloquent than the lecturer's factual historical corrections in this scene is Ugwu's puzzled reaction to his employer's mention of 'strange places' (p. 10) such as the Congo, which confront in passing contemporary Western attitudes that still tend to view the African continent as a monolithic whole. In this way, an ideological statement is unobtrusively embedded into the feelings of the focalizer and, ever so slowly, 'fact' is turned into 'truth'.

Even if one should be wary of generalizing across the diverse reading experiences of Adichie's novel, it can rather safely be asserted that, in the above scene, the reader's likely recognition of Odenigbo's 'wide piece of paper' as being a map rests on deductions triggered by a series of contextual elements – among these, the character's question to his houseboy, 'Do you know where Congo is?' (p. 10); the fact that the interrogative sentence occurs in a conversation during which the lecturer is imparting knowledge to his young servant; the reader's awareness that geographical information is displayed on a map, and so on. In cognitive linguistics, elements that cluster together in this manner to activate knowledge are known as 'headers', that is, triggers that invoke particular 'schemas'. Schemas, broadly speaking, are '[c]onnected bits of general cultural information based on verbal and non-verbal experience' (Wales, 2011: 376) – in other words, they form background knowledge that is stored and organized in people's minds, and which is used by individuals to interpret texts and situations.[2] Over the last few decades, schemas have enjoyed great popularity in cognitive stylistics, the area that focuses on readers' mental processing of texts. However, because schemas are in part determined by individuals' cultural and social experiences, even stylisticians working within the Euro-American mainstream have cautioned against indiscriminate applications of this theoretical concept in the elucidation of interpretative mechanisms (e.g., Jeffries, 2001: 337–9). One can easily see how, in the field of African literary studies, such (over-)generalizing hazards are further amplified. For example, in *Half of a Yellow Sun*, Ugwu's fear that 'somebody would bring palm wine' (Adichie, 2006b: 9) to the father of the girl he is attracted to is unlikely to be processed equally successfully by all types of readers – chances are the statement will be instantly decoded by those familiar with Igbo culture, for whom the 'bringing palm-wine' header is part of a culturally specific 'marriage proposal' schema, while others are likely to make an educated guess based on the narrative context.

Nonetheless, schema theory can be useful in analysing Adichie's book, since it *is* possible to piece together a profile that will fit the overwhelming majority of those reading the original version of the novel, regardless of their location or origin. All of them can indeed be assumed to be literate, to have a certain command of English resulting from exposure to Western forms of culture and education and, because they live in the globalized world of the twenty-first century, they can be expected to have a level of familiarity with technological advances and Western-influenced social conventions that may have eluded rural Igbo teenagers in the early 1960s. It is precisely on the vastly different schemas accessible to contemporary readers, on the one hand, and Ugwu, on the other, that much of the humour found in the first chapter of *Half of a Yellow Sun* relies. For instance, on the first evening of the boy's stay in Nsukka, his careful examination of the 'layers of cloth on top of [the bed]' (Adichie, 2006b: 9 – another case of underlexicalization), and his eventual decision to sleep on those sheets rather than between them, is likely to generate amusement for those whose knowledge of such household items is broader than the character's. Similarly, the boy's decision to remove pieces of roasted chicken from the fridge and put them in his shorts' pockets to give away to his relatives at a later stage (p. 8) will probably provoke a – perhaps slightly condescending – chuckle on the part of the knowledgeable reader.

Importantly, as often in Adichie's work, such humorous incidents serve more serious purposes as well. Ugwu's compulsion to secure the chicken in case it should disappear from the fridge is a revealing comment on the scarcity of such luxury items as meat in his own home; furthermore, Odenigbo's stocked-up fridge starkly contrasts with the deprivation suffered by all the members of his household during the war that breaks out a few years later. Other minor domestic incidents found in the opening chapter work in a similar manner. Among these is Ugwu's ironing and accidental burning of one of his employer's socks. Despite Odenigbo's initial annoyance at his houseboy's clumsiness – expressed in the form of a fleeting reprimand, forgotten as quickly as it is uttered (p. 14) – it is clear that the item has little value to the easy-going middle-class academic, and that Ugwu's panicked reaction and ensuing hour-long worry over the incident is entirely disproportionate. However, the excessiveness of Ugwu's response is somewhat put into perspective when Odenigbo has 'only ... two shirts and pairs of trousers' to wear after the family have fled to Abba during the Biafran conflict (p. 187).[3] Even earlier in the book, Odenigbo's relative affluence is rather starkly contrasted with the modest living conditions of Olanna's aunt and uncle in the northern city of Kano, where they share a single room with their adult daughter.

The ways in which different geographical and temporal settings found in the novel interact to generate meaning can be intuited relatively easily without recourse to the notion of schema. This begs the question whether the cognitive concept might in fact be no more than a handy – some might say fancy – shorthand term to describe a self-evident reading process. This statement may hold some truth if one's only intention is to perform a cursory analysis of isolated elements, but a more extended examination shows the value of schemas to lie elsewhere. By focusing attention on the mechanics of textual interpretation, they shed light on just how systematically *Half of a Yellow Sun* forces readers to reassess assumptions reinforced in the early pages of the book. For example, when the gardener Jomo tells Ugwu not to go near his bag because he 'might find a human head there' (Adichie, 2006b: 16), contextual knowledge allows readers to establish that the warning issued by the good-natured gardener, 'a small man with a tough, shrivelled body' (p. 15), is jocular and absurd – though, remarkably enough, Ugwu himself 'had not entirely doubted [him]'

(p. 16). However, schemas cease to operate according to prediction when, after the first massacres perpetrated in the North, Olanna flees Kano by train and is invited by a woman to look into a calabash, which is unexpectedly revealed to contain a 'child's head' (p. 82). The sudden materialization of the horrific image casually summoned by Jomo illustrates an important point: as political conflict degenerates into slaughter, expectations built on sound contextual knowledge are defeated, and what was previously barely conceivable for both readers and characters enters the realm of 'reality'. In more theoretical terms, this process of mental alteration is known as 'schema refreshment' (Cook, 1994) and consists in the 'restructuring or tuning of existing schemas, such that we see the world differently as a result' (Jeffries and McIntyre, 2010: 133). Interestingly, schema refreshment is a 'cognitive variant' (p. 133) of the better-known technique of defamiliarization discussed above, which bespeaks the extent to which Adichie's novel relies on taking its readers outside their cognitive and emotional comfort zones. Even if the notions of 'schema refreshment' and 'defamiliarization' are bound to present only an imperfect picture of a myriad of complex reading experiences, they do gesture towards a helpful conceptualization of the elusive potency of literature, which Adichie has expressed in less theoretical terms: 'Books are immensely powerful. Inherently powerful' (2012: 5).

If many literary texts wield their powers by compelling readers to interrogate some of their pre-existing schemas, they also inevitably take some ideologies for granted. This statement aims to draw attention not so much to the process of 'schema affirmation', found in 'literary texts' which 'reinforce our worldview by reflecting our [existing] schematic knowledge' (Jeffries and McIntyre, 2010: 133), as to the more puzzling fact that texts sometimes '[draw] you into a viewpoint that is not necessarily your own' (Jeffries, 2001: 339). The 'burnt sock' incident mentioned above can serve as a basis to illustrate this. As previously stated, readers are unlikely to entirely subscribe to Ugwu's assessment of the gravity of the situation, and they will therefore view with some measure of amusement the protagonist's concern over the damaged item, his blaming of the minor domestic incident on 'evil spirits' (Adichie, 2006b: 14) and his ensuing search for *arigbe*, the 'herb of forgiveness' (p. 17) that will 'soft[en] Master's heart' (p. 16). Still, they will also probably have a certain amount of sympathy for the boy, and will thus be unlikely to wish him to be dismissed because of his blunder. This benevolent desire not to see the protagonist lose his job rests on a basic assumption: that Ugwu has the 'good fortune' (p. 4) of working in Odenigbo's house. Remarkably, in different circumstances, Western readers in particular might have regarded a situation involving a deprived 13-year-old doing full-time domestic work for a middle-class man as a dubious instance of child labour.

The phrase 'child labour' is used here with deliberate provocativeness – the caricature only helps to emphasize a rather more subtle point regarding the workings of ideologies. As Jeffries has rightly pointed out, contemporary Western societies promote the belief that 'children should be looked after and are not required to work 13-hour days in factories' (2010a: 9). This ideology is so widely held in the West that it has become 'naturalized' – i.e., that it is made to appear '"common sense" to members of the community' (p. 9). However, Jeffries continues, this particular ideology may appear surprising to 'Victorian families who relied on children's wages', or to 'families in the developing world who do so today' (p. 9). The central point emphasized by the linguist is that different societies, across time and space, tend to naturalize different ideologies.[4] Such a culturally-based ideological divergence largely explains the slightly awkward conversation that took place between Chimamanda Ngozi Adichie and the American radio host Leonard Lopate shortly after the release of *Half of a Yellow Sun*:

Lopate: Odenigbo sends him [Ugwu] to school, but he calls Odenigbo 'Master', Odenigbo addresses him as 'my good man', and I wondered whether the idea of having a houseboy might not be uncomfortable for an intellectual and a revolutionary like Odenigbo …

Adichie: No, I don't think so at all. I think that what's important in this case is how he treats Ugwu, and he comes to treat him really as a son in some ways, as an adopted son, and so gives him opportunities and wants to bring him up, wants to educate him … I grew up the daughter of a professor – having a houseboy really wasn't having a slave; it was in some ways that you had a sibling who, yes, wasn't quite on the same level as you, but who was given respect, and who was educated, and who was given opportunities.

Lopate: Even though he does call Odenigbo 'Master'...
Adichie: Yes, but then, class is a part of all societies, isn't it?

(Adichie, 2006c)

The writer's reference to the common denominator of 'class' does more than adroitly skirt the interviewer's embarrassing question, as this notion holds the key to interpreting – and eventually legitimizing – the relationship between Odenigbo and Ugwu. However, it seems to me that even more significant insight can be gained by reversing the equation proposed by Adichie in the interview, and by wondering to what extent the bond between the master and his houseboy as it is presented in the novel does not in fact validate the author's *idiosyncratic* vision of class in her country of birth.

Before this line of argument is pursued, it must be emphasized that *Half of a Yellow Sun* does not gloss over the existence of levels of social privilege in Nigeria, and that it presents the lecturer's generosity towards his houseboy as the exception rather than the norm. Indeed, Ugwu rapidly comes to realize that 'He [is] not a normal houseboy' (Adichie, 2006b: 17), and that his colleagues in other households are given none of the material privileges and intellectual stimulation offered by his own master (p. 17). Ultimately, the contrast between the treatment enjoyed by Ugwu and the less enviable situation faced by his counterparts largely reinforces the idea that 'Odenigbo and Olanna raise [their houseboy] as a son' (Marx, 2008: 615) – a sentiment that pervades scholarly studies of Adichie's novel. Naturally, the fact that the book promotes the possibility of a filial relationship between the master and his servant does not mean that this ideology of social permeability will be unilaterally absorbed by readers; Lopate's reaction above is a case in point. Nevertheless, as Herman and Vervaeck suggest, '[i]f a narrative is convincing, the ideology it both conveys and helps reproduce stands a good chance of being accepted tacitly by the reader' (2007: 218). The stylistician's interest thus lies in pinpointing how narrative devices and literary techniques are deployed to naturalize these ideologies.

Once again, the exchange between Lopate and Adichie cited above provides a useful starting point. Says Lopate: 'Ugwu calls Odenigbo "Master", Odenigbo addresses him as "my good man".' This is not entirely correct, for even if the word 'Master' is indeed continually used to refer to the lecturer in the sections in which Ugwu serves as the main focalizer, the houseboy never directly addresses his employer as such in conversation, instead preferring, on his aunt's advice, the vocative 'sah' (Adichie, 2006b: 4), which reflects the West African pronunciation of 'sir'. The name given by Odenigbo to his houseboy, on the other hand, is accurately reported by Lopate, since the academic repeatedly uses the English phrase 'my good man' when talking to his employee in Igbo. This distinctive vocative has already attracted the attention of at least one critic, who sees in the term an intertextual echo of Robinson Crusoe's reference to his servant as 'my man Friday' (Ngwira, 2012: 47). Whether or not one subscribes to this interpretation, Odenigbo's use of 'my good man' does to some extent betray his 'internalization of Western education' (Ngwira, 2012: 47), if only because the old-fashioned phrase marks a codeswitch to the colonial language. Interestingly, while the term of address places Ugwu in a position of social inferiority, it simultaneously connotes a form of respect, as it is typically used when speaking to adult males rather than young teenagers. The vocative therefore recognizes the existence of class boundaries even as it challenges established social conventions. Odenigbo further defeats expectations associated with his rank by inviting his houseboy to call him by his first name:

> 'Odenigbo. Call me Odenigbo.'
> Ugwu stared at him doubtfully. 'Sah?'
> 'My name is not Sah. Call me Odenigbo.'
> 'Yes, sah.'
> 'Odenigbo will always be my name. *Sir* is arbitrary. You could be the *sir* tomorrow.'
> 'Yes, sah – Odenigbo.'
>
> (Adichie, 2006b: 13, italics in original)

By asking his servant to address him as an equal, Odenigbo acts in accordance with his progressive convictions. His mention that Ugwu 'could be the *sir* tomorrow' also attests to his belief in class mobility and, as Ngwira notes, this prediction anticipates the boy's future status as an intellectual and the author of 'The Book' about the Biafran War (2012: 48). Perhaps even more striking in the above passage is the fact that Ugwu initially resists such possibility of social ascension. Despite two attempts at complying with his master's request – both of which end in the comical juxtaposition 'sah – Odenigbo' (Adichie, 2006b: 13, 16) – he can never bring himself to call his master by his first name. For the young Ugwu, the route to social prestige rather lies in emphasizing his employer's respectability in front of members of the working class:

> Ugwu really preferred *sah* [to Odenigbo], the crisp power behind the word, and when two men from the Works Department came a few days later to install shelves in the corridor, he told them that they would have to wait for Sah to come home; he himself could not sign the white paper with typewritten words. He said *Sah* proudly.
> 'He's one of these village houseboys', one of the men said dismissively ...
>
> (13, italics in original)

Ugwu's attempt at vicariously drawing on his master's prestige results in his stigmatization as a rural servant. The incident exposes the boy's idea of social sophistication as illusory and, in the process, mocks his exaggerated deference to his employer's status. Importantly, the episode also draws the boy's attention to the usefulness of mastering the art of writing for, as the rest of the passage makes clear, it is above all his unfamiliarity with the simple form-signing protocol that attracts the workers' scorn. No doubt the event is to be regarded as one of the many steps in Ugwu's coming of age, but its significance also lies in the way it encourages readers to distance themselves from the boy's rigid class-conscious worldview. Indeed, the scene makes a social comment *on* the character as much as it apprehends the situation *through* his point of view. This, I would argue, is facilitated by a shift from internal to external focalization: the narratorial voice temporarily dissociates itself from the perspective of the protagonist when it reports that 'He said *Sah* proudly' (p. 13). Even if it is impossible to isolate the narrator's and the character's voices on a purely formal linguistic basis in this short sentence, one can nevertheless obtain indications as to the type of focalization employed by performing a simple narratological test: that which consists in rewriting this third-person passage in the first person. Following Shlomith Rimmon-Kenan's concise instructions, 'If this is feasible – the segment is internally focalized, if not – the focalization is external' (2002: 76–7).

The test is not foolproof, for a statement that would read 'I said *Sah* proudly' in the context of the incident narrated above can only be discounted in 'elusive terms of verisimilitude' (2002: 77). Still, Ugwu's assessment of his own behaviour in such a clear-headed and mildly ironic manner looks improbable enough to conclude that the original statement smacks of narratorial intervention.

In short, vocatives are devices used in the novel in two different ways: first, they (predictably) give indications about the characters' relationship with each other and about their broader views of social conventions; second, they are one of many elements used by the narrator to exploit the possibilities of the polyphonic text. The latter point is worth emphasizing, as it allows for a reassessment of the final words of the novel, which make up the last segment of the series of fragments entitled 'The Book': 'Ugwu writes his dedication last: *For Master, my good man*' (Adichie, 2006b: 433, italics in original). Even if the final pages of the novel contain several clues that Ugwu, and not would-be novelist Richard, is indeed the author of 'The Book', it is only at this point that the houseboy is unambiguously revealed to be the writer figure who has been bearing witness to the history of Biafra in the vignettes interspersed between the chapters of the novel. Understandably, this crucial narrative twist has been copiously commented on by critics. For instance, some scholars see Ugwu's emergence as a writer as 'marking the exit of the Western subject [Richard] from narrative control' (Novak, 2008: 40; see also Walder, 2010: 132, for a similar comment). Others, in line with this view, additionally regard the disclosure of the real author of the historical narrative as a 'surprising reversal' (Palmberg and Holst Petersen, 2011: 99) similar to that which occurs at the end of Achebe's *Things Fall Apart* (2001 [1958]: 152), where the District Commissioner is revealed to have plans to write a book entitled *The Pacification of the Primitive Tribes of the Lower Niger* (see also Hawley, 2008: 21; Whittaker, 2011: 115–16; Simoes da Silva, 2012: 463–4). Adopting a more class-oriented perspective on Ugwu's development into a writer, another scholar observes that the novel 'summon[s] a most unlikely subject, a houseboy, to make visible an alternative subjectivity' (Ouma, 2012: 45). What all these stimulating readings have in common is their insistence on notions of disruption and change within the narrative – they speak of 'exit[s]', 'reversal[s]', 'alternative[s]'. Such substitution of perspectives is also perceptible in the vocative used in the second part of the dedication, '*my good man*', which appropriates the phrase used by the lecturer to address his houseboy and thereby signals that Ugwu, like Odenigbo before him, 'is now a member of Biafra's *intelligentsia*' (Simoes da Silva, 2012: 463, italics in original).

A closer look at the polyphonic mechanisms of the text allows for an adjustment of these accounts. While the houseboy's reference to his mentor indeed represents a handing over of authority from one man to the other, the phrase 'my good man' above all stands out as a direct invocation of Odenigbo's voice. As Bakhtin reminds us, '[l]anguage is not a neutral medium that passes freely and easily into the private property of the speaker's intentions; it is populated – overpopulated – with the intentions of others' (1981: 294). Therefore, even under Ugwu's pen, the phrase 'my good man' is bound to remain laden with some of the values it had acquired in Odenigbo's speech, making the houseboy's rise to authorship appear not only as an actualization of the fact that 'the subaltern can, and in fact should, speak' (Krishnan, 2013: 199), but also as a triumph of the moral and social standards embodied by the lecturer himself. This is significant for, after honestly interrogating the naivety and potential hypocrisy of Odenigbo's intellectualism, the novel eventually ends where it started – that is, with a celebration of the nurturing and enabling role of the liberal, academic middle class in the process of social equality and postcolonial resistance in Africa. Even if this position is ethically defendable, probably even laudable in the eyes of many, it nonetheless remains an ideology that has been naturalized in the pages of the book. To emphasize the relative nature of this particular social worldview, suffice it to recall Ngũgĩ's indictment of the same class of Western-educated, English-speaking intellectuals in his *Decolonising the Mind* (1986), or the ungenerous attitudes of the majority of academics towards their domestic helps within *Half of a Yellow Sun* itself.

The other half of Ugwu's dedication, '*For Master*', is also worth examining through a polyphonic lens. With the exception of one instance where Ugwu's aunt uses the word in direct speech to refer to Odenigbo in his absence (Adichie, 2006b: 4), the term 'Master' is found only in narrative passages in the sections focusing on Ugwu. The appearance of the term at the end of the book therefore not only recalls the perspective of Ugwu's younger focalizer-self, but it is also inextricably linked to the *narrator*'s voice.[5] Significantly, then,

Ugwu's first use of the term in the 'real' world of the novel aligns his speech with the narrator's and cements the link between the two perspectives. In this way, the dedication 'For Master, my good man', which at first sight stands out for its almost oxymoronic quality (calling attention as it does to the different, mutually exclusive social statuses of the younger and the older Ugwu), in fact partakes of the alignment, in a single polyphonic statement, of what Bakhtin (1981: 304) calls three different 'axiological belief systems' (that is, ideological viewpoints): Odenigbo's, Ugwu's, and the narrator's. Polyphony, in other words, eventually works to promote a specific, single-minded vision of Nigerian society that is most likely in line with the author's own.

If this social worldview finds expression through some of the novel's narrative developments, it is also supported by specific stylistic choices. These techniques often allow ideologies to be carried across effectively because they rely on pragmatic inferences rather than purely semantic interpretations. One such device, exemplification, plays a role in the naturalization of the 'houseboy' ideology introduced above. It has already been established that Odenigbo's intellectual and material generosity, as well as his invitation to be addressed on a first-name basis by Ugwu, contributes to enhancing the representation of the domestic worker's position as one of privilege and opportunity, rather than one of servitude and exploitation. This ideology, I wish to argue, is also reinforced by passages such as the following: 'He [Ugwu] opened his eyes, overcome by a new wonder, and looked around to make sure it was all real. To think that he would sit on these sofas, polish this slippery-smooth floor, wash these gauzy curtains' (Adichie, 2006b: 5). The first sentence unambiguously establishes Ugwu's sense of marvel at what he perceives to be the luxuriousness of his surroundings – the impression, which the reader is invited to share, is only tempered later when the narrative, focalized through the wealthy Olanna (reflecting on her snobbish mother's opinion of Odenigbo's house), describes it as 'basic' (p. 35, italics in original). Stylistically more elusive is the second sentence, which contains a list of three items that are separated by commas and which display roughly equivalent grammatical structures (either a verb followed by a noun phrase acting as direct object, or a verb followed by a prepositional phrase acting as adverbial). The fact that these exemplifying elements are separated only by commas, with no final coordinating conjunction such as 'and', creates a potential structural ambiguity, in the sense that the list of different items is not syntactically distinct from a construction of equivalence built via apposition. To clarify this point with a non-literary example: the above instance of exemplification is not structurally different from an appositional structure such as *'the rock of our family, the love of my life, the nation's next first lady'*, used by Barack Obama to refer to one single person – his wife Michelle – in his victory speech after the 2008 American presidential elections (Jeffries, 2010a: 73, italics in original). The point is not that Adichie's sentence is in any way semantically ambiguous, for it is clear that 'sit[ting] on these sofas', 'polish[ing] this slippery-smooth floor', and 'wash[ing] these gauzy curtains' are distinct activities. However, as Jeffries has shown, this type of exemplification without a final conjunction can be used for rhetorical purposes. She illustrates her point with an example from Martin Luther King's famous 'I Have a Dream' speech: 'With this faith we will be able *to work together, to pray together, to struggle together, to go to jail together, to stand up for freedom together*, knowing that we will be free one day' (Jeffries, 2010a: 72, italics in original). As Jeffries aptly notices, the items in this list are 'not entirely distinct': 'going to jail or praying may both be one aspect of the "struggle", and standing up for freedom is surely a summary of all the others' (p. 72). In the above-mentioned example from *Half of a Yellow Sun*, the three enumerated elements are somewhat similarly associated. They all contain references to domestic items ('sofas', 'floor', and 'curtains') – that is, entities that belong to the same semantic field and that are easily associated as parts of a whole. Meanwhile, the equivalence between the verb phrases contained in the list is encouraged by the absence of a coordinating conjunction. As a result, the leisurely activity of 'sit[ting] on these sofas' is put on the same level as the houseboy's chores ('polish[ing] this slippery-smooth floor', 'wash[ing] these gauzy curtains'); by pragmatic association, these tasks are presented as being equally desirable as 'sit[ting] on these sofas'. Consequently, it is strongly suggested – without being directly stated – that Ugwu will engage in a range of pleasurable activities in Odenigbo's magnificent home.

If exemplification can be a covert carrier of ideology, its stylistic potential can also be exploited for ironic effect. This is the case in the second segment dedicated to 'The Book', in which the (as yet anonymous) writer, then still assumed to be Richard, is shown discussing the colonizers' view of the country that would become Nigeria: 'The British preferred the North. The heat there was pleasantly dry ... The humid South, on the other hand, was full of mosquitoes and animists and disparate tribes' (Adichie, 2006b: 115). Unlike the list discussed above, the instance of exemplification 'mosquitoes and animists and disparate tribes' cannot be associated with an appositional structure, considering the double presence of the coordinating conjunction 'and', which suggests accumulation. However, the text explores a related pragmatic expectation that has already played a role in the first example, namely that lists are usually *'homogenous referential ensemble[s]'* (Dubois and Sankoff, 2001: 285, italics in original) – in other words, that they display some internal cohesion. Since the first item is 'mosquitoes', which are parasites that evoke human discomfort and, in the West African context, illness, the list triggers the pragmatic inference that 'animists' and 'disparate tribes' are also nuisances and inferior forms of life found in excess in the South of the country. An ironic effect is thus achieved by exploiting the dialogic potential of the novelistic form: words that are loaded with colonial undertones – 'animists' and 'disparate tribes' – are given an additional layer of meaning by being compiled into a single indiscriminate, and therefore nonsensical list. This incoherence is used to mock the dubious logic of colonial discourses, and to denounce the dehumanizing treatment of African peoples at the hands of the British colonizers.

This derisive effect is enhanced by the mention that the South of the country is 'full of' these undesirable parasites. This expression undeniably betrays the colonizers' perspective and ideology, as do evaluative phrases such as 'pleasantly dry'. The colonial oppressors' voice is therefore present within the narrator's account of 'The Book', a fact that is even more visibly marked in the explanations that follow the passage quoted above:

> The Yoruba were the largest [tribe] in the Southwest. In the Southeast, the Igbo lived in small republican communities. They were non-docile and worryingly ambitious. Since they did not have the good sense to have kings, the British created 'warrant chiefs', because indirect rule cost the Crown less.
>
> (Adichie, 2006b: 115)

Clearly, the idea that the Igbo are 'non-docile' and 'worryingly ambitious' is a projection of what the *British* thought of this people, as
is the fact that Igbo 'did not have the good sense to have kings'.
Interestingly, these observations, along with the fact that 'indirect
rule cost the Crown less', do not reflect the official position of the
colonial authorities, but rather expose the hidden political and
economic motivations behind the imperial enterprise. Since these
thoughts are refracted through the fictional author (or the novel's
narrator), who almost certainly does not subscribe to the views being
denounced, the above passage is clearly a double-voiced structure, of
the type identified by Bakhtin as a 'hybrid construction': 'an utterance that belongs, by its grammatical (syntactic) and compositional
markers, to a single speaker, but that actually contains mixed within
it two utterances, two speech manners, two styles, two "languages",
two semantic and axiological belief systems' (1981: 304). Of prime
importance to the stylistic effect produced by intentional novelistic
hybrids such as this is 'the collision between differing points of view
on the world that are embedded in these forms' (p. 360). In other
words, two axiological belief systems are 'set against each other dia-
logically' (p. 360), and it is from this clash that the irony emerges.

More recent linguistic theories also subscribe to such a fundamentally polyphonic view of irony. As Elizabeth Black suggests in her
discussion of Wilson and Sperber's work, '[t]he ironist ... echoes an
opinion while dissociating herself from it' (Black, 2006: 114). This
'dissociative' aspect is not always detected by readers whose preconceptions intersect with the views being mocked (p. 119), but *Half
of a Yellow Sun* deploys specific stylistic and narrative techniques to
maximize the chances of the irony displayed in 'The Book' being carried across successfully. One device used to achieve this is the nonsensical association of 'mosquitoes and animists and disparate tribes'
discussed above; another is the inclusion of the harrowing image of
the child's head in the calabash following the massacres perpetrated
by the northern Hausa (Adichie, 2006b: 82) before reporting on the
British opinion that Northerners are 'superior' to, and more 'civilized' than, the Southern ethnic groups (p. 115).

While one can often assert which statements in the segments
devoted to 'The Book' are intended as echoes of colonial discourses,
it is all but impossible to disentangle the voice of the fictional writer
of the historical narrative from that of the third-person narrator of

the novel, who introduces the views of the author of 'The Book' using expressions such as 'He discusses' (p. 115), 'He argues' (p. 204), and 'He writes' (p. 258). In spite of this, it can be assumed that at least some level of hybridization is to be attributed to the fictional writer figure, if only because no such similar ironic effect pervades the chapters of the novel chiefly focalized through the younger Ugwu, Olanna or Richard. Interestingly, the heavily ironic style of 'The Book' is one of the novel's earliest clues that the author of this imaginary work is *not* Richard, the English protagonist of *Half of a Yellow Sun*. Even though this character is an aspiring novelist, the only prose of his that readers are invited to experience directly is some rather mediocre journalistic work, which he himself perceives as a 'temporary' (p. 55) occupation until 'he [writes] that brilliant novel' (p. 55):

> It is imperative to remember that the first time the Igbo people were massacred, albeit on a much smaller scale than what has recently occurred, was in 1945. That carnage was precipitated by the British colonial government when it blamed the Igbo people for the national strike, banned Igbo-published newspapers, and generally encouraged anti-Igbo sentiment. The notion of the recent killings being the product of 'age-old' hatred is therefore misleading. The tribes of the North and the South have long had contact, at least as far back as the ninth century, as some of the magnificent beads discovered at the historic Igbo-Ukwu site attest.

(p. 166, italics in original)

This excerpt from Richard's work is representative of its general tone. Even if the anti-colonial point put across is similar to that developed in 'The Book', the above passage contains no traces of ironic distance; it neatly isolates voices that do not reflect the author-character's own stance using quotation marks ('age-old'), and is largely consistent in its use of register, unlike the fragment reporting on 'The Book', which regularly lapses into informal discourse (e.g., 'they did not have the good sense to have kings': p. 115). The most noticeable difference between the two extracts, therefore, is not one in political content but one in style. The first part of Richard's article, in particular ('It is imperative ... misleading'), bears such close resemblance to a textbook example of politically committed journalism that it can be considered an occurrence of what Bakhtin calls 'stylization' – 'an artistic representation of another's linguistic style' (1981: 362). Like the intentional novelistic hybrids discussed above, stylizations conceal multiple voices, in the sense that they always include the voice 'that *represents* (that is, the linguistic consciousness of the stylizer)' – here, the third-person narrator – and 'the one that is *represented*, which is stylized' (p. 362, italics in original) – here, the character-author. Unlike the hybridized account of 'The Book', the stylization technique works *at the expense* of the fictional writer featured in the text. Even if Richard's journalistic speech is not caricatured to the extent of being obviously parodic, it is stylistically conventional, largely monologic in its uncompromising condemnation of the British colonial power, and far from possessing the bitingly ironic tone lent to the author of 'The Book'. The point, in short, is that Richard is simply not a very good writer, a fact whose implications extend well beyond his inability to produce an aesthetically sophisticated text.

Based on this observation, what I wish to argue is that, throughout the novel and in increasing measure, the English character is coupled with different types of registers typically associated with monologic and authoritarian discourses. These are symptomatic of his inability to acquire the critical distance needed to produce an engaged, yet sound and level-headed, account of the Biafran War. Put together, these multiple associations between the protagonist and discourses of authority contribute to discrediting his competence as a postcolonial intellectual, thereby legitimizing one of the novel's key ideological claims, namely that '[t]he war isn't [Richard's] story to tell' (Adichie, 2006b: 425). In the final part of this chapter I will, first of all, trace how precise linguistic choices work in combination with narrative incidents to put across this particular view. Then, I will consider how the novel, by recurrently zooming in on the meaning of the personal pronoun 'we', often used by Richard to refer to the people of Biafra, comments on issues of inclusion within (and exclusion from) Biafran identity. Finally, I will discuss some of the critically disputed aspects of the novel's conclusion, which, as already mentioned, legitimizes the older Ugwu's position as the recorder of Biafran history.

In the above excerpt from Richard's article, the adjective 'magnificent' alerts the reader to the character's use of a potentially questionable register. Admittedly, Richard's well-intentioned piece contrasts with the overtly racist response given by the editor of the English newspaper to which he sends his article, who would rather find out if Nigerians 'mutter[ed] any tribal incantations while they did the killings', or '[ate] body parts like they did in the Congo' (Adichie, 2006b: 167). However, the protagonist's fervent advocacy of all things Igbo clearly epitomizes the flip side of the colonial coin. His passion for ancient Igbo-Ukwu art, which he consistently describes in overblown such terms as 'stunning' (p. 111) and 'marvellous' (p. 111), is imbued with 'noble savage' sentiments that critic Madhu Krishnan, following Graham Huggan, has rightly identified as a manifestation of the 'postcolonial' or 'anthropological exotic' (Krishnan, 2012: 31). As Krishnan has convincingly shown, Richard's 'fetishization of the [Igbo-Ukwu] pots' betrays his yearning for 'the conceptual purity of an abstract African identity' (2012: 31), a desire also expressed in his attraction to his Igbo girlfriend Kainene, whom his mind associates with the Igbo-Ukwu artefacts on at least two occasions (Krishnan, 2012: 33–4; Novak, 2008: 40). The most explicit clues that Kainene, like the pots, 'stand[s] in for the land' (Krishnan, 2012: 31) are found only at a relatively late stage in the novel (Adichie, 2006b: 310, 407), but the link between the continent and the female character is suggested far earlier in the text. After the young woman has just sarcastically called Richard 'a modern-day explorer of the Dark Continent' (p. 62), the very next paragraph depicts him as '*explor[ing]* the angles of her collarbones and her hips' (63, my italics), shortly after which he associates his sexual desire for his girlfriend with an attempt to '*discover* something that he knew he never would' (p. 65, my italics). These terms, especially in the context set up by Kainene's description of Richard, collectively recall the language typically used in colonial travel writing, leaving little doubt as to the narrator's sentiments towards the English character. As much is also made clear by the mention, on the same page, that Richard finds Kainene 'inscrutable' (p. 65), an adjective bound to summon up associations with Conrad's *Heart of Darkness* (Krishnan, 2012: 32).[6] Remarkably, these words occur in the narrative several dozen pages ahead of the scene where the poet Okeoma overtly accuses Richard of reproducing condescending colonial attitudes towards Africa (Adichie, 2006b: 111); the narrator, in short, ever so subtly lends weight to the Igbo character's allegations before they have even been formulated. In addition to these inconspicuous lexical clues, the novel includes

several narrative episodes that similarly position the English protagonist as a colonial explorer of sorts. A case in point is Richard's
attendance of a traditional festival during which he writes down his
observations in a notebook – a gesture strongly reminiscent of early
anthropological methods. Language and narrative occurrences, in
sum, work hand in hand to problematize Richard's admiration for
Igbo culture and, as will become clear in what follows, his later
claim for Biafran identity.

Because Richard's brand of exoticization involves romanticization,
it is hardly surprising to see his early politically committed writing
morph into more insistently *'flowery'* prose (p. 306, italics in original). When Kainene's friend Colonel Madu asks the Englishman to
write articles to support the Biafran war effort, the first piece that he
produces is described as follows:

> His first article was about the fall of Onitsha. He wrote that the
> Nigerians had tried many times to take this ancient town but the
> Biafrans fought valiantly, that hundreds of popular novels had
> been published here before the war, that the thick, sad smoke of
> the burning Niger Bridge had risen like a defiant elegy.
>
> (p. 305)

The second sentence in this excerpt, introduced by 'He wrote', is
modelled on some of the passages reporting on the writing of 'The
Book'. Even if this somewhat mischievously tricks the reader into
thinking that Richard is the author of the historical fragments, the
tone of the Englishman's piece once again contrasts with the wry
irony displayed in 'The Book'. This time, uncompromising rhetoric
is replaced with an admiring assessment of the Biafran army's brav-
ery in battle ('valiantly') and a wistful mention of 'thick, sad smoke'
rising like a 'defiant elegy' – an expression evocative of the lyrical
mode. Crucially, both the smoke rising from the bridge and the
contemplative manner in which the image is evoked situate Richard
as an *outsider* observing the events from a safe distance, rather than
a direct participant in the action.[7] That this distance fuels a sense
of romanticization is also suggested by the fact that, while writing his piece on the fall of Onitsha, Richard revealingly 'imagine[s]
himself as the young Winston Churchill covering Kitchener's battle at Omdurman, a battle of superior versus inferior arms, except

that, unlike Churchill, he sided with the moral victor' (p. 306). The comparison with Winston Churchill is, of course, hardly incidental. Not only does Richard share the older man's family name (p. 36) and does he greatly admire him (p. 236), but Winston Churchill, in addition to being a war correspondent, was also a soldier and, most famously, a politician – two types of figures typically associated with discourses of authority. Under the guise of his naive romanticism, Richard is therefore depicted as a potentially overbearing figure with a strictly authoritarian worldview, whose rigidity also manifests itself in his unwavering support of Biafra. The fact that he congratulates himself on choosing the side of the 'moral victor' is symptomatic of his fervent and uncompromising belief in the righteousness of Biafran ideology; his steadfastness, significantly, leaves no room for examining the potential shortcomings of the actual realization of the Biafran project of independence.

The association between Richard and the figure of the soldier-politician finds its most eloquent expression in a scene set much later during the war, which sees him leading two American journalists around refugee camps. Although one is likely to share Richard's irritation at the obscenity of the journalists' comments – for example, seeing starving children roasting rats, one of the men observes that 'Niggers are never choosy about what they eat' (p. 370) – one cannot fail to perceive some truth in one of the journalists' remark that Richard's denial of the existence of a Biafran 'propaganda machine' makes him sound like 'Radio Biafra' (p. 371), the station that relayed the views of the authorities led by the Biafran leader Colonel Ojukwu. In line with this, the novel itself goes as far as suggesting, albeit indirectly, that Richard has become a type of Ojukwu figure. Indeed, when one of the journalists insistently enquires about the death of an Italian oil worker, Richard is lent the following exasperated thought: 'Thousands of Biafrans were dead, and this man wanted to know if there was anything new about one dead white man. Richard would write about this, the rule of Western journalism: One hundred dead black people equal one dead white person' (p. 369). This consideration bears more than a passing resemblance to Ojukwu's Ahiara Declaration, in which he virulently denounced the Western world's indifference to the millions of Biafran dead, and the commotion that broke out after 18 Westerners were 'caught' by the Biafran troops: 'For 18 white men, Europe is aroused. What have they said about our millions? ... How many black dead make one missing white?' (Ojukwu, 1969: 5–6).

What the novel appears to question is not the validity of Ojukwu's and Richard's shared concern, but rather the latter's right to appoint himself as spokesperson for the Biafran nation while continuing to enjoy the privileges of his racial and cultural background. This also seems to be the message conveyed by his temporary retreat into another type of typically authoritative discourse: that of religion. To Richard, 'considering the fall of Port Harcourt', where he lives, is a 'blasphemous' thought (Adichie, 2006b: 309); he further vows not to bring up in conversation a move away from the city to 'absolve himself from the blasphemy' (p. 309). Later, he revealingly reflects on people's betrayal of Biafra as a 'sacrilege' (p. 314). Interestingly, these religious terms do not denote Godly devotion as much as they refer to the unacceptable violation of sacrosanct principles, of which Richard appoints himself guardian, much like Eugene Achike in *Purple Hibiscus*. The religious and the political are linked on an even more explicit level with the appearance of a minor character, Inatimi, whose 'god', we are told, 'was Biafra': 'His was a fervent faith in the cause' (p. 319). The fact that Richard 'resent[s]' the man (p. 319) – ostensibly because Kainene admires him – seems to indicate that the Englishman aspires to more than participation in the Biafran community, but rather makes an illicit claim for exclusive ownership of Biafranness.

The novel exposes this position as not only illegitimate, but also ultimately untenable, by disenfranchising its English character towards the very end. After Kainene has disappeared while trading across enemy lines, a distraught Richard cannot contain the jealousy that he has been harbouring towards Colonel Madu ever since his first meeting with the man. As Richard is about to hit the soldier, the following intention flashes across his mind: 'he wanted to say, come back here and tell me if you ever laid your filthy black hand on her [Kainene]' (p. 430). Semantically speaking, the adjective 'black' is entirely unnecessary, and it unmistakably indicates that Richard, when overcome with the most visceral feelings of jealousy and grief, reverts to the racism that characterizes hegemonic Western attitudes towards Africa (see Novak, 2008: 40, Cooper, 2008: 147, for similar interpretations). As for the adjective 'filthy', it can only be understood as metaphorical but, similarly, its combination with the term

'black' evokes the stereotype that depicts black men as sexual preda-
tors. This implicature is triggered effortlessly. In Bakhtinian fashion,
the implied author simply 'makes use of words that are already populated with the social intentions of others and compels them to serve
[her] own intentions' (Bakhtin, 1981, 299–300).

Thus, in just two short adjectives and one swing of the fist,
Richard's self-proclaimed African identity is revealed to be a fragile,
fabricated construction. In the process, the larger ideological message
of the narrative emerges: no matter how strong one's desire to belong
to a community, the forces of collective history and racial prejudice
can never be entirely escaped. Somewhat ironically, in resisting the
colonization of Biafranness by a socially privileged white individual,
the novel might be seen to endorse the essentialist views of cultural
and racial identity that have justified colonialism itself. In keeping
with this, Brenda Cooper has maintained that Richard's eventual
exclusion from the Biafran narrative amounts to a reversion to an
'intrinsic, ethnic view' of culture (2008: 147). This point is debatable, in the sense that the impulse behind the novel is precisely to
suggest that identities – be they appropriative or exclusionary – are
not shaped against a blank historical canvas. Biafran secession was
but the result of a long and complex colonial history, a fact that
exposes the naivety of Richard's belief that '[h]e would be Biafran in
a way he could never have been Nigerian' because 'he was here at
the beginning; he had shared in the birth' (Adichie, 2006b: 168). No
individual, the novel intimates, can shed centuries of history to fulfil
a personal need to belong.

Significantly, the legitimacy to speak for Biafra that is withdrawn
from Richard is carried over to Ugwu. Whereas the narrative portrays
the Englishman sinking into an incoherent entanglement of authoritarian types of speech, the young houseboy undergoes the reverse
process and develops a capacity to gauge different discourses from a
critical vantage point. In the early stages of the novel, he is presented
as an avid eavesdropper who fantasizes about having Odenigbo's
knowledge and intellectual standing, and who 'imagine[s] himself
speaking swift English, talking to rapt imaginary guests, using words
like *decolonize* and *pan-African*, moulding his voice after Master's'
(p. 20, italics in original). Even much later in the narrative, his
understanding of the war still imperfect, Ugwu tries to impress his
girlfriend by 'repeat[ing] Master's words ... with authority, as though

they were his' (p. 295). The domestic servant starts out by mimicking his master's words undiscerningly, in the hope of capitalizing on their prestige; during the conflict, he naively becomes enraptured with Biafran ideals to the extent that he wishes to join the fighters (p. 179). It is only towards the end of the novel, after he has been faced with the realities of the war as a soldier, that he loses interest in the 'shabby theatrics of the war reports, the voice that forced morsels of invented hope down people's throats' (p. 399). With this rejection of the hegemonic discourse of the authorities comes the development of his ability to apprehend the multifaceted nature of reality, and reflect on it using his own 'orchestration of discourses'. This dialogism finds expression, as already mentioned, in the ironic passages from 'The Book' examined above, but also in the poem 'Were You Silent When We Died?', which Ugwu 'models after one of Okeoma's' texts (p. 375).

The poem is the result of Ugwu's earlier frustrated attempts at drawing inspiration from the Igbo poet in the shaping of his own voice (p. 397). Ugwu's positioning as heir to the writer, who was killed in battle during the war, carries all the more symbolic weight as all of Okeoma's works were lost during the conflict (p. 391). More generally, Ugwu's piece also gives insight into the novel's conception of the links between history and literature. The insertion of a poetic text in 'The Book', until then assumed to be largely historical in orientation, signals a blurring between the figures of the historian and the artist also effected by Adichie elsewhere (see Tunca, 2012: 245–6). That the novelist intends this cross-disciplinary connection to be perceived as a metafictional comment on her own writerly practice can only be indirectly inferred, but what can far less controversially be stated is that Adichie, in *Half of a Yellow Sun*, ultimately invests her writer character with the moral authority to recount the history of Biafra. In this respect, the itinerary followed in the novel by the title of the poem, 'Were You Silent When We Died?', is highly symbolic of this legitimation. This sentence, first uttered by Colonel Madu in the form 'They simply cannot remain silent while we die' (p. 305), is appropriated as 'The World Was Silent When We Died' by Richard, who intends to use it as the title of his work about 'Biafra's difficult victory' in the war (p. 374). The Englishman then mentions these words to Ugwu, who is 'haunted' (p. 396) by them and reuses them for 'The Book', while also rephrasing them as a question in the title of his poem. The interrogative form carries its own significance, as it directly addresses Western readers, who are thereby encouraged to reflect on the shallowness of their fleetingly empathetic responses to a war followed only in glossy magazines and behind television screens (p. 375).

Above all, the boomerang trajectory of Madu's formulation seems to embody the novel's stance on the ownership of the first-person plural pronoun 'we' as it is used in relation to Biafra. Since this grammatical word is a deictic – that is, a word whose reference is determined by the context in which it appears – its meaning is often subject to either interpretation or debate. In the novel, the pronoun 'we', along with its object form 'us' and its possessive equivalent 'our', is foregrounded an almost dizzying number of times, whether by means of italicization or through its appearance in the characters' own reflections. For instance, when Kainene takes Richard to her house and casually remarks that 'I did wish it was closer to the sea, so we could have a better view', Richard is overjoyed 'because she had said *we*. *We* meant both of them; she had included him' (p. 76, italics in original). In a different situation, Ugwu tells his mother that '"We use [toothpaste] to clean our teeth." Ugwu felt proud saying *we*' (p. 91, italics in original). In these examples, the metalinguistic use of 'we' – that is, its occurrence as an item whose meaning is commented on – reflects the protagonists' desire for, respectively, emotional and social inclusion. Unsurprisingly, as the narrative progresses, the pronoun 'we' acquires additional connotations. A case in point is Kainene's response to Richard's mention of his wish to entitle his book 'The World Was Silent When We Died':

> She arched her eyebrows. 'We? The world was silent when *we* died?'
>   'I'll make sure to note that the Nigerian bombs carefully avoided anybody with a British passport', he said.
>
> (p. 374, italics in original)

The forceful practicality of Richard's reply in fact conceals fallacious reasoning. Even if his presence in Biafra exposes him to the air raids of the Nigerian army, somewhat qualifying his earlier enjoyment of relative safety, this fact alone cannot be used to legitimize his appropriation of Biafran identity. Indeed, the danger mentioned by the protagonist also applies to foreign aid workers in refugee camps or, to cite an example mentioned in the novel, to Count Von Rosen, the 'Swedish aristocrat who bombed Nigerian targets with his own small plane' (pp. 309–10). Disregarding any possible counterarguments, Richard seems bent on using 'we' and 'our' to perform his own inclusion within Biafran identity. His mention of 'our new forest markets' (p. 312), or his reference to the 'saboteurs in our midst' (p. 313), all appear to express his deep-seated belief in his own legitimacy.

Yet a closer look at the text invalidates this assertion. When Richard is appointed as the two American journalists' guide around the refugee camps, his aversion to the men is obvious from the start. The encounter is recounted as follows:

> When he had met them at the airport and handed them their passes and told them he would be their guide and that the Biafran government welcomed them, he had disliked the redhead's expression of scornful amusement. It was as if he were saying, *You are speaking for the Biafrans?*
>
> (p. 369, italics in original)

At first sight, this passage simply seems to illustrate Richard's recurring irritation at not being recognized as a legitimate spokesperson for the Biafran 'cause'. But what is easily missed in this excerpt is the implication of the precise words used to formulate Richard's thoughts: 'It was *as if* [the journalist] were saying ...' (my italics). Recall that the conjunction 'as if' is a term of estrangement – Richard is, in fact, *interpreting* the redhead's facial expression from an external vantage point, and expressing annoyance at the man's attitude even before his own legitimacy has been explicitly challenged. As it turns out, the journalists do think of Richard as an expatriate Englishman rather than a Biafran, as indicated, for example, by their conspiratorial warning to him not to bring sexually transmitted diseases 'back home' (p. 369), or by their surprise at the fact that Richard 'keep[s] saying *we*' (p. 372, italics in original) when talking about the accomplishments of the Biafran army. Nonetheless, this does not detract from the fact that Richard's instantaneous defensiveness mirrors his deep insecurities; in other words, his immediate prickliness may indicate that he is not as confident about the validity of his claim to Biafran identity as his constant use of 'we' suggests.

This impression is reinforced when the above passage is read alongside an earlier incident. Recalling Madu's war tales told in the first person plural, Richard perceives the soldier's 'we', used to refer to the Biafrans, to be 'edged with exclusion. The deliberate emphasis, the deepened voice, meant that Richard was not part of we; a visitor could not take the liberties of the homeowners' (p. 304, italics in original). Once again, Richard's feeling of being considered an outsider relies on his interpretation of elusive clues – here, elements of stress and intonation – which he assumes, but can in fact not possibly *know*, to be 'deliberate'. Moreover, as the character's vision is influenced by his jealousy towards the soldier, it is impossible to ascertain whether Richard's account of events is reliable at all; even Madu's 'emphasis' on the pronoun 'we', and the 'deepened voice' in which the word is supposedly spoken, may be a figment of the Englishman's imagination. Whatever the answer, the character's obsession with issues of belonging reveals his insecurity, exposing his insistent use of 'we' as profoundly self-delusory. This, in turn, reinforces the ideology already conveyed by the narrator – namely, that Richard's identification with the Biafran nation is, ultimately, appropriative and illegitimate.

It is Ugwu, through his writing of 'The Book', who eventually emerges as the rightful owner of the Biafran 'we'. This fact has not gone undisputed either. Because the houseboy has participated in the gang rape of a waitress during the war, Cooper calls him a 'problematic role model for post-war Nigeria' (2008: 150); focusing more closely on the way the novel attempts to impose the self-evidence of its conclusion, Masterson adds that 'the relationship between individual redemption and collective recuperation through writing appears strained' (2009: 154). This critical resistance seems to indicate that, in this particular instance, Adichie may have been slightly less successful than elsewhere in putting across her ideological point. No doubt, the novel's insistence on 'the restorative, curative and resistant potential of [Ugwu's] new craft' (Masterson, 2009: 155) stems at least partly from the Nigerian author's personal belief in the power of writing, as outlined in the lecture on realist literature cited at the beginning of this chapter (Adichie, 2012). Yet it is also striking that the novelist, who states that she 'tr[ies] very hard not to start off [her] writing with ideology', has admitted that the ending of *Half of a Yellow Sun* was 'the one place where [she] just couldn't help slipping in [her] politics' and give voice to her 'very firm, ardent belief that people should be allowed to tell their own stories' (2009b). Put differently, the author's desire to push forward her political agenda may have led her to slightly rush Ugwu's 'redemption' (Adichie, 2006b: 397) towards the very end. Interestingly, with the scholarly debate mainly focused on the ethics of the houseboy's 'atone[ment]' (p. 397), the social implications of his rise to authorship have been largely disregarded. Ugwu, says Adichie, is 'not a privileged Nigerian' like Odenigbo and, 'in some ways', he 'earns the right to tell the story' (2009b). In this statement, and in the dedication that ends the novel ('For Master, my good man': 433), a key ideology is unobtrusively slipped in: Ugwu's legitimacy as spokesperson for his people is only cemented through his inclusion in the intellectual middle class.

And thus my analysis of ideology in Adichie's novel comes full circle. At the beginning of this chapter, I argued that some of the stylistic techniques deployed in the first chapter of *Half of a Yellow Sun* contributed to the naturalization of a set of ideologies. Chief among these ideas were the acceptability of the concept of the young 'houseboy', and the potential of the academic middle class in fostering the intellectual development of the underprivileged Nigerian youth. In the opening of the book as elsewhere in the novel, these meanings emerge from the *dialogic* construction of the text, in which the voices of the chapters' respective focalizers are filtered through the third-person narrator's gaze and speech. Because of this narrator's overarching presence, I have suggested that, beyond the diversity of the individual characters' experiences or worldviews, the novel is above all a discursive unit – or, as Bakhtin would say, 'a structured artistic system' (1981: 300) – that serves the narrator's (and, by extension here, the implied author's) creative and political agendas. My brief incursion into schema theory has outlined that narrative events also enter into dialogue with each other to create new meanings; the entire novel, in fact, may be read as an attempt to allow these combined meanings to generate new perspectives on the Biafran War, and thus 'refresh' readers' existing schemas. It is no coincidence that Adichie herself perceives the generation of new ideas as one of the purposes of her craft: 'If literature can affect the way one person thinks', she says, 'then perhaps it has helped' (Adichie, 2004b).

To some extent, then, literature partakes of the art of persuasion, and it is therefore hardly surprising that *Half of a Yellow Sun* recurrently exploits the rhetorical potential of particular stylistic devices. It is in this light that the technique of exemplification was examined. It is used in the book to quietly reinforce the aforementioned social ideologies but also, more conspicuously, to lend forcefulness to the irony used in the vignettes summarizing 'The Book'. These excerpts are not only polyphonic, but they can also be viewed as an instance where the narrator and the fictional author of the literary-historical work conspire to use double-voicedness as a critical tool against the former colonial power. The sense of distance inherent in the ironic reporting of the colonizer's opinion prefigures the fact that Ugwu, who is revealed to be the author of 'The Book', develops precisely such an ability to understand, gauge and critique the different discourses that have shaped Nigerian history.

The Englishman Richard, on the other hand, seems unable to capitalize on the potential of the dialogic text in his writing; rather, the discursive power of double-voicedness seems to be used by the narrator at the protagonist's expense. He is in turn characterized as a colonial explorer, a religious dogmatist, a soldier, a politician, and eventually a repressed racist. The typically monologic discourses of authority associated with the character form a pattern that casts doubt on the legitimacy of his well-intentioned attempt at claiming the Biafran narrative. The novel even suggests that Richard himself may be aware of the illicit nature of his vicarious victimhood, and that he overcompensates for his sense of insecurity by obsessively including himself in the Biafran 'we'.

Methodologically speaking, this chapter has attempted to lend weight to the idea formulated by stylistician Paul Simpson that, '[b]y developing a particular style, a producer of a spoken or written text privileges certain readings, certain ways of seeing things, while suppressing or downplaying others' (1993: 8). Evidently, awareness of these textual mechanics may offer guidelines for interpretation, but Simpson's statement by no means suggests that fictions have a unique meaning, or that the ideological foundations of a novel like *Half of a Yellow Sun* can simply be laid bare. In fact, it may even be the very task of a successful literary work to open up dialogic spaces where ambiguity and uncertainty prevail. When, after his return from the war, Ugwu learns that his mother has died, he exclaims that 'God will never forgive' the Hausa, only to be told by his father that she was not killed by the 'vandals', but that she died because of 'the coughing' (Adichie, 2006b: 420). How is Ugwu's statement meant to resonate within the dialogic text? Is his inability to forgive the Hausa's crimes not somewhat incongruous, considering his own active involvement in the atrocities committed during the war? Is his invocation of divine judgement a comment on whom forgiveness should eventually be left to? Or does the father's response intimate that neither side should be too rash in apportioning blame? Alternatively, does the fact that, while formulating his reply, the father 'look[s] around fearfully, although he and Ugwu were alone' (p. 420), rather suggest that the Biafran defeat has plunged the Igbo people into a paranoid silence that would take years to be broken? In examples such as these, neither the extent of the narrator's intervention nor the precise nature of the author's intention can be neatly determined; the literary text is bound to remain an ambiguous, unstable intertwinement of voices. But this, after all, may be precisely the point: 'What literature should do', says Adichie, 'is to ask questions, and not give answers' ('Out of Nigeria', 2009).

4
Art is a Journey
Metaphor in Ben Okri's *The Landscapes Within* and *Dangerous Love*

'I'm like a painter that's got so many hidden secrets', Ben Okri once said about himself in an interview. This observation was meant to underline the fact that his work contained 'details, many of which you are not going to see the first three times you read it' (2012a: 106). But anyone acquainted with the Nigerian author's writing will recognize the wider significance of the comparison too. The connections between Okri's work and the art of painting are indeed numerous. To cite but a few, his 2002 novel, *In Arcadia*, features as a central motif Nicolas Poussin's oil on canvas *Les Bergers d'Arcadie*, an image used as a stepping-stone to the exploration of wider themes such as man's everlasting quest for happiness. His 2012 collection of poems *Wild* contains a piece written 'After Velasquez' (2012b: 75), which more specifically muses on the Spanish artist's painting of Venus gazing into a mirror. Even more recently, in 2013, Okri wrote a poem entitled 'Diallo's Testament', commissioned by the National Portrait Gallery in London and inspired by William Hoare's painting of the former slave Ayuba Suleiman Diallo (Okri, 2013).

Long before all these achievements, at the age of 14, the young Ben Okri took a piece of paper and painstakingly attempted to draw the objects found on the mantelpiece at his family home. Once he had finished the drawing, he wrote a poem. He comments: 'I looked at the drawing and it was terrible and I read the poem and it was alright. And that day I decided I was going to be a writer rather than a painter' (2011a). A decisive choice was made then, but it was only a few years before the two art forms met again in Okri's creative quest, in the shape of his second novel, *The Landscapes Within* (1981), which focused on the life and artistic aspirations of Omovo, a young painter residing in Lagos. To the author, this early book remained much like an unfinished sketch, which he decided to revisit by rewriting the narrative under the title *Dangerous Love* in 1996. In an 'Author's Note' included at the end of this revised version, Okri expressed the hope that he had been able to 'redeem' his early work for, by his own admission, '[t]he many things [he] wanted to accomplish [in *The Landscapes Within*] were too ambitious for [his] craft at the time' (1996: 325).

A superficial reading of the two novels rapidly shows that *Dangerous Love* is broadly similar to *The Landscapes Within* at the level of the plot: the characters involved are the same, and the chronology of events is almost identical. More thorough comparative analyses have revealed that the fundamental differences between the two books more markedly lie in the addition or recasting of certain statements made by the narrator or the characters, in the precision of some theoretical considerations about art, and in the protagonist's awareness of his social responsibility as an artist (see e.g. Costantini, 2002: 95–126; 2005; Fraser, 2002: 30–6; Tunca, 2004; O'Connor, 2008: 38–49). Importantly, however, the significance of the rewritten opus lies not only in these conspicuous changes, but also in some 'hidden secrets' that need to be unearthed from the text. This chapter will revolve around one such concealed element, namely the use of metaphor in the two novels, and will be divided into three main parts. First, by way of introduction, I will outline some of the significant changes that have taken place between *The Landscapes Within* and *Dangerous Love*, starting with the books' titles, so as to contextualize the points to be raised later. Then, moving on to the central, stylistic section of the chapter, I will briefly introduce conceptual metaphor theory, on which the linguistic part of the analysis will rely, and which is generally acknowledged to be 'the most influential and widely used theory of metaphor' today (Kövecses, 2010: vii). I will undertake a comparative study of specific metaphors in the two novels and show how, while the books share common ground, the second version exploits the device more creatively, and more consistently, than the first. Following this, I will attempt to demonstrate that the variations in Okri's treatment of metaphor bear considerable relevance to the understanding of a major theme in the novels: the conceptualization of the artistic process. In the final part of the study, I will try to build on these findings and consider how the stylistic analysis undertaken can serve as a basis to reassess one of the novels' central characters, Omovo's lover, Ifeyi(n)wa.[1] Examining the ending of *Dangerous Love*, I will then conclude that the artist-hero's evolution between the two versions of the narrative largely parallels the writer's own development.

The first alteration made by Okri to his early novel strikes the eye even before one opens the book, since the author has changed the title from *The Landscapes Within* to *Dangerous Love*. The title of the first version, as suggested within the narrative itself, refers to the 'landscapes of [the] mind' (1981: 168), that is, the imaginary realm, as opposed to the 'landscapes without' (1981: 206), that is, the physical world. The title of the revised version has a much more sentimental resonance, but the relationship between art and love in the novel has also been modified. As several critics have observed, the two themes are intertwined much more closely in *Dangerous Love* than in *The Landscapes Within* (Jowitt, 1996: 63; Kerrigan, 1996; Costantini, 2002: 97).

In both novels, the main character, Omovo, becomes romantically involved with Ifeyi(n)wa, a young woman who left her village for Lagos after marrying an older man named Takpo. While the account of the lovers' relationship remains 'fragmentary and undeveloped' in *The Landscapes Within* (Fraser, 2002: 34), Omovo and Ifeyi(n)wa's physical attraction and spiritual connection acquire a far more significant dimension in *Dangerous Love*, as the substantial expansion of the characters' climactic love-making scene indicates (1981: 214–15; 1996: 212–14). In the rewritten book, love no longer plays a secondary role in Omovo's psychological development, but rather provides a central source of inspiration, in a manner strikingly similar to the epiphanies that lie at the origin of his artistic creativity – to the extent that, in the revised version of the novel, 'art and love … may indeed amount to the same thing' (Kerrigan, 1996).

The intertwinement of love and art in *Dangerous Love* is evidenced by their common 'dangerousness', a feature emphasized in the revised novel by its inclusion in the title. The connection between these types of love, in their romantic and artistic guises, is underscored by Jowitt:

> The two themes [i.e. Okri's 'interest in the artist's consciousness' and 'the conventional love story'] interact in an obvious, public

way that by sketching Ifeyiwa Omovo attracts attention to their relationship; but at a deeper level too they are meant to connect because the image of Ifeyiwa takes over as the inspiration for Omovo's creativity, though not until she has disappeared and met her death.

(1996: 63)

Jowitt aptly highlights that the 'dangerous love' (Okri, 1996: 86) that gives the novel its name can be seen to include Omovo's attraction to Ifeyi(n)wa, but also the risk entailed in the act of painting, for the young man's creations often lead him into trouble: in the instance cited above, his sketching of Ifeyi(n)wa attracts the attention of her husband; in another case, one of Omovo's canvasses, entitled 'Drift', is perceived by the authorities to be an insult to the leaders of the country, which results in his being interrogated by the police. Moreover, as this chapter will attempt to demonstrate, the painter's artistic journey as a whole is a risky endeavour, for he ventures beyond the boundaries of physical reality to explore the plight of his society. In this respect, Omovo's captivation with the unhappy Ifeyi(n)wa is partly attributable to his wish to acquire a complete understanding of the world, including its cruelties. Omovo, in a revealing confession after the young woman's death, tells his journalist friend Keme: 'Maybe I also loved her because she suffered. A dangerous reason to love' (Okri, 1996: 320). In this sense, Omovo's irresistible pull towards Ifeyi(n)wa testifies to his desire to 'bear witness' (p. 265) to his country's suffering.

The prominent position occupied by Ifeyi(n)wa in the painter's life and imagination is but one manifestation of the development that Okri's female character has undergone since *The Landscapes Within*. In my view, the significance of the young woman in *Dangerous Love* has been underestimated in critical studies of the novel, which tend to focus only on her relationship with Omovo or assess her in terms of her failures. In an otherwise compelling analysis, Costantini views Ifeyi(n)wa as a 'resigned victim' who 'misses all her chances to develop' (2002: 103) and 'endangers, rather than helps, the male protagonist' (p. 104). I will argue against such a view of the character, who is not the passive object of Omovo's love, but aspires to become an individual in her own right, despite her eventual lack of success. Ifeyi(n)wa *does* attempt to grow, as her desire to get an education suggests, but her efforts repeatedly end in frustration. She is never given a chance to blossom, for she is continually hindered by the actions of her male relatives. After her father's suicide, the elders of her family force her into a loveless marriage, to which she eventually resigns herself following her brother's death (1981: 98–9; 1996: 79–80). Furthermore, her jealous, domineering husband refuses to let her complete her secretarial course. In other words, Ifeyi(n)wa is restrained by her gender and her financial situation, both of which are symptomatic of wider social issues.

The problems that plague Nigerian society and their interaction with the artist's search for creative responses undeniably feature more prominently in *Dangerous Love* than in *The Landscapes Within* (see e.g. Costantini, 2002: 120). The more elaborate treatment of the complex interplay between the physical and imaginary universes, between the collective and private spheres, is, for example, illustrated in the revised novel by the advice given to Omovo by his mentor, an old painter named Dr Okocha. Okocha indeed tries to help his pupil to overcome his inhibitions and translate his painful life experiences into art by exhorting him to 'live deeply, fully' (1996: 310). As the addition of the elderly painter's words of guidance shows, a more experienced Okri writes with greater insistence on the importance of learning from one's ordeals to arrive at a more profound comprehension of the world.

In sum, *Dangerous Love* places an increased emphasis on the relationship between physical and mental landscapes with the ultimate aim of providing a more complete view of the artistic process. The revised version of Okri's novel also extends its scope diachronically by paying attention to historical landscapes. Both *The Landscapes Within* and *Dangerous Love* broach the topic of the Biafran War, but the latter does so in considerably more detail by expanding on Omovo's and his friend Okoro's traumatic memories of the conflict. The importance of history in the understanding of the present is also highlighted in *Dangerous Love* by the addition of the theme of slavery, a collective experience seen as a key element in the exploration of the past.[2] The artist, wandering between past and present, between the real world and that of the imagination, feels compelled to attend to all those who have suffered throughout history. He has thus, as unequivocally stated in *Dangerous Love*, 'chosen the most terrible path' (1996: 267).

The noun 'path', as it is used above, refers to a course taken in life. The term may appear unremarkable in itself, but it is not the result of a random choice of words. Rather, as cognitive linguists George Lakoff and Mark Turner have shown, such terms have a metaphorical value – more specifically, they may be interpreted as linguistic expressions of the conceptual metaphor LIFE IS A JOURNEY.[3] The fact that the metaphorical quality of the word 'path' is hardly noticeable at all substantiates the same authors' observation that 'metaphor is an integral part of our ordinary everyday thought and language' (Lakoff and Turner, 1989: xi). This idea, first developed by Lakoff and Johnson in their seminal study *Metaphors We Live By* (1980), deserves to be briefly explained here, for it finds interesting applications in the novels under examination, and particularly *Dangerous Love*. The theories developed by Lakoff and his colleagues will indeed allow me to highlight the potency of some of Okri's lexical choices, and help to gain a fuller understanding of the artist's task as it is consistently presented in the revised version of the book.

As Lakoff and Johnson remind us, metaphors are stereotypically regarded as creative figures of speech, 'device[s] of the poetic imagination and the rhetorical flourish' (1980: 3), but the two scholars go on to debunk this view and demonstrate that, on the contrary, metaphorical linguistic expressions pervade everyday language, and make manifest what is known as 'conceptual metaphors'. By way of example, one of the first concepts examined in their study is that of TIME, which is viewed (at least in Western cultures) in terms of the conceptual metaphors TIME IS MONEY, TIME IS A LIMITED RESOURCE, and TIME IS A VALUABLE COMMODITY (p. 8). This is reflected in contemporary English by expressions such as 'spend time', 'invest time' and 'use time profitably', among others (p. 8). Importantly, as Lakoff and Johnson argue, we do not simply talk about time in terms of a valuable commodity or act as if it were one, we also '*conceive of* time that way. Thus we understand and experience time as the kind of thing that can be spent, wasted, budgeted, invested wisely or poorly, saved, or squandered' (p. 8, italics in original). Metaphor, in sum, 'is not simply a matter of words or linguistic expressions but of concepts, of thinking of one thing in terms of another' (Kövecses 2010: xi). To be more precise, metaphors such as TIME IS MONEY consist of two 'conceptual domains', one of which is understood in terms of the other. This set of correspondences is known as a 'mapping', involving a 'source domain' (here, MONEY) from which metaphorical expressions are drawn to understand another conceptual domain, known as a 'target domain' (here, TIME).

Since conventional metaphors abound in language, works of literature are also replete with them. *The Landscapes Within* and *Dangerous Love* are no exceptions. For example, when Omovo is working on a charcoal drawing called 'Related Losses', an apparently unexceptional sentence appears, in slightly different versions, in both novels:

(1) In the end he felt he had captured something more strange and real than the original sensations. (1981: 7)
(1') He felt he was capturing something more strange and real than the actual event ... (1996: 6)

The verb 'capture' primarily denotes the action of 'catch[ing] by force, surprise, or stratagem' but, in both (1) and (1'), the verb is used, in the domain of ART, in the conventional metaphorical sense of 'represent[ing], catch[ing], or record[ing] (something elusive, as a quality)'.[4] The conceptual metaphor underlying Okri's linguistic choice could be formulated as REPRESENTING IS CATCHING. If the use of the verb 'capture' in (1) and (1') may be said to be so deeply entrenched in ordinary speech that its metaphorical quality is almost imperceptible, the verb 'trap' in the following quotation from *Dangerous Love* is much more unusual:

[Omovo] began to think about the concrete basis of all ideas, and about the long silent phases it had taken him to trap the scumscape [i.e. a nearby scumpool that he has painted] on canvas, when his mind clouded.

(1996: 71)

The term 'trap' – which replaces the verb 'put' in *The Landscapes Within* (1981: 88) – can be said to refer to the same process as the verb 'capture', but it is not ordinarily used in the domain of ART to denote representation. In this sentence, it rather brings to mind the physical act of 'catching', using subterfuge. Thus, while the understanding of 'representation' in terms of 'capture' is a conventional one, the term realizing the mapping in this extract is not. This may be considered an example of metaphor 'elaboration', which consists in describing an existing element of a metaphorical mapping in an unconventional way (see e.g. Lakoff and Turner, 1989: 67–8; Kövecses, 2010: 53–4). Such examples discreetly signal that Okri uses the conventional metaphor REPRESENTING IS CATCHING as a foundation for the creation of a richer poetic image, particularly in *Dangerous Love*.

Of course one can hardly argue that a poetic reworking of the conventional metaphor REPRESENTING IS CATCHING has taken place on the basis of the sole replacement of the verb 'put' by the variant 'trap'. To prove that this verb is part of a coherent metaphorical system, one should – and, I believe, can – substantiate the interpretation suggested by the presence of 'trap' with further evidence extracted from *Dangerous Love*. For instance, in a passage that occurs as Omovo is drawing Ifeyi(n)wa, reference is not only made to the act of 'catching', but notions of space and movement are also introduced:

> [Omovo] decided also to capture her sensuality, her curves, the promise of her thighs, the definition of her breasts ... he was soon lost in work, lost in her pose which best coincided, at that moment, with the private image he had of her.
> Omovo worked fast. There was so much he wanted to catch which appeared in his mind and moved away so rapidly.
>
> (1996: 146)

The verb 'capture' is used again in its usual metaphorical sense, as is the verb 'catch', which is also often found in the artistic context – a painter, for example, can be said to 'catch the expression of a face'. The expression 'lost in work', which contains the preposition 'in', a grammatical word indicative of a spatial location, may be considered another conventional metaphor – one that presents an activity (here, work) as a container (cf. Lakoff and Johnson, 1980: 31). Far less common is the fact that the images and moods which Omovo wants to capture actually 'move away'. As Kövecses reminds us (2010: 91), metaphorical mappings are always partial; in the instance examined here, the fact that the subject of the drawing may be in movement is not part of the conventional metaphor REPRESENTING IS CATCHING. The novel, in other words, poetically exploits a conventional conceptual metaphor by introducing an 'unused' element of the source domain, a technique known as 'extending' a metaphor (Lakoff and Turner, 1989: 67; Kövecses, 2010: 53). As a result, the original metaphor is apprehended in a new light: the verb 'move away' introduces a sense

of dynamism, and images are presented, quite literally, as mobile entities that leave the visual field of the artist's inner eye. The introduction of such dynamic concepts suggests a shift from the conventional
REPRESENTING IS CATCHING metaphor to the more generic poetic metaphor ART IS A CHASE. Interestingly, the addition of movement before
the action of 'capturing' in *Dangerous Love* is echoed on the narrative
level. In *The Landscapes Within*, Omovo asks Ifeyi(n)wa to strike a pose
to be able to sketch her (1981: 149–50), while in the revised version of
the novel, he starts by drawing her in movement, as she 'perform[s]
the ordinary actions of washing and drying clothes' (1996: 145). He
then manages to 'capture her sensuality' when she 'stop[s] moving'
(1996: 146), as if the couple had indeed been engaged in a pursuit
until the artist manages to get hold of his subject.

As the sentences analysed above illustrate, the novels, and especially *Dangerous Love*, engage both in the extending and elaboration
of conventional conceptual metaphors. They sometimes do both
within the space of a single sentence:

(2) It [the painting] had to be coaxed, attuned to, grasped, captured.
(1981: 72–3)
(2′) It had to be coaxed, attuned to, grasped, released. (1996: 59)

The Landscapes Within uses the conventional 'captured' (applied to
the painting, which metonymically stands for what it contains), and
both versions of the book feature the verb 'grasp'. 'Grasp' could be
considered an elaboration of the metaphor REPRESENTING IS CATCHING,
since this verb is not conventionally used in the 'capture' slot, even
though both 'grasp' and 'capture' are near synonyms denoting the
act of seizing. Alternatively, since 'grasp' also has the conventional
metaphorical sense of 'seizing intellectually', i.e. 'comprehend-
ing', its presence here may be regarded as a linguistic expression
of another conceptual metaphor, UNDERSTANDING IS GRASPING (Lakoff
and Turner, 1989: 129). Another verb used in both versions of the
sentence, 'coaxing', denotes 'cajoling', often with the intention of
persuading a person or an animal to do something, as, for instance,
approach. For this reason, 'coaxing' can also be read as a component
of the CHASE domain, though it is not usually an element mapped
onto the target domain of ART – 'coaxing', in other words, partakes
of the extending of the metaphor ART IS A CHASE. 'Attune to', on the

other hand, denotes the act of bringing oneself in harmony with something – the word is not conventionally applied to the domains of either ART or CHASE, but in fact originates from the field of music, where it means 'bringing into musical accord'. Using terminology from conceptual metaphor theory, one could argue that the sentence 'combines' the metaphors ART IS A CHASE and VISUAL ART IS MUSIC, a creative technique that provides yet another way to apprehend the artistic process and thus 'go beyond our everyday conceptual system' (Kövecses, 2010: 55). Crucially, the main metaphor used in the extract, ART IS A CHASE, is further extended in the revised version of the novel, where the conventional 'captured' used in *The Landscapes Within* has been replaced by the non-equivalent 'released'. This change gives decisive insight into Okri's conception of the nature of the artist's unusual chase. Unlike the outcome of a physical pursuit, which typically leads to the imprisonment or death of the entity being chased, people or objects temporarily fixed in the artist's mind do not die or become caged. Rather, they undergo a transformation which offers them an imaginary release.

Transformation through art is a key concept in both *The Landscapes Within* and *Dangerous Love*. Omovo's dissatisfaction with his painting 'Drift' may be said to stem from its failure to transform reality. While the picture is a competent visual imitation of the scumpool, it does not, as Costantini observes, 'render the regenerative power that lies at the very core of rot' (2002: 115). Omovo's inability to transform his subject through art lies in the execution of the painting, for his desire to initiate change is perceptible in both versions of the narrative. When his brother, Okur, tells him that an onion, despite its many layers, contains 'nothing' at its centre, Omovo intuitively feels that 'there had to be "something"' (1996: 203, see 1981: 207 for an earlier version). The idea of transformation is hinted at in *The Landscapes Within*, as Omovo senses that 'he should start creating the destruction of nothings' (1981: 207), but is stated explicitly only in *Dangerous Love*, in which Omovo understands that 'it [i]s only by the application of vision, only by making things, that we c[an] *transform* the negative "nothing"' (1996: 203, my italics). This reformulation is not the sole indication of the increased use of the leitmotif of transformation in *Dangerous Love*. One final comparative example will suffice to establish the greater systematicity of metaphorical correspondences in the revised version of the novel. After Omovo discovers the mutilated body of a young girl in a park (1981: 58–60; 1996: 45–7), he cannot stop thinking about the incident:

(3) When he thought of the girl a strange thing happened inside him. He felt as though he was in a way guilty; and with this sensation the urge to do the painting reached fever pitch. (1981: 95)

(3') As he thought about the girl, he felt guilty. He felt he should be doing something about it. But he was powerless. He felt in curious need of redemption. He felt that his powerlessness, and the powerlessness of all the people without voices, needed to be redeemed, to be transformed. With this feeling his urge to do the painting reached fever pitch. (1996: 76)

In both *The Landscapes Within* and *Dangerous Love*, Omovo experiences a feeling of guilt, which is the expression of the sense of responsibility placed on him by his discovery of the young girl's body. As the protagonist says himself, 'the moment you see something is wrong you have a responsibility' (1996: 321). In *The Landscapes Within*, this sensation induces his urge to paint, but in *Dangerous Love*, the need to *transform* his powerlessness and that of 'all the people without voices' (1996: 76) brings about artistic stimulation. The double occurrence of the noun 'powerlessness' after the adjective from which it is derived suggests both the omnipresence of the feeling and the overpowering urge to transform the sensation that arises from its ubiquity. The idea of transformation is doubled with that of 'redemption', which, in both its religious and secular senses, carries with it the promise of release, either from blame or from sin. In *Dangerous Love*, one can therefore once more establish the existence of links between painting, transformation and deliverance, an association that suggests that the poetic extension of the ART IS A CHASE metaphor is used consistently.

The transfiguration brought about by art is not unidirectional, for the artist too is transformed in the process of creation. This fact is clearly perceived by Dr Okocha when he advises Omovo on how to deal with the memory of a dead Igbo man that the young painter saw during the Biafran War:

The original experience must be the guide. But what you make of it, what you bring back from it, the vision, call it what you will, is the most important thing. What you forget returns in a hundred other shapes. It becomes the true material of invention. To learn how to remember creatively is to learn how to feel. But to paint that dream of yours [i.e. Omovo's dream about the dead Igbo man] will mean a long descent into yourself. It will also mean learning how to think differently. I am happy for you, for you are young and you are on a threshold ... This is one painting that will change you. Craft is important. The greater the idea, the greater the craft you need. But in finding the right colours, the right shapes, to capture that dream you will begin to discover unsuspected dimensions within you.

(1996: 99–100)

This meta-artistic passage introduces several new metaphorical elements. While the idea of 'capture' is still present, the ART IS A CHASE metaphor is combined with, or even superseded by, the broader idea that ART IS A JOURNEY. Several words, used metaphorically here, are typically associated with the JOURNEY domain or, more generally, are evocative of movement in space, exploration and progress towards a goal: the original experience acts as a 'guide', forgotten memories 'return', painting means 'a long descent' into oneself, the artist discovers 'dimensions' within himself. The critical stage which Omovo has reached is also described in spatial terms, as he is said to be 'on a threshold'. This image once more situates Omovo on a boundary: besides attempting to cross the border between reality and the imagination, he is also about to take a critical step across the edge of known territory to explore new 'landscapes within'.

The metaphorical use of space-related words in Dr Okocha's advisory speech creates for the reader a mental image of Omovo wandering through space, following a guide and trying to cross boundaries in an effort to capture a memory. This scenario surfaces again later in the novel, when Omovo dreams that he is pursuing his dead mother:

He followed her through the maze and she kept eluding him, kept disappearing around corners just as he caught sight of her. And because he couldn't reach her he spoke to her, saying:

'O mother who suffered so much in such silence, why did you travel without teaching me how to reach you? Stop escaping from me, running from me ... I am in danger of getting lost. Guide me through this maze.'

(1996: 168–9)

Omovo's vision shares some striking similarities with the artistic quest previously described by Dr Okocha. As in the journey depicted by the old painter, Omovo is, in his dream, physically moving towards a goal that takes the form of a memory. In the artistic expedition, the experience that must be the 'guide' is Omovo's imperfect recollection of a dead Igbo man, particularly his eyes, which, the young painter says using another spatially connoted word, 'will never leave [him]' (1996: 99). In the dream described above, Omovo asks his mother, who, although deceased, is 'always there' (p. 19), to take on the role of 'guide'. Just as he 'can't remember exactly how [the man's eyes] look' (pp. 98–9), so he can't 'reach' his mother, whom he manages to 'catch' only by sight. Because Omovo's artistic initiation is still in progress, he is as yet unable to traverse the boundary between life and death, even though he fleetingly gestures towards the crossing of this threshold by dreaming his deceased mother into being.

In the extract, the motif of the journey is more generally applied to both death and life. The fact that Omovo refers to his mother as having 'travel[led]' may be seen as an expression of the conventional DEATH IS DEPARTURE metaphor (see e.g. Lakoff and Turner, 1989: 7). This metaphor recurs in the description of the events unfolding in the dream, for Omovo's mother literally 'escap[es]' and 'run[s]' away from her son. As for the domain of LIFE, it inherits from that of the JOURNEY the idea that a 'guide' may help Omovo to 'feel his way towards some sort of orientation' (Okri, 1996: 76) in the 'maze' in which the protagonist finds himself.

The metaphor of the 'maze', already found in *The Landscapes Within*, presents the path taken on the journey of existence as a labyrinth, and the many windings of the tortuous structure as obstacles to progress in life. On the labyrinthine path of life, one runs the risk of getting 'lost' – as Omovo fears in his dream – and, eventually, of becoming 'trapped'. A few lines in Omovo's notebook, which prefigure his most significant epiphanic moment at the end of the novel (1981: 272; 1996: 293–5), describe this progressive entrapment: 'lost in the cities – lost in the offices – lost in traffic jams – trapped in the mazes of daily life – the maze of our history' (1996: 156). 'Lost' and 'maze' both have spatial denotations in English but, significantly, they can refer to states of mental confusion as well. Such literal and metaphorical interpretations also apply to the idea of being 'trapped', since one may be physically trapped in a location or figuratively trapped in a situation. These conventional metaphors, especially the idea of entrapment, are ubiquitous in *Dangerous Love*, in which almost all the major characters are 'trapped' one way or another. Ifyeyi(n)wa's mind is 'trapped in a maze of desires, of pain, of compromises, and of love' (1996: 86) and 'her act of compromise [i.e. her marriage] ha[s] forever caged her buoyant spirit' (p. 80); Dele, one of Omovo's friends, is 'momentarily trapped by his inability to articulate what he mean[s]' (p. 112); Keme wants to leave town because he feels 'trapped' in Lagos (p. 152); and Omovo himself is 'trapped by his own emotions' (p. 26), 'trapped in his room' (p. 276), 'ambushed by images' (p. 203), 'want[s] to escape from the traffic jam of our lives' (p. 277), and so on.[5]

The idea that Omovo must try to 'capture' his environment but is, at the same time, 'trapped' in it like all the other protagonists, points to the fundamental ambivalence of many of the elements contained in the ART IS A JOURNEY and ART IS A CHASE metaphors. While Omovo runs the danger of becoming 'trapped' by getting 'lost' in the maze of life, his being 'lost' in work (p. 145) and 'lost' during the dream he has in Badagry, in which he literally wanders through the maze of history (p. 286), leads to imaginary exploration, not immobility. Similarly, the act of remembering can help one to save the dead from the abyss of time or it can, conversely, trap one into the past. Omovo is disturbed by the mutilated young girl who follows him in his dreams (p. 151), but he eventually becomes her guide of sorts by transforming the traumatizing image through art, when he paints her at the end of the novel. Omovo's friend Okoro, on the other hand, may have 'escape[d] injury and death' as a child soldier during the Biafran War (p. 108), but he is trapped by haunting memories which he tries to flee by attending parties and seducing women. His past eventually catches up with him in a most literal way in *Dangerous Love* when he is run over by a military vehicle. As Costantini rightly notices, '[t]he military lorry that runs him over is an ironic manifestation of the spectre of the war that he has failed to exorcise' (2002: 106). Physical escape too is presented as an ambivalent course of action. It can be, as with Dele's plan to abandon his pregnant girlfriend and leave for the USA, a means of shaking off one's responsibilities; it can result in homelessness, as suggested by Omovo's brothers' endless roaming after their violent argument with their father; or it can, conversely, give access to an experience of spiritual exploration, as Omovo's trip to Badagry demonstrates. Another element with conflicting interpretations is the metaphor of the traffic jam, already evoked above. Indeed, for all its associations with immobility, the 'go slow' is inseparable from the activity of the city. It inspires Omovo with a painting in which he captures the maze of life in almost allegorical fashion, much like Okri himself in his novels:

> In his painting the city became a demented maze ... All roads lead into the maze of the city. The chaos and the frustration of the city. But the only ways out lead to the forests of the interior and to the seas.
>
> (1996: 155)

In this painting, Omovo manages to 'convey the dramatic gestures of Lagosians in their frozen angled positions' (p. 155), which testifies to his increasing ability to convey the 'chaos' of the city to life in pictorial representations. This growing understanding of three-dimensionality and dynamism leads, quite naturally, to the use of the spatial metaphor of the 'maze'. The fact that 'All roads lead into the maze of the city' suggests how easy – inevitable even – it is to become 'trapped' in Lagos. The coordinating conjunction 'But' at the beginning of the last sentence in the extract indicates that the 'ways out' do not lead to safe harbours either. The first destination, the forest, is the well-known site of esoteric manifestations in the West African storytelling tradition and, in *The Landscapes Within* and *Dangerous Love*, it is the place where Omovo stumbles upon a ritualistic religious ceremony (1981: 220 -1; 1996: 218 -21). The second destination, the sea, is also an ambivalent space in the novels. In *Dangerous Love*, it is used to elaborate the ART IS A JOURNEY metaphor: '[Omovo] had sworn to set his sails to the fortunes of art. How was he to know what cruel and difficult seas his ship would travel?', 1996: 265). In these sentences, 'set his sails to the fortunes of art' presents navigation as artistic exploration, while the 'cruel and difficult seas' associate the sea with danger.

In short, *Dangerous Love*, even more markedly than *The Landscapes Within*, is based on the ART IS A CHASE and ART IS A JOURNEY metaphors. The first metaphor presents the act of artistic creation as a pursuit in which the painter attempts to catch a subject in order to transform it, then release it, thereby giving it spiritual liberation. This process also transforms the artist. The second metaphor, linked to the first, more generally evokes the process of maturation, and suggests that life is an expedition, either through a maze or across boundaries. Getting lost on the path of existence may lead either to exploration and discovery or, conversely, to a state of entrapment.

So far, I have tried to show that these two metaphors more heavily bear upon the representation of the artistic process in the second version of the novel than in the first. In what follows, I would like to argue that awareness of these conceptual metaphors, associated with other elements of literary interpretation, can help to reassess the role played by one of the major characters in the narrative, namely Ifeyi(n)wa. Methodologically speaking, this examination shows how the conclusions of stylistic analyses can be built *upon* to shed further light on narrative incidents – the whole enterprise, one might say, advocates a type of disciplinary mongrelization.

As has already been hinted at, Omovo's lover Ifeyi(n)wa plays a major role in helping the young man towards a transformation of reality through painting. Most obviously, her beauty inspires the artist; moreover, she occupies an important position in Omovo's imaginative retrieval of the mutilated girl, even more so in *Dangerous Love* than in *The Landscapes Within*. Indeed, when the painter tries to recreate the dead girl's features on canvas at the end of the revised novel, he 'keep[s] Ifeyiwa's face in mind', and he later 'complete[s] ... seven Ifeyiwa paintings' (1996: 314), two facts that are absent from the earlier version of the book. Connections between Ifeyi(n)wa and the girl are suggested in both *The Landscapes Within* and *Dangerous Love*, but they are established much more explicitly in the latter:

(4) She thought of the mutilated girl Omovo had seen in the park. (1981: 249)
(4') She thought of the dead, mutilated girl in the park. She felt a little like that girl, mutilated and no-one noticing. (1996: 254)

The comparison between Ifeyi(n)wa and the mutilated girl may be said to anticipate the young woman's own fate, for she too is destined for a senseless death, in the dispute between her village and the neighbouring one. Ifeyi(n)wa, like the young girl, is the victim of a 'sacrifice' – a word mentioned in *Dangerous Love* in relation both to the child (1996: 134) and to Ifeyi(n)wa (1996: 282). It is important to note that in (4'), Ifeyi(n)wa is not just compared to the young girl, but 'feels' like the child. She is, in other words, not merely an object, but she is given emotional depth, and therefore possible volition – a textual change in line with the development of her character in *Dangerous Love*. Ifeyi(n)wa fulfils this potential as an agent by acting as a guide to Omovo, not only in the imaginary sphere but also in reality. On several occasions, the metaphor ART IS A CHASE is transformed into a 'love is a chase' motif in the physical world. Thus, when the young couple leave their homes to meet away from the prying eyes of their neighbours, Ifeyi(n)wa systematically leads the way out of the compound, followed by Omovo (1996: 124–5, 206–7). Just like the artistic journey, the pursuits between the lovers are riddled with obstacles. In the first instance Omovo is blocked by a lorry and loses sight of Ifeyi(n)wa before she calls out to him (1981: 132–3; 1996: 124–5). In the second case, she confuses Omovo by leading him through a maze of streets:

> She had been walking so quickly, taking the most unusual detours, dipping into compounds and emerging at other streets through mysterious corridors, that when they re-emerged at their street he didn't recognise it for a while.
>
> (1996: 206)

Ifeyi(n)wa's meandering leads Omovo to see his own environment 'with a stranger's eyes' (p. 105). For the young painter, who believes that defamiliarization can help him to 'see more clearly' (p. 105), Ifeyi(n)wa acts as a guide, a teacher even, in this case. Their walk through the streets of Lagos ends in the room of a prostitute, where the two characters have sexual intercourse, an experience whose intensity – rendered in both versions of the novel by the presence of an unusually long sentence (1981: 214; 1996: 214) – is reminiscent of the ecstasy of artistic achievement. The quotation above also evokes a passage from Omovo's dream in Badagry, in which he '[finds] himself wandering down a corridor ... through strange towns down whose streets slaves were dragged screaming' (1996: 286), following an old woman of whom he later loses sight. The dream continues:

> In one city he saw Ifeyiwa fleeing down the streets. He pursued her, but she outran him, and when at a closed-off road he finally

caught up with her – she turned into a shadow and melted through the walls.

(p. 287)

The motif of the chase between Omovo and Ifeyi(n)wa is reproduced in the artist's revelatory dream, in which he wanders through time and space. Because the young woman vanishes, just like Omovo's mother 'disappear[s] into the maze, lost to him forever' (p. 169) in his earlier dream, Ifeyi(n)wa's evaporation may be interpreted as Omovo's unconscious awareness of the death which, unknown to him, she has already met. Alternatively, her mutation into a shadow may be viewed as an anticipation of her 'transformation' by the artist, which Omovo achieves only later.

Considering the importance of change in the artistic chase, Ifeyi(n)wa's transformation in Omovo's dream is a rather striking addition in *Dangerous Love*. In my view, this detail is not incidental, for it is corroborated by several similar references. When the young woman dresses up for a meeting with Omovo, the latter is 'astonished at her *transformation*' (p. 125, my italics). Later, Omovo finds her eyes hardened by her painful experiences and voices the concern that she 'keep[s] *changing*' (p. 210, my italics). After Ifeyi(n)wa is threatened by her husband Takpo in a dark forest, it is reported that she 'felt that the night had *changed* her in some way. She felt as if a door which she never knew existed had opened within her. She felt curiously light and freed of something' (pp. 235–6, my italics). The opening of a door, which also appears in Omovo's dream, is yet another spatial indicator associated with discovery, while Ifeyi(n)wa's feeling of freedom can be related to the liberation from entrapment which the artist achieves through his work. Crucially, then, these ideas of transformation and liberation provide clues to Ifeyi(n)wa's status as the object of the painter's inspiration, and also point to her own potential as an artist.

Already in *The Landscapes Within*, Ifeyi(n)wa possesses an intuition shared only with the artist figures of the novel. For instance, her obsession with drowning and the fact that she is 'afraid of water' (1981: 136), an element that cannot be dissociated from either life or death, may signal her keen perception of their interrelatedness. In *Dangerous Love*, such clues are developed and multiplied. In the revised version of the novel, Ifeyi(n)wa no longer fears water itself, but is 'afraid of the sea' (1996: 129). The image suggests even more strongly the inseparability of life and death, since the ocean, which may either kill or provide sustenance, is more readily evocative of these two concepts than mere 'water' is. The metaphor of the sea also gains a new dimension considering the comparison of artistic discovery with a voyage across the ocean. Ifeyi(n)wa's apprehension may indeed indicate that she senses the danger of such an exploration. Moreover, in *Dangerous Love*, the young woman's artistic inclination is explicitly conveyed by her desire to become a writer. As she tells Omovo, 'I've often thought of writing poems ... But I don't know how' (1996: 211). If Ifeyi(n)wa never becomes a fully-fledged artist, it is not for lack of vision, for she has, like Omovo, an acute understanding of the human condition. As she is about to leave the compound to return to her village, she perceives the ghetto-dwellers as 'ghosts and shadows without voices' (p. 256), and is shocked at the realization that 'no one could see alternatives, the other ways to the seas that Omovo's brother's poem had talked about' (p. 256).[6] Her perceptions clearly indicate that she has the ability to cross the boundaries of the physical world and that she senses the necessity to undertake the journey mentioned in the poem. Therefore, Ifeyi(n)wa's return to her village to escape her marriage need not be interpreted as a sign of defeat, but rather, it can be regarded as a search for such a 'way to the sea'. Her trip, then, much like Omovo's painting of the young girl after his traumatic experience, can be viewed as an attempt to complete a cycle of suffering, and actively pursue the 'vision of how she could live, of the person she could be' (p. 281). Even though Ifeyi(n)wa falls short of completing her journey, she refuses to remain trapped in Lagos and she dies a traveller, as she tries to cross the boundary to her village – a narrative fact that has particular resonance in view of the ART IS A JOURNEY metaphor. Ifeyi(n)wa also dies on another dangerous frontier for, as she hears 'a man's gruff voice' in the dark, she thinks it all 'a horrible dream' and 's[ees] her dead father staring at her' (p. 281). She thus expires on the treacherous boundary between reality and the imagination, and is never allowed to give concrete expression to her creative aspirations.

Ifeyi(n)wa, however, undergoes a process of artistic reincarnation thanks to her lover Omovo. On the one hand, as already mentioned above, she is the subject of a series of paintings executed by the artist; on the other, her association in the novel with the young girl in the park means that her presence also haunts Omovo's 'Related Losses', which represents the child. As a central figure in the painter's imagination, Ifeyi(n)wa accompanies Omovo on the road towards artistic accomplishment – a path that is, in many ways, the novelist's too. At the end of *Dangerous Love* (and not in *The Landscapes Within*) Omovo makes a number of changes to his 'Related Losses', an act which is strikingly reminiscent of Okri's reshaping of his early book:

> [S]even years later, after [Omovo] had completed his seven Ifeyiwa paintings, when he had seen more, suffered more, learned more, and thought he knew more, he made certain changes to 'Related Losses', vainly trying to complete what he knew was beyond completion, trying to realise a fuller painting on a foundation whose frame was set forever. Succumbing to the dangerous process of looking back, making himself suffer a long penance for a past artistic shame at a work unrealised by youthful craft, and under the pretext of wanting to re-educate himself in the form, he quite radically altered the painting. He ... allowed the girl's body more dominance. He made a phantom figure brood above her, the figure of an ancestor or of the unborn. Then he painted for the girl a bright yellow dress. He made her mutilation obscenely beautiful, as if she were giving birth to a monstrous mythic force; a messy, almost messianic birth from a flowering wound ... Then, finally, he created for her a sweet pair of eyes, a beautiful little nose ... and thick proud lips, sensual, silent, beyond speech, self-communicative.
>
> (1996: 314–15)

The dead body giving birth evokes regeneration, reconciliation between life and death, a cyclic representation of existence. Ugliness and beauty are reunited in the oxymoronic 'obscenely beautiful' mutilation, as an echo of Omovo's fascination with the unattractive aspects of the world; the past and the future are also interwoven, as suggested by the confusion of an 'ancestor' with 'the unborn'. One detail, perhaps, establishes a direct link between Omovo's revision of his painting and Okri's rewriting of *The Landscapes Within*: just as Omovo 'paint[s] for the girl a bright yellow dress' (1996: 315), so Okri gives Ifeyi(n)wa a yellow dress in *Dangerous Love*, which she did not have in the earlier book, and which is insistently mentioned in the revised version of the novel (e.g. 1996: 125, 134, 138–9, 141). Furthermore, the girl represented in Omovo's painting is finally given a face in the more accomplished work, something which the artist had failed to do in the first version. By developing the character of Ifeyi(n)wa, Okri may also be said to have given her a face in *Dangerous Love*. The young girl and the woman, both of whom are reincarnated in Omovo's work, replace the faceless dead of the first version of the painting (and of the novel) as symbols of the country's suffering. They have been captured on canvas and, in metaphorically overcoming their anonymous death, they have undergone an imaginary release.

That the terms 'captured' and 'release' should appear in my own sentence summarizing Omovo's commemorative painting is no coincidence – these words are, as I have attempted to show, central elements in the metaphors ART IS A CHASE and ART IS A JOURNEY used in relation to the artistic process in *The Landscapes Within* and *Dangerous Love*. The artist, more insistently and consistently so in the later version of the book, initially feels haunted, trapped, by his subject, before managing to capture it on canvas, thereby giving it – and himself – an imaginary liberation. The paradox suggested by the association of capture and release perfectly embodies the complexity, and the almost ungraspable nature, of artistic creation.

As Lakoff and Johnson (1980) assert, the link between language and conceptualization is a deeply rooted, sometimes unconscious one. It therefore comes as no surprise that, in *Dangerous Love*, the aforementioned metaphors extend beyond the fictional content of the book to the 'Author's Note' appended to the novel:

> I came to see that novel [*The Landscapes Within*] as the key to much of my past work, and perhaps also to my future, and became sure that it would not let me go until I had at least tried to redeem it. Many years passed before I took up the raw material again and from that grew this new work. *Dangerous Love* is the fruit of much restlessness. I hope that I have, at last, managed to free its spirit.
>
> (1996: 325)

Already the word 'key' introduces an inconspicuous reference to space, since the metaphor indicates that the finding of answers is akin to the opening of a door or a container. That Okri's early novel 'would not let [him] go' is strongly reminiscent of the feeling of entrapment felt by his painter-hero, while the act of trying to 'free [the] spirit' of his work is suggestive of attempts at artistic liberation also undertaken by Omovo. Asked about the rewriting of *The Landscapes Within* in an interview, Okri further expressed the hope that, now he had revised his earlier book, he 'c[ould] be let out of prison ... and be a free man' (1997: 47). Read together with the last sentence of the 'Author's Note', this statement emphasizes that the realization of an artistic enterprise results in the liberation of both the artist and his subject. The attainment of this sense of freedom, however, does not signify 'perfection' (p. 47), but it is simply a stage in an expedition that is 'beyond completion' (1996: 315). Ultimately, Okri seems to suggest, creation is an unending journey and the artist, perhaps, a traveller, walking on a road to infinity.

5

'Bi-textual' Poetics

Investigating Form in Chris Abani's *Becoming Abigail*

At a literary event held in Venice, Italy, in March 2008, poet and novelist Chris Abani received a fairly unremarkable request from the floor: to read from his poetry. As the writer did not have any of his collections of poems at hand, he instead shared with the audience a short chapter of his novella, *Becoming Abigail* (2006b). Before doing so, he offered the following comment: 'It's the same [as poetry]. I'll read so you can hear the music' (Abani, 2008).

The anecdote may be unfamiliar, but Abani's reaction should not come across as entirely unexpected to seasoned readers of his fiction. Indeed, his prose is regularly described by critics as 'poetic' and 'lyrical', two adjectives that have been applied with unusual frequency to *Becoming Abigail*. That these labels have elicited vigorous nods of approval but little in-depth discussion so far is hardly surprising, since the book displays conspicuous features (including fragmented syntax, abundant imagery, and deeply emotional passages) that are routinely considered 'poetic' or 'lyrical' in the (stereo)typical, non-technical senses of the terms. Added to this, the novella's musicality, to which Abani alludes above, can also be said to partake of its 'poetic' or 'lyrical' nature.[1] The question worth investigating, then, is not so much whether *Becoming Abigail* can be regarded as loosely 'poetic', considering that the answer is obviously affirmative, but rather how the so-called 'poetic' elements affect the way the book can be construed and, ultimately, why the author has found it necessary to choose a hybrid, poetry-infused prose form to convey his protagonist's experience. Abani's toing and froing between the genres of prose and poetry throughout his career is well known – borrowing a word used by his Jamaican writer friend Colin Channer to describe him, he sometimes refers to himself as 'bi-textual' (Abani, 2009b: n.p.). But what has hardly ever been explored is how, and to what effect, the two genres converge in single texts that Abani has authored. Elucidating this matter in relation to *Becoming Abigail* demands, of course, that one first establish precisely what, in more strictly scientific terms, motivates the description of the novella as 'poetic'.

The beginning of an answer to these questions can be found in Abani's essay 'Abigail and My Becoming' (2006a), in which the writer reflects on the genesis of his novella. The book was originally inspired by two separate news items that he encountered while living in Britain in the 1990s. The first report featured the 'pulped face' of a Nigerian girl, who had been beaten into submission by the relatives who had brought her to England to work as a servant. The second story was that of a young Moroccan woman in France who had become romantically involved with the judge presiding over her immigration case, a scandal that led to her eventual suicide. The 'ghosts' of these two women, Abani explains, started to 'haunt' him, and the 'ectoplasmic traces' that they 'had left on [his] psyche' (2006a) first led him to write the short story 'Jazz Petals' (1996). In this text, which is (at least factually) hardly related to the young women's predicaments, the lesbian heroine, Jasmine, 'comes out to her mother in a scene where she has colored her hair purple', an incident that mirrors the passage 'in which Abigail [in the novella] comes out to her father, this time not sexually, but as a human being' (2006a). Apart from this shared concern with the affirmation of identity, and disregarding a few common details,[2] the echoes between the early story (told in the first person) and the novella (recounted by a third-person narrator) are, by and large, relatively faint.

After 'Jazz Petals', Abani 'returned to the haunting, to the ectoplasm' once more: 'This time it had a shape, a form, and a name: Abigail' (2006a). The result was the short story 'Becoming Abigail' (2000a), which inherited only minor features from 'Jazz Petals', such as the – perhaps not entirely felicitous – association between 'petals' and the heroine's labia, a somewhat clichéd image abandoned in the 2006 novella. 'Becoming Abigail', however, clearly prefigures its book-length incarnation, as both versions of the narrative follow a Nigerian girl obsessed with her mother, a woman who died while giving birth to her. In both texts, the main character is sent to London by her father to stay with a cousin by marriage, Peter, who attempts to force her into prostitution and sexually abuses her; in both works too, the protagonist starts a consensual relationship with a middle-aged social worker named Derek, but their affair is exposed, leading the girl to presumably commit suicide by jumping into the River Thames.[3]

By Abani's own admission, the 2000 version of 'Becoming Abigail' was 'only the dim outline of a form still barely glimpsed', as in hindsight he realized that, when writing the story, he 'still did not have the compassion for this voice, the words for this kind of tenderness' (2006a). The writer's acknowledgement of the limitations of his early self is strongly reminiscent of Ben Okri's backward glance in his 'Author's Note' to *Dangerous Love*, in which he states, as already mentioned in Chapter 4, that '[t]he many things [he] wanted to accomplish [in *The Landscapes Within*] were too ambitious for [his] craft at the time' (1996: 325). The similarity between the two writers' declarations is more than a mere coincidence. In the essay 'Abigail and My Becoming', Abani not only cites his first reading of Okri's *The Landscapes Within* as the defining moment that 'made [him] want to stop writing thrillers and write literary fiction', but he also reveals that Okri, in revising his early novel, 'taught [him, i.e. Abani] something about the courage of being the kind of artist you want to be' (2006a). Just as Okri decided to come back to the work that had 'haunt[ed] ... [him] through the years' (1996: 325), so Abani felt the urge to repeatedly 'respond' to his own literary 'ghosts' (2006a).

While the short story 'Becoming Abigail' is stylistically more conventional than its successor (most notably in its use of syntax), Abani already likened the earlier version to 'a poem' (2006a). This term, along with its related adjective 'poetic', may have escaped clear-cut formal definition since the modernist experiments of the twentieth century, but contemporary stylisticians still concur in characterizing the poetic form as that which exhibits the highest level of linguistic 'deviation' (e.g. Short, 1996: 10; Jeffries and McIntyre, 2010: 31). 'Deviation', in a nutshell, is 'the occurrence of unexpected irregularity in language'; it 'results in foregrounding on the basis that the irregularity is surprising to the reader' (Jeffries and McIntyre, 2010: 31). This notion of 'deviation', inherited from Russian formalism, is not unproblematic in that it presupposes divergence from, or violation of, a linguistic 'norm' which 'itself is very much a relative concept' (Wales, 2011: 110). Moreover, the effect of 'foregrounding', or 'throwing into relief' (p. 166) produced by deviation inevitably involves 'an element of subjectivity of response' (p. 167). However, provided that one consider foregrounding theory as a guide to interpretation rather than a rigid set of rules, the approach constitutes a valuable methodological ally.

The principle at work is simple: it rests on the idea that 'the foregrounded features of a text are often seen as both memorable and highly interpretable' (Jeffries and McIntyre, 2010: 31). As mentioned above, foregrounding effects can be achieved by unexpected irregularity in language, but also by 'unexpected *regularity*', known as parallelism (p. 32, italics in original). While instances of deviation and parallelism occur most frequently in poetry, they can also be found in fictional and non-fictional prose, and some of them were indeed discussed in previous chapters of this book. For example, Kambili's inclination not to cast her father in the role of 'Actor' during the beating he inflicts on his family in *Purple Hibiscus*, or the instances of underlexicalization in *Half of a Yellow Sun*, are illustrations of such linguistic arrangements that trigger foregrounding effects. Admittedly, not all instances are equally salient: as Geoffrey Leech notes, deviation, just like parallelism, is 'a matter of gradience' (2008: 17).

It is because the occurrences of deviation and parallelism found in poetry tend to occupy higher levels on the scale of prominence that the theory of foregrounding is most productively applied to such types of texts. A short example from Abani's own poetry will illustrate this. The prison poem 'Killing Time', in which the I-persona is submitted to torture, ends with the following line: 'terror drips down my legs' (2000b: 40). The collocation used in this clause is semantically deviant, since the feeling of 'terror' is an abstract concept that cannot literally 'drip' like a liquid. This deviation prompts the reader to interpret the clause metaphorically, and to recognize relatively easily that 'terror' actually stands for a physical manifestation of fear that can drip down someone's legs, i.e. urine, or perhaps diarrhoea. However, a clause such as 'urine drips down my legs' would have been a poor substitute, since it lacks the suggestion offered by the metaphorical expression that the 'terror' experienced by the speaker is so intense, so palpable that it can be equated with a physical entity. The linguistic deviation used by the poet, in short, adds a layer of meaning that a simple non-metaphorical formulation would not have conveyed.

Such unconventional metaphorical expressions, along with other foregrounded elements, occur particularly frequently in *Becoming Abigail*. In fact, part of the reshaping of the short story into the novella seems to have consisted in a move away from the semantically transparent in favour of a more oblique imparting of meaning. For instance, where the early text stated that '[Abigail's] light complexion was a throwback from that time a Portuguese sailor had raped her great-grandmother' (2000a: 247), the novella more circuitously recounts that 'her light complexion was a throwback from that time a Portuguese sailor had mistaken her great-grandmother's cries' (2006b: 26). The expression 'mistake her cries' is unlikely to cause problems of understanding for the reader, who will in all probability process this rather conventional association of words successfully – perhaps even entirely unconsciously – and recognize it as a veiled reference to rape. However, the phrase is unmistakably 'deviant', for it is doubtlessly not *literally* accurate. Regardless, even, of the euphemistic nature of the expression, it is evident that the sailor of the story cannot in all good faith have 'mistaken' the woman's cries of distress for a manifestation of pleasure. The passage can therefore be said to be deviant in that it flouts pragmatic principles of communication, according to which speakers must provide information that is, among other things, sufficient in quantity and truthful in quality.[4] This instance of deviation is worth pointing out, for 'mistake her cries' is not just a more 'arty' or aesthetically pleasing way of talking about rape. Rather, the phrase involves a shift in perspective: whereas the term 'rape' forthrightly reflects the viewpoint of the great-grandmother, and most likely that of the narrator, the alternative expression 'mistake her cries' feigns to provide absolution for the European colonizers and tradesmen who assaulted indigenous women with impunity for centuries. As such, the phrase comments both on the sailor's immorality and on colonial society's hypocrisy in ignoring or condoning the crimes committed by Europeans in Africa. The 'deviant' item, in short, has a discernible artistic function.

Deviation seems to be part and parcel of what might be termed the novella's aesthetics of violence. Whereas the above example only relatively inconspicuously gestures towards the disturbing immorality of the abuse committed by men against women, the following passage is far more likely to cause readers to flinch:

> She [Abigail] had been ten when her first, fifteen-year-old cousin
> Edwin, swapped her cherry for a bag of sweets. The caramel and
> treacle was the full measure of his guilt. Then while stroking her
> hair tenderly, he whispered softly.
>   'I will kill you if you tell anyone.'
>
> (Abani, 2006b: 28)

While the shocking events described in this passage would suffice
to make most readers recoil, the narrative impact of this scene is
increased by a series of 'deviant' stylistic choices. First of all, the
sexual abuse of Abigail by her cousin is not at all described in terms
of an assault, but of an exchange ('swap') involving two items: her
'cherry' and 'a bag of sweets'. The first term, a crude reference to
the hymen and, by extension, a girl's virginity, is a deviant lexical
choice in this context, as it belongs to a far more colloquial register
than that found in the rest of the extract, or indeed in the rest of
the book. Moreover, 'cherry' does not appear with any of its usual
collocates (typically 'lose', 'take', or the rather crass 'pop'), but is
rather disturbingly juxtaposed with the verb 'swap', suggesting that
a 10-year-old girl's virginity is a commodity that can be traded for
merchandise of equivalent value. Further, the fact that the item that
the 'cherry' is being traded for is 'a bag of sweets' triggers associations with the original meaning of the word 'cherry', a fruit that one
might more reasonably expect a child to trade in for sweets. Thus,
the novella presents as an innocent childhood transaction an act
of indescribable moral and physical violence, casting doubt in the
process on the exact nature of the assault. Indeed, even though some
form of duress is evidently involved, it is impossible to determine
whether Edwin had to physically restrain Abigail, or whether the
girl had sexual intercourse with her abuser following his assurance
that she would be given 'caramel and treacle' after the act.[5] The second interpretation is all the more disturbing as it may hint at some
measure of willingness on Abigail's part – the verb 'swap', after all,
is an action denoting intention. This suggestion, in turn, prompts
unsettling questions about the extent of the young Abigail's innocence, and about her intuiting of the fact that masculinity defines
itself 'through violence ... over women's bodies' (Abani, 2007b),
as it already did in her great-grandmother's time. Whatever one's
precise understanding of the text, the combination of the incident

recounted in the extract and of the language used to portray it is suggestive of an uneasy collision between the worlds of childhood and adulthood. Childhood, the book revealingly states much later, 'was perhaps the one thing Abigail had never really had, and yet truly needed' (2006b: 111).

As the scene depicting Edwin's abuse of his younger cousin progresses, instances of deviation accumulate. The words 'stroke', 'tenderly', 'whisper' and 'softly' all evoke affection and tenderness; the last three, especially, do not belong to the lexical fields of rape or sexual abuse, which typically contain words denoting violence, or physical and emotional pain. So numerous are the deviant lexical choices in the first lines of the passage quoted above that the positively connoted concepts of childhood and affection become the new norm through which the passage is read. As a consequence, Edwin's violent threat at the end, 'I will kill you if you tell anyone', is foregrounded as a case of internal deviation (Levin, 1965), that is, 'deviation against a norm set up by *the text itself*' (Short, 1996: 59, italics in original). The foregrounding is not only the result of a sudden change in the type of vocabulary featured, but also of the speech type used. By way of illustration, compare the excerpt from *Becoming Abigail* with the version found in the 2000 short story: 'Then, while stroking her hair tenderly, he whispered softly that he would kill her if she told anyone' (2000a: 248). In contrast to this early version, the novella uses direct speech, which conveys a greater sense of immediacy since it is theoretically *'unmediated by the reporter'* (Short, 1996: 289, italics in original). What is more, Edwin's intimidating words, being in direct discourse, are more evidently foregrounded in the textual environment of the novella, as they form the first and only instance of such speech type in the entire chapter. This double case of internal deviation – the clause 'I will kill you' after a string of words evoking tenderness, and the use of direct discourse – helps to bring home the chilling brutality of the young man's act.

Physical violence takes many forms in *Becoming Abigail*. Some of it is self-inflicted, such as the protagonist's burning and cutting of her own body. Yet the text does not present this act as pathological self-mutilation, but rather as a quiet gesture of self-affirmation: 'This burning wasn't immolation. Not combustion. But an exorcism. Cauterization. Permanence even' (2006b: 34). Once again, the stylistic impact produced by this passage partly lies in the use of deviation, most visibly on the level of syntax. Impressionistically, one might say that one has the feeling of being faced with a series of still shots. This effect is generated by the presence of at least three linguistic features. First, most of the sentences are, quite obviously, very short – rather than strings of words linked by commas, what we have here are brief structures separated by full stops. As Leech and Short remind us, the full stop is 'the "heaviest" punctuation mark', that which 'has the greatest separative force'; it allows 'each piece of information' to be 'asserted with the maximum force' (2007: 174). The full stops, in short, neatly separate the shots. The still frames themselves are created using two further techniques. Most of the sentences in the extract are not only very short, as previously mentioned, but they are also verbless – such structures, because they are 'irregular' in form, are known as 'minor sentences'. As Jeffries and McIntyre point out, '[t]he loss of the verbal element of a clause has the effect of placing the remaining words outside any normal time-frame and results in a kind of timelessness' (Jeffries and McIntyre, 2010: 51-2). In other words, the syntactic structure of the last four sentences de-emphasizes their potential narrative aspect and enhances their descriptive value, hence the 'photographic' effect. Further, all the nouns in the short excerpt are instances of nominalization, which is to say that they are abstract nouns derived from other word types, such as verbs or adjectives. For example, 'exorcism' actually refers to the action of 'exorcizing', and therefore has a distinctly verbal origin; 'permanence' denotes the state of being 'permanent', which is a descriptive adjective. Stylistically speaking, nominalization, especially when applied to verbs, typically 'render[s] static the potentially dynamic or active' (Wales, 2011: 291). In this passage, the absence of dynamism makes it difficult to construe the protagonist's gesture as an act of violence committed upon the body; instead, what is enhanced through language is the stillness and symbolic significance of the ritual. This sense of the static is further conveyed by the fact that the successive nouns are in fact appositional: 'burning', 'immolation', 'combustion', 'exorcism', 'cauterization' and 'permanence' all refer to a single act. The extract, in brief, does not actually contain a progression in time.

Another stylistic feature, even more decisive to the understanding of the above passage, is the exploitation of the phenomenon of 'negated opposition' (Jeffries, 2010a: 55). This label simply refers to constructions of the 'X not Y' type – e.g. 'black not white', 'hot not cold'. In the variant used here – 'not X but Y' – the opposition is triggered by the co-occurrence of the negator 'not' and the conjunction 'but' (Jeffries 2010b: 36). Importantly, the pairs of opposites constructed via such structures 'may or may not be conventionally recognized' (Jeffries, 2010a: 55) – that is, these constructions may involve elements that are not in a semantic relationship of antonymy outside the text in which they appear. As a consequence, discourses can construct a particular 'version of the world' by using oppositions (p. 51); more precisely, 'texts have the capacity ... to set up *new* synonymies and oppositions, sometimes between words that we would *never* relate to each other out of context' (p. 52, italics in original). The passage from *Becoming Abigail* is a case in point. 'Immolation' and 'combustion', on the one hand, are opposed to 'exorcism', 'cauterization' and 'permanence', on the other, even though these sets of items are by no means conventionally recognized antonyms. Hence, the last three elements – 'exorcism', 'cauterization' and 'permanence' – emerge as being 'the opposite of destruction by fire'. They are, thus, given new meanings by virtue of their textual environment. This fact, added to the conventional definition of the three terms in question, turns a potential act of self-mutilation into a range of positively connoted processes associated with change and renewal: symbolic healing, the driving away of malicious spirits and, most importantly, coming into being – one of the major themes of the novella, as indicated by its title.

As already hinted above, the fact that the terms 'exorcism', 'cauterization' and 'permanence' are collectively opposed to 'immolation' and 'combustion' results in them becoming bound in a relationship of near synonymy. The setting up of semantic relationships between these words is further encouraged by the fact that they occur in succession in the text, and that they appear in minor sentences that each contain a single noun. Using the more precise terminology introduced at the beginning of this chapter, one might say that the structural similarity between the sentences leads the sole nouns contained in them to become foregrounded as components of parallel constructions. Such equivalent structures, as is widely acknowledged, 'invite the reader to search for meaning connections' (Short, 1996: 14), and they may also reflect the author's difficult quest 'to express the inexpressible' (Widdowson, 1975: 44). In line with this, 'exorcism', 'cauterization' and 'permanence' can all be regarded as glimpses into the linguistic shape of what the author has called the 'haunting', the 'ectoplasm' (Abani, 2006a) – something that is 'of its very nature ineffable' and 'beyond exact description' (Widdowson, 1975: 43).

The different strands of this micro-analysis converge towards one central argument: the poetic prose used in the excerpt above, and elsewhere in the book, leads to the creation of what Abani has called a 'conceptual ... framework ... generated by the narrative' itself (2006a). In the universe brought into being by the text, Abigail's existence is literally inscribed through ritualistic markings of the body, which are presented as a form of healing. This marking is first initiated by external agents, a fact only disclosed in a memory recounted towards the end of the novella. When Abigail is a child, her father takes her to an old 'witch' who, in an attempt to 'exorcize this devil' – that is, Abigail's 'longing for death and the ways of the dead' – cuts 'a straight line' and 'a wave' on the girl's face, 'the hot metal [of the knife] cauterizing' (2006b: 112). The lexical similarity between this passage and the previous one – both speak of exorcism and cauterization – is no coincidence, as it points to one of the key dynamics in the conceptual framework mentioned above. Since cauterization is the destruction of tissue to heal a wound, while exorcism is the killing of a malevolent spirit or ghost to restore to their own body the person inhabited by it, both concepts emphasize the interaction between destruction and regeneration.

This interplay is paradigmatic of the novella's interweaving of traditionally discrete notions in Western thought such as absence and presence, invisibility and visibility, death and life. The effacement of these binaries has not constituted the focus of scholarly analyses of *Becoming Abigail* so far, but existing studies have nonetheless provided substantial insights into the significance of Abigail's marking of her own body. For instance, Ashley Dawson has retraced the evolution of the protagonist's rituals, and has rightly observed that she first 'struggles to recover her lost mother' (2010: 185) by collecting anecdotes about her that she writes down 'in red ink on bits of paper which she [sticks] on her skin', in the hope of '[becoming] her mother and her mother her' (Abani, 2006b: 34). As Abigail grows older, Dawson continues, she 'begins to struggle increasingly to forge her own identity'; '[h]er acts of self-signification with fire offer her a means of marking

and mourning her lost mother on her body' (2010: 185). Also noticing a development in Abigail's rituals, another commentator, Pietro
Deandrea (2009), emphasizes the fact that, although she 'has used
her body as a writable surface since she was a child', she first did so
'lightly' (by 'trac[ing]' the 'outlines' of the stories about her mother
'on her skin with soft fingers': Abani, 2006b: 45), but then through
'more pain-inflicting practices' (Deandrea, 2009: 678). Both scholars
certainly concur in seeing the burns on Abigail's body as intimately
linked to her sense of self: Deandrea speaks of 'identitarian bodily
marks' (p. 678), while Dawson states that '[h]er physical inscriptions
remind her of who she is' (2010: 186). As the two critics point out,
this link between Abigail's physical brandings and her sense of identity assumes major significance when she is chained to a doghouse
by her cousin Peter and repeatedly raped by him. As the sexual abuse
to which he subjects her 'threaten[s] to obliterate the tattoos that
made her' (Abani, 2006b: 95), the girl, '[u]nable to stand it anymore',
'[invokes] the spirit of Abigail' and bites off Peter's penis (p. 97).

Evidently, the metaphorical purport of the writer's representation
of the young Abigail's body has escaped neither of the critics cited.
Examining the protagonist's relationship with men – to whom, the
novella states, she was a 'foreign country' (p. 27) – Deandrea rightly
identifies the presence of a 'metaphor reminiscent of the female-
body-as-conquered-land trope' (2009: 676). Dawson also comments
on the metaphorical connection between geography and identity,
and writes that, like Abigail's observation of the ancient 'maps' that
she is obsessed with, her 'willed rituals of remembrance ... are a
means of charting the world on her body, an assertion of loss but also
of an ordering of self' (2010: 185). These remarks are incisive indeed,
but they do not tell the whole story, for the portions of texts describing Abigail's self-inscriptions lend themselves to a multiplicity of
metaphorical readings. Such is the case of a passage in which Derek
discovers the marks that the girl has burned into her skin:

> He ran his hands over her, stopping as his fingers encountered
> the bubbles of Braille ... And he traced her in that moment, the
> map of her, the skin of her world, as she emerged in pointillism.
> Emerging in parts of a whole. Each. Every. He wondered what
> would form should he draw a line between each dot.
>
> (Abani, 2006b: 53–4)

This short excerpt does not invalidate Deandrea's and Dawson's analyses, but rather points to the partial delineation of the author's artistic strategies so far. This passage alone relies for its interpretation on an intricate network of poetic metaphors that is woven into the narrative and that would, in fact, require an entire study unto itself. For example, the description of Abigail's burns as 'bubbles of Braille' associates her markings with a form of *linguistic* expression; more subtly still, the fact that this language is used by the blind may suggest that Derek is, after all, not so different from all the other men in Abigail's life, who had never 'seen her' (2006b: 26). At the same time, Derek's connecting of the dots on his lover's body evokes innocence rather than malicious intent, as the act is reminiscent of a children's game – and the social worker is, indeed, described as a 'man-child' (p. 54) in the passage that follows on from this one. Moreover, Abigail's body is briefly assimilated to a map which Derek traces into being; yet, the term 'pointillism' is rather suggestive of *painting*, equating the body to a canvas. Elsewhere in the book, it is Abigail who 'trac[es] the outline of Derek' (p. 79) in her mind, and not the other way round; in another passage still, she observes a map until her mother emerges '[i]n true cubist form' (p. 72). Thus, the heroine is alternatively, and sometimes at once, artist and canvas, topographer and map. She is, more precisely, 'the cartographer of dreams. Of ghosts' (p. 72), but she is also repeatedly described as a ghost herself – in other words, she is shown attempting to capture the intangible, but she is herself presented as incorporeal. In the passages cited above and throughout the novella, the physical and the imaginary, or the concrete and the ineffable, are repeatedly linked through metaphor. Thus far, the paradoxical quality of this duality has remained largely unexplored.

The novella's metaphorical network is both sinuous and slippery, sustained as it is by a language at once 'diaphanous and poetic', and a 'lyricism' that is 'elliptical, almost evasive' (Ehrenreich, 2006). It might seem almost a contradiction in terms to describe as trans-lucent a style that relies so heavily on foregrounding by means of deviation and parallelism, but this paradox in fact largely accounts for the elusory impression left by the novella as a whole. Capturing such elusiveness, the book's own blurb describes the prose of the narrative as 'spare yet haunting and lyrical'; in the same vein, a reviewer has called *Becoming Abigail* 'ethereal' (Casey, 2007). But what, exactly, makes Abani's text so ungraspable, besides its pervasive reliance on metaphor and its thematic exploration of ghosts? A closer look at the enigmatic opening of the novella may help to partially elucidate this question:

> And this.
>   Even this. This memory like all the others was a lie. Like the sound of someone ascending wooden stairs, which she couldn't know because she had never heard it. Still it was as real as this one.
>   (Abani, 2006b: 17)

The first sentence of the book starts with the coordinating conjunction 'and', thereby presenting itself as the continuation of something that is, in fact, unwritten. Opening a text with the second part of a coordinated structure constitutes an example of discoursal deviation, since it defies 'the general assumption in language that one should begin at the beginning' (Short, 1996: 37–8). Having slightly unsettled its readers in this way, the text then introduces a demonstrative pronoun, 'this' (whose referent is as yet unknown), and then begins a new paragraph, recalling the poetic use of line breaks. In the second sentence, the deictic 'this' is brought into focus by means of the adverb 'even', pointing to the extreme or unexpected character of the element being discussed. The word 'even' draws readers' attention to 'this' but, disconcertingly, they are not given any clue as to the type of thing or event whose surprising or extreme nature is being emphasized. The veil is partly lifted with the introduction of 'This memory', though the assertion that this element is 'a lie' may again be viewed as destabilizing, as it is semantically deviant. Since a 'memory' denotes a thing, person or event remembered, the very word refers to a reflection on something that happened in actual fact; a 'lie', on the other hand, suggests the opposite. The text, in other words, first withholds the identity of its topic, and then describes it as something based on reality, only to withdraw this claim straight away. A similarly puzzling effect is produced by the next sentence, which contains an auditory evocation of an action ('ascending wooden stairs') that is actually a non-experience for the protagonist. The other two verbs in this sentence, 'know' and 'hear', are both negated ('couldn't know', 'never heard') and thus do not refer to existing states or perceptions either. Then, the text goes on to affirm, 'it' (presumably 'This memory') 'was as real as this one' (presumably the imagined memory of the 'sound'). The comparative structure 'as real as' triggers the presupposition that the 'sound', which was previously identified as a non-experience, is in fact 'real', which suggests that what has not been experienced can nonetheless be 'real'. The novella thereby challenges the traditional view that what is 'real' must necessarily be based in our actual experience of the outside world. Imagined memories, the book seems to be saying, can constitute reality; or, more radically still, everything that constitutes our memory of reality is, to an extent, an invention.

The first few sentences of the novella alone provide a number of cognitive and conceptual challenges that render nearly impossible any firm hold over the text. This sense of the ungraspable is heightened when Abigail's untrue-real memory is described:

> A coffin sinking reluctantly into the open mouth of a grave, earth in clods collected around it in a pile like froth from the mouth of a mad dog. And women. Gathered in a cluster of black, like angry crows. Weeping. The sound was something she had heard only in her dreams and in these moments of memory – a keening, loud and sharp, but not brittle like the screeching of glass or the imagined sound of women crying. This was something entirely different. A deep lowing, a presence, dark and palpable, like a shadow emanating from the women, becoming a thing that circled the grave and the mourners in a predatory manner before rising up to the brightness of the sky and the sun, to be replaced by another momentarily.
>
> (Abani, 2006b: 17)

This passage starts with a personification of the coffin, which is said to descend 'reluctantly' into the grave, an image that lends the consciousness of living beings to an object that is connected to death. Further, both the inanimate earth and the humans gathered around the grave are associated with animals experiencing emotionally-related states of mind (the former is 'like froth from the mouth of a mad dog'; the latter are 'like angry crows'). Like the initial personification, these similes bring together human, animal and mineral elements that are regarded as belonging to discrete categories in European philosophy; the trope can therefore be said to gesture towards a similar collapsing of boundaries as the opening lines discussed above. As much is also suggested, for example, by the description of the sound emitted by the woman as a 'lowing', which is an animal cry.

The real difficulty of this passage, however, resides elsewhere. Simile is, by definition, the establishment of a connection between different elements on the basis of some perceived similarity, a function that indeed appears to be performed in the two examples pointed out above. Yet the other similes in the extract seem to work in a rather less transparent way. First, the sound of the women weeping is described as 'a keening, loud and sharp, but not brittle like the screeching of glass or the imagined sound of women crying'. The simile does not really help readers to forge a more precise mental representation of the sound, as the trope is appended to the element that describes the keening in terms of what it is *not*. Most striking is the second part of the simile, which states that the women's wailing lamentations are 'not brittle like ... the imagined sound of women crying'. Interpreted literally, this means that the sound being described is not like itself. This might create puzzlement, but it quickly becomes obvious that such a narrowly literal reading must be left aside, for the keening (which is by definition high-pitched) is then identified as a 'deep lowing' – that is, a sound that stands at the opposite end of the tonal scale. It is by then entirely clear that the textual universe does not operate according to the rules of conventional Western logic. Rather, it invites its readers to consider that things are unlike themselves, and that these things are at once particular entities and their opposite. These riddles unarguably contribute to making the text elusive yet, at the same time, they also provide the key to unlocking its 'conceptual framework', as will be detailed below.

In Abigail's invented memory, the mysterious keening/lowing then morphs into 'a presence, dark and palpable, like a shadow', marking a transition from the sense of hearing to those of touch and sight.[6] This shadowy presence eventually becomes a 'thing' that circles the grave, vulture-like, in a 'predatory' manner, which once again positions the entity being described as simultaneously object-like and animate. This mysterious, possibly malevolent presence may or may not be the ghost of Abigail's mother; what can more conclusively be established in light of the above examination is that the opening sequence of the novella provides a blueprint for the entire narrative, in which untrue things are real, things are but are not, the border between the animate and the inanimate is abolished, and the abstract morphs into the concrete. Significantly, some of these connections are echoed in Abani's circuitous description of the character of 'Abigail' in his 2006 essay on the genesis of his book:

> When I went to Berlin ..., the wall had fallen. Yet there was still the notion of a conceptual wall, perhaps in this way more impenetrable because of its invisibility. The wall is a yellow line in the road. I stepped over it many times, ignoring the angry cars. On either side I was Chris. One [sic] either side I was not Chris.
> This was Abigail.
>
> (Abani, 2006a)

Abani captures the substance of his protagonist through the seeming paradox of 'being and not being', while moving across an invisible 'conceptual wall' – a 'line' separating two worlds. In the novella, Abigail straddles a similar frontier when she stands on the Greenwich meridian, 'the line that cut the earth into two time zones' (Abani, 2006b: 50). As Jason Weaver points out, 'the International Date Line at Greenwich' is 'a symbol of colonial over-mapping of the world' (2008), but Abigail's standing on the meridian also emphasizes her own ghostly liminality – she is described in the book as 'trapped forever between the two' worlds separated by the line (Abani, 2006b: 50). Greenwich surfaces again in the narrative a few pages later, when Abigail, having shown Derek the dots on her breasts representing herself and her lover, adds: 'In the middle is Greenwich' (p. 53) – the image at once evoking connection, balance, symmetry, and but also separation.

Both the elusive condition of 'being and not being' and the image of the line present in Abani's essay are central to the novella as a whole, and they are worth exploring in some more detail as they relate to the relationship between form and content in the book. This argument may seem a little fuzzy, so let us clarify it somewhat by anticipating its conclusion: the novella's thematic import is sustained by, or indeed enacted through, the very form of the text. To give this claim its necessary substance, let us start by quoting Chapter 17, which is made up of a short, enigmatic fragment:

> And this was the shape of her desire:
>   To be a white bird beating its wings against night. Beating until that was all. To be. Yet not the bird. Or night. Or the air. Or the beating.
>   To be a white bird.
>
> (2006b: 73)

The words opening this section, 'And this', echo those found at the start of the novella, though here they are not followed by a full stop but by the expected explanation of what the demonstrative pronoun 'this' stands for. Any illusion of conventionality, however, rapidly dissipates with the accumulation of deviations, most noticeably on the syntactic and semantic levels. The minor sentences and the repetition of the state verb 'to be' are consistent with the figurative rather than narrative nature of the segment. The semantic deviations found in the passage work in similar fashion. Most obviously, Abigail's desire to be a white bird, '[y]et not' to be the bird, a seemingly contradictory wish eventually summarized again as 'To be a white bird', cannot be understood literally, and is therefore likely to generate associations with the earlier images of the ghost that is yet is not, and of the protagonist that is at once human and incorporeal. In sum, the numerous poetic features in this passage incite readers to interpret the fragment in a symbolic rather than purely logical light, hence encouraging them to leave the paradox at its heart unresolved, and the metaphor open. The image of the 'white bird beating its wings' invites a range of interpretations – the bird may be a dove, an egret or an owl; it may summon up associations with freedom or (in)visibility in the dark; it may rely for its decoding on the numerous other birds mentioned in the novella, or it may even be based on an unrelated cultural reference.

Developing this argument further, one could go as far as suggesting that the precise symbolism of the passage is subordinated to the 'poetic function' of the text – the function that, through the inclusion of devices such as deviation, repetition and parallelism, 'promot[es] the palpability of signs' (Jakobson, 1960: 356). Metre and rhyme are two well-known techniques that are used to achieve this effect, by foregrounding patterns of rhythm and sound. Abani follows no set verse metre rules, but he nonetheless exploits the rhythmic potential of language in similar ways. For instance, the sequence 'Or night. Or the air. Or the beating' (Abani, 2006b: 73) is marked by syllabic expansion between the different sentences, so that the natural prose rhythm tends to blend with the metrical regularity of poetry. This is made possible by a grammatical deviation, which takes the form of a missing definite article in front of the noun 'night'. This deviation also allows for a rhythmic effect in the phrase 'beating its wings against night'. The sound parallelism in this phrase is perhaps best captured with a musical analogy: the seven syllables can be divided up into three bars, each starting with a stressed syllable, with the first two bars containing a triplet.[7] In both of the cases just mentioned, the inclusion of the uncountable poetic form 'night' also has a potential semantic impact, as it presents darkness as a mass without boundaries rather than a unit that can neatly be isolated, thus possibly reinforcing the engulfing quality of the space against which the bird is beating its wings. That a single grammatical deviation can have both rhythmic and semantic effects confirms, if need be, that focusing on the manifestation of the 'poetic function' in a text does not mean disregarding meaning altogether in favour of form. What is rather put forward for consideration is that, to fully gauge the artistry involved in a passage such as the one quoted above, one should not only attempt to understand the words that constitute it, but also to 'hear the music' it produces, as Abani recommended at the Venice event mentioned at the beginning of this chapter. The passage from *Becoming Abigail* in relation to which the writer made this comment is, significantly, precisely the one that I have just examined.

Importantly, the interplay between written signs and sound patterns in the novella is by no means limited to the excerpt discussed above. The book is indeed infused with assonances and alliterations, found in phrases such as 'slap of slipper' (2006b: 29), 'fresh like a new fern unfurling' (p. 30), 'carried clear across the water' (p. 39), '[a] line is a lie' (p. 113), and '[r]evenge is a raven' (p. 117). There is no need to venture on the slippery slope of sound symbolism – which would suggest a systematic association between the phonetic features of these words and their meanings – to ascertain the significance of these occurrences in the author's stylistic strategy. Suffice it to say that the repetition of sounds results in foregrounding, which itself attracts the reader's attention to the oral and physical rather than purely referential nature of language. This statement on the concreteness of the text may appear to work against the multiple evocations of 'ghostliness' and 'incorporeality' found earlier in this chapter; however, this is not a contradiction, but rather a tension within the novella that I wish to emphasize. Abani, commenting on the evolution of his character, has stated that, as Abigail 'begins to gain an agency over her body', the body, 'which was ephemeral before', 'begins to solidify' (2006c). One of the strategies implemented to signify this coming into being is that 'the names become clearer' – for instance, Abigail's surname, Tansi, is revealed towards the end of the book (2006c). In line with this, what I would like to suggest is that the entire novella actually uses its poetic strategy to work towards its own physical incarnation. Like Abigail, who writes down anecdotes about her mother on pieces of paper, the text too seeks to 'create memory, make it concrete, physical' (Abani, 2006b: 45). The assonances and alliterations mentioned above are one way of achieving this; another technique is found in a passage depicting Abigail after her father has committed suicide by hanging. Sitting 'on the floor beneath him', 'his toe brush[ing] her cheek with every turn', she feels its uncut nail cutting her face:

> Sharp enough to cut. Cut a small line. Line linking her to him. Him held only by that line falling. Falling from the ceiling in hemp. Hemp becoming flesh. Flesh the fluid of him, leaking. Leaking down his leg. Leg ending in the toe. Toe brushing her cheek with a cut. Cut the line. Cut the line. Line. The rope. Rope-saw-rough voices. Voices calling. Falling heavy in the dust around her. Her sitting on the floor. Floor where his crumpled body was laid on the hard of concrete. Concrete falling away into the soft of loam and he falling. Falling into Abigail. Abigail, her, sitting on the floor. Losing him. Him losing her. Her. She. She the reason for him doing this. This love. Love calling to love.
>
> (pp. 81–2)

What stands out most clearly in this passage is the presence of ana-diplosis, that is, the '[r]epetition of the last word of one ... clause to begin the next' (Lanham, 1991: 10). When words are not repeated in their exact form, sentences are often linked by words that are phonetically close (cf. 'calling. Falling'), or that belong to the same grammatical category and have a common referent (cf. 'Her. She'). An entire sentence, 'Cut the line', is also repeated – its duplication is likely to evoke the repetitive movements of the people sawing the rope to bring down the body. This explanation suggests that the iteration of 'Cut the line' follows the principle of iconicity, which is to say that the text 'mim[es] the meaning that it expresses' (Leech and Short, 2007: 188). The instances of anadiplosis occurring after each other may be said to follow such a mimetic principle too, since the chain of sentences contained in the excerpt reproduces the trajectory of the gaze moving upwards from the dead man's toe to the rope falling from the ceiling, and then downwards again to the cut on Abigail's face. By contrast, the short minor sentences in this passage and the many pauses brought about by the full stops separating them rather evoke the idea of fracture, which the man's suicide indeed effects in Abigail's life, as his death precipitates her move to London.

In short, the passage deploys stylistic techniques that highlight a pervasive link-and-rupture motif, which is represented on the literal level by the 'line' (that is, the rope) being cut, and on the figurative level by the disruption caused in Abigail's existence by the death of her father. This connection between link and rupture is also symbolized by the cut on the protagonist's face – a literal rupturing of the skin that nonetheless represents a '[l]ine linking her to him' (Abani, 2006b: 81). Significantly, this image evokes the association between cutting and symbolic healing suggested by Abigail's bodily markings and by the lines drawn on her face by the old witch. Thus, the interaction between destruction and regeneration is once again underscored; in the post-suicide scene, the annihilation of the father's body is similarly paired with an ambiguous sense of renewal. In the passage that comes immediately after the one quoted above, Abigail 'dip[s] her finger in the pool of him' (p. 82) and tastes her father's urine, before soaking her hands, her face and her entire body in it. To an extent, the act could be said to express Abigail's desire to fuse with her father, a wish akin to her obsession to become one with her mother. But the girl's actual gesture, the description of the fluid as 'water' that is '[t]he salt of him' (p. 82), and the intense feeling of 'joy' (p. 82) provoked by the action, more insistently recall the religious ritual of baptism, which is synonymous with birth and purification. Ultimately, the ambiguity of the relationship between Abigail and her father is captured in the phrase '[l]ove calling to love' (p. 82), whose loop-like structure might signify the strength of their bond, but which might also refer to Abigail's loving recognition of 'the reason for him doing this' – that is, the father's love for his daughter, expressed through a suicide that prevents him from acting on his incestuous impulses towards the girl.[8]

My double use of the modal 'might' in the preceding sentence signals a measure of cautiousness that is both deliberate and necessary, for the analysis put forward rests on the supposition that the sentence beginning and ending in 'love' must be read against the many instances of anadiplosis that precede. In other words, the assumption underlying my claim is that the circularity of the sentence is a form of internal deviation that calls for interpretation. In line with this, the entire examination of the above scene in fact rests on the *perceived* iconicity of anadiplosis. The mimetic association is, I believe, justified, but it remains based on a principle rather than a rule. The purpose of this self-reflexive parenthesis – too important to be footnoted – is to remind critics relying on iconicity to heed the warning given by Leech and Short who, despite recognizing the 'undoubted iconic suggestibility of language', caution that this principle may be used 'as a *carte blanche* for justifying private and whimsical responses' to literary texts (2007: 195, italics in original). In the end, it falls upon individual analysts – and their readers – to determine the precise point at which the 'capacity to see connections' (p. 195) starts morphing into a form of methodology-induced hallucination.

These cautionary words must not detract from the fact that, in some cases, the textual evidence is so considerable that it simply *cannot* be denied interpretation. In *Becoming Abigail*, repetition is a device used with such insistence that it inevitably comes to confer meaning upon the text. For instance, the protagonist's deep understanding of the death of her father is described with an iterated phrase: 'Loss: She knew this. Knew this. Knew this' (Abani, 2006b: 82). The verb 'know' is also repeated by Abigail and Peter's wife Mary when the protagonist is chained to a doghouse, and the older woman attempts to warm her up with an electric blanket: 'And Abigail would nod and whisper: I know. I know. I know ... And Mary would echo: I know. I know. I know' (p. 92). In the examples cited above, repetition clearly has an expressive rather than a referential function. Abigail's words to Mary may translate as forgiveness of her relative's inability to actually rescue her; Mary's echoed response may signal deep empathy with the younger woman's plight, as well as her own attempt to deal with her guilt and desperation. Abigail's words, spoken in a 'hoarse rasp' (p. 92), also carry the last fading traces of human dignity left in 'a girl slowly becoming a dog' (p. 92).

In many ways, repetition is used in the novella to signal – even cement – existence, humanity, *being* itself. That the verb 'know' should be repeated so many times supports this reading, for this word is a factive predicate – that is, a verb that commits the speaker to the truth of what follows, and therefore situates the complement phrase in the realm of mental existence. The verb is also one of cognition, which by definition signals consciousness – and, potentially, individuality and agency. Such an interpretation may clarify the repetition of 'know' not only in the passages above, but also in a brief chapter set as Abigail is smoking by the Thames at night, shortly before jumping into the river:

> Sometimes there is no way to leave something behind. Something over. We know this. We know this. We know this. This is the prevalence of ritual. To remember something that cannot be forgotten. Yet not left over. She knew this. As she smoked. She knew this. This. This. This. And what now?
>
> (p. 59)

This excerpt foregrounds several sentences through repetition ('We know this', 'She knew this', and the minor sentence 'This'), as if to ensure the imprinting of the subjects and the object of knowing, as well as the existence of this state of consciousness itself. The device is of particular importance because of its juxtaposition with the mention of 'ritual', a word that recalls Abigail's numerous attempts to be seen by her father, by others, and by herself, through the assertion of her physical existence. The textual repetitions, just like the actions constituting rituals, appear to serve a *performative* function; the multiple mentions of the words bring their referents into being. This association between ritual, repetition and the spoken word is also encapsulated in the idea of the 'mantra', mentioned in the narrative as Abigail recites the names of London underground stations 'as if they were a mantra that would reveal all to her' (p. 78). As is widely known, this type of sacred utterance plays a central role in religions such as Hinduism and Buddhism – spiritual traditions in which the writer has a particular interest (Abani, 2006c). Significantly, mantras serve to attain a state of extreme concentration, of full consciousness – that is, a state of pure *being*.

The above paragraph reformulates in more detail my initial hypothesis that the form of the novella literally enacts its content. By drawing the reader's attention to the physical aspects of the language used to create the character of Abigail, the book almost takes on an incantatory function, as though it were itself a ritualistic chant willing its ghostly protagonist into being. To an extent, the entire narrative can also be regarded as a fictional equivalent to the 'second burial' of Igbo tradition, given by a newly rich relative to '[a] person who lived poor and was buried poor' (Abani, 2006b: 107). The wealth of words offered by the writer to his character is obviously not a literal one, but the spirit remains the same: it is a 'second chance' given to the dead (p. 107). This, significantly, ties in with Abani's conception of art: 'The creative process', the author has stated in a recent essay, 'is a ritual of remembrance' (2013).

The writer's bearing 'witness' to Abigail, 'seeing' her through the literary medium is also what he calls an 'act of love' (Abani, 2013), but one that spurns romanticization by cultivating ambiguity. Abigail's 'becoming' is not cast in simplistic sentimentalism – her affirmation of identity through self-mutilation illustrates this, as does her relationship with the social worker Derek, which is represented as tender, empowering for her, yet not devoid of the disquieting lust that attracts a middle-aged man to a 14-year-old. However, Derek does, to an extent, fulfil Abigail's desire to be 'seen' (Abani, 2006b: 54); being forcibly separated from him by the authorities is what turns her into a 'ghost' once more (p. 110). In this sense, her suicide can be read as the ultimate act of agency, and therefore self-affirmation, even if it is one that precipitates her own physical erasure. This gesture may even give the novella what might provocatively be called a 'happy ending'. '[H]appy endings,' Abani insists, 'aren't pretty endings. They're beautiful endings, they're inevitable endings.' The author continues: 'the death of a character can actually be a beautiful ending', because it can provide 'a resolution', 'a release' (2009a). So it is for Abigail, who can only come into being by, paradoxically, ceasing to be. Thus, the dividing line between absence and presence, invisibility and visibility, death and life is, once more, disrupted. Yet again, what Abani has termed the 'this or that' mode characteristic of the Western mindset is challenged by a more typically African, 'this and that' paradigm (cited in Ranzenberger, 2014).

In many ways, the sense of haunting described by Abani in his essay 'Abigail and My Becoming' is a painstaking search for the exact words to that will do justice to the elusive, 'ectoplasmic traces' (2006a) of human suffering and dignity that dwell in a writer's consciousness. Put differently, this haunting is a patient search for *form*. It has been my argument in this chapter that Abani's 'bi-textual' poetics are an integral part of this artistic quest. Whether it takes the form of linguistic deviations used to convey the full horror of sexual violence; minor sentences and oppositional constructions designed to reveal the restorative force of bodily rituals; deviant similes employed to suggest the unreality of the imagined memories that shape our existence; rhythmic patterns expressive of a paradoxical desire to be yet not to be; or repetitions aimed at conjuring the heroine into being – all these formal features are part and parcel of what constitutes the character of Abigail. Without the elements that make up this poetic prose, the heroine simply would not exist in our imagination in the many different ways that she does. Because, as Abani says, 'there are always casualties to memory', it is imperative to try and forego the erasure of those marginalized by official histories, by conferring them agency, if only through literature. Or, perhaps, *especially* through literature, for art, as Abani once said, 'is the one hope that we have' (2008).

6
Children at War
Language and Representation in Uzodinma Iweala's *Beasts of No Nation* and Chris Abani's *Song for Night*

A metaphor that is insistently used to talk about the connections between the writers and works that make up individual literary movements is that of genealogy. Literary traditions, it seems, are families, and Nigerian fiction is no exception: Chinua Achebe is regularly labelled the 'father' of the Nigerian novel (or indeed of African literature as a whole), Chimamanda Ngozi Adichie is considered by many to be his literary 'daughter', and authors born after 1960 are often said to be part of the third 'generation' of Nigerian writers. Applying this image of the family tree to the literary works themselves, one might regard Ken Saro-Wiwa's civil war novel *Sozaboy* (1994 [1985]) as the ancestor of Uzodinma Iweala's *Beasts of No Nation* (2005a) and Chris Abani's *Song for Night* (2007a). One could even extend the familial metaphor, and describe these two offspring as non-identical twins – siblings that both take after their shared forebear, but in rather different ways.

Thematically speaking, *Beasts of No Nation* and *Song for Night* have much in common. Both books recount the experiences of boy soldiers involved in African civil wars, and describe acts of extreme violence (such as killings and rapes) in which the protagonists participate, and which disturbingly bring these characters some level of pleasure. The two narratives also share a series of formal features, including a first-person narrator, the use of the present as the main tense of narration, and the inclusion of flashbacks to the protagonists' lives before the war and in the early stages of the conflict. As will be detailed below, both books also deploy stylistic strategies that overtly challenge the conventions of realism, though it is also here

146

that the novels' dizygotic traits start to show, as their linguistic take on their common subject is radically different. This is hardly a controversial claim, yet one that has not often been made directly, perhaps because of its sheer obviousness. Its interest, however, lies in the specifics that it hides. So far, critical studies involving both novels have mostly privileged 'top-down' approaches, in the sense that, on the one hand, they have compared and contrasted these books with a number of other works that are part of the growing corpus of child soldier narratives; on the other hand, they have broadly situated the novels in relation to non-literary theoretical discourses, most notably those on human rights. Several of these analyses have put forward claims that are both discerning and provocative, some of which will be detailed below to allow readers, if need be, to become acquainted with the critical context in which my own examination takes place. This chapter will build on previous studies, but it will approach Iweala's and Abani's novels from a different methodological angle, as it will seek to assess whether a 'bottom-up' approach – based on the analysis of specific textual and linguistic features – might yield insights that refine, supplement, perhaps even dispute, those already offered by the existing criticism. More specifically, my analysis will attempt to appraise how the novels' narrative and stylistic strategies differ, and to what extent the devices used in the books impact on the representation of civil wars that they offer. Put yet another way, my interest lies in determining what makes *Beasts of No Nation* and *Song for Night* singular works of art.

The question of representation briefly evoked above has been broached repeatedly by commentators in recent years. Broadly speaking, debates have revolved around two aspects of the problem: the first relating to the geographical and historical specificity of fictional child soldier narratives, the second pertaining to the representability of the traumatic experiences addressed by the texts. The first issue has been raised against the background of ongoing discussions about the stereotypical depictions of Africa often promoted in the Western media, and supposedly perpetuated in literary works from the continent as well. In this context, the genre of the child soldier narrative itself already presents a potential problem since, as Dinaw Mengestu points out, 'the brutal existence of a child soldier dovetails neatly with depictions of Africa both as a place born of hell and misery and as a continent that, like a child, can be saved' (2007, cited in Schultheis, 2008: 33). In indirect response to Mengestu's valid point, Eleni Coundouriotis sees the possibility of warding off this danger to lie in 'proper contextualization' (2010: 203) – that is, in writers' 'explicit' identification of the 'historical setting' of their narratives (p. 197). Whereas the critic approvingly assigns this quality to Adichie's *Half of a Yellow Sun* (2006b), both *Beasts of No Nation* and *Song for Night* fall short of meeting her standards, partly because of their 'unspecific setting ..., although Iweala and Abani use Ibo names for their characters' (2010: 204, n12).[1] Discussing what she perceives to be the undefined location and temporality of the action in *Song for Night*, Coundouriotis further notes that 'there are references to Lexus cars' (these vehicles were introduced on the international market in the 1980s), a fact indicating that 'it cannot be Biafra in 1967' (p. 195). These comments, I believe, call for two separate remarks.

First, although Abani's strategy is indeed more oblique than Adichie's, *Song for Night* is far from being as geographically or even temporally unspecific as Coundouriotis suggests. Among other things, an entire chapter in the novella revolves around 'a legend of the Igbo' (Abani, 2007a: 69–74); the book alludes to 'pogroms against the Igbos' (p. 93), a term often used to refer to the massacres that precipitated the Biafran War; the narrative includes a character's recounting of a 'racist jok[e]' (p. 91) involving an Igbo, a Yoruba and a Hausa (pp. 90–1); the story is partly set in a 'Sabon Gari', a Hausa word used to refer to a 'foreigners' ghetto' (p. 92); and, even more revealingly, the book explicitly mentions 'the first colonial capital of Calabar', which was then 'moved to Lagos' (p. 70). Taken together, these accumulated references firmly locate the narrative in Nigeria. However, the geographical indeterminacy identified by Coundouriotis *does* apply to Iweala's novel, as does her comment that 'the fighting [in *Beasts of No Nation*] is never explained in terms other than basic survival. You fight to live; war is a total condition, a way of life, not a cause in the name of something' (2010: 196). Yet, while the scholar connects her statement to a larger argument deploring that such narrative strategies '[tend] to obscure the political context' (p. 197), one might just as well respond that this kind of obfuscation is precisely the point – Iweala and, to an extent, Abani might wish to intimate that those too young to be directly involved in political debates end up being the individuals who pay the highest price. The two writers make this suggestion in rather different ways.

Beasts of No Nation features a narrator – aged 'anywhere from 9 to 12' (Iweala, 2005b) – obviously not old enough to understand the political implications of the conflict in which he is involved. *Song for Night*, on the other hand, has My Luck, its 15-year-old narrator, more maturely reflect that '[i]t has been three years of a senseless war, *and though the reasons for it are clear*, ... none of us can remember the hate that led us here' (Abani, 2007a: 19, my italics). Abani's novella, in other words, clearly withholds its narrator's historical knowledge, possibly indicating that facts alone do not suffice to understand or justify the 'hate' that brought about the war.

Coundouriotis' second remark – about Abani's inclusion of possible anachronisms in *Song for Night* – is more intriguing, especially when read alongside Hamish Dalley's perceptive observation that My Luck 'compares a comrade to "a *Star Wars* Ewok" [2007a: 130], drawing on cultural knowledge inaccessible until more than ten years after Biafra's demise' (2013: 446). The two critics interpret these chronological 'inaccuracies' in a different light: Coundouriotis sees them as partaking of 'the ways in which the memory of the Nigerian Civil War grafts onto [Abani's] awareness of West Africa's more recent wars' (2010: 195), whereas Dalley considers it an element justifying a reading of the book as a trauma narrative that mimics the temporal collapse associated with extreme experiences of suffering (2013: 446). Interestingly, Dalley in particular refrains from seeing these anachronisms as artistic flaws – this is judicious in my view, considering that the novella contains a few too many supposed inconsistencies for them to be purely accidental.[2] Of interest to the argument that I wish to pursue in this chapter is that these details point to a fundamental tension within Abani's text. When Coundouriotis states that the anachronisms mean that 'it cannot be Biafra' (2010: 195), one is tempted to reply that it cannot possibly be anything else either, for no three-year war has taken place in Nigeria since the civil conflict of 1967–70.

Put differently, insistence on 'rationality' and on the accuracy of historical data may not be the best way to approach a text that features a narrator who, as the ending of his tale makes clear, is in fact already dead. The type of poetic licence that characterizes *Song for Night* more interestingly highlights the potential of literary inventiveness to escape the clichés evoked by Mengestu above. As Alison Mackey convincingly argues, books like Abani's and Iweala's 'side-step generic expectations by employing relational and indirect narrative strategies that register a highly critical sensibility, thus potentially challenging complacent readings' (2013: 100). While Mackey's analysis of the representational techniques used in child soldier narratives focuses on writers' deployment of devices that 'complicate [the] easy or uncritical consumption' of these texts by Western audiences (p. 100), Kenneth W. Harrow interrogates the very possibility of 'conveying to the reader an event whose excessiveness defies the language of representation' (2013: 4). He pertinently asks: 'can we express the failure to represent an image ... without resorting to representation?' (p. 5). This question is not merely rhetorical; rather, it captures the aporia at the heart of *Beasts of No Nation* and *Song for Night*, both of which wrestle with the conundrum of how to put into words experiences that 'can hardly be described or grasped in any human language' (Giommi, 2011: 181).

This idea of representation is intimately linked to the debates around geographical and historical specificity outlined above, for all of these issues circle around the subject of writers' adherence to – or, conversely, challenging of – the conventions of literary realism. Both *Beasts of No Nation* and *Song for Night*, in their choice of narrative strategy, emphatically spurn the rules of mimesis. One way in which Iweala does this is by giving his narrator, Agu, an Igbo name (meaning 'leopard', as several commentators have already noted), while setting his tale in a country that is clearly not Nigeria at the time of the Biafran War – the government is said to be situated in the North (Iweala, 2005a: 51), a character is nicknamed 'Rambo' after the hero of a 1982 film (p. 54; both are of these details are noted by Hodges, 2009: 7) and, unlike Abani's novella, Iweala's book does not provide toponymic information that would firmly anchor the story in Biafra at the time of the war. Iweala's most overt challenge to realism, however, lies in his creation of an invented idiom for his first-person narrator. As has rightly been observed, this unusual use of English recalls Ken Saro-Wiwa's *Sozaboy*, a novel written in what its author, in his introductory note to the book, has famously described as '"rotten English", a mixture of Nigerian pidgin English, broken English and occasional flashes of good, even idiomatic English' (1994 [1985]: n.p.). According to Saro-Wiwa, this idiom was 'the result of ... [his] closely observing the speech and writings of a certain segment of Nigerian society' (1994 [1985]: n.p.). Echoing this, Iweala states that the language of his novel is 'based loosely on the way that people speak, or that [he's] heard people speak, in Nigeria' but that he, as a writer, 'wasn't trying to be accurate and have [his] characters speak in pidgin English' (2006). Thus, while Agu's idiolect contains elements of Nigerian English and Pidgin, it needs to be noted that Iweala – much like Saro-Wiwa – wasn't aiming for sociolinguistic accuracy. This point is an important one to make, for expectations of 'authenticity' have tended to skew early critical assessments of the novel. Consider, for instance, the following comments by Nigerian writer and critic Molara Wood:

> Praised for its innovative use of language, *Beasts of No Nation* however shows the potential pitfalls when an American-educated author ... attempts to render the Pidgin English of a barely educated West African boy traumatized by war. The language of the novel has impressed many Western reviewers, but one could argue that they are not well-placed to determine the success or otherwise of the use of non-standard English. One such critic noted the 'staccato-like Pidgin English, mangled and bent by African inflection'. However, if the language is mangled by anything, it is the author's handling of 'African inflection', or the lack of it, that is responsible ... This is Pidgin written by someone who does not show an intimate familiarity with the form.
>
> (2008: 147)

Wood is right on at least two counts. First, critics such as the one cited in her review (Anderson Tepper, writing for the *Washington Post*, 2005) have insistently described the language of *Beasts of No Nation* using the label 'Pidgin English', and some have expressed an enthrallment with the 'Africanness' of Agu's idiolect that all but recalls the Western fascination with the Yoruba-inflected English of Amos Tutuola's *The Palm-Wine Drinkard* in the 1950s. Second, the idiom used by Iweala indeed bears only a slight resemblance to Nigerian Pidgin, a linguistic code which, as has been repeatedly demonstrated, is not a variety of English but a distinct language with coherent rules that is largely unintelligible to the non-Nigerian speaker of the former colonial tongue (see e.g. Faraclas, 1996; Deuber, 2005; Zabus, 2007: 56). However, Wood also implies that the artificiality of Iweala's language necessarily means that the idiom is flawed.

It is on this point that she and I part company. I believe that, in the case of Iweala, the problem rather lies on the side of those numerous critics – Western and otherwise – who have insisted on using the 'Pidgin' label, even in hedged terms such as 'a form of pidgin English' (Owomoyela, 2008: 120). As will become clear in this chapter, my view is that the narrative's sociolinguistic *in*accuracy and, hence, departure from realism are precisely what allows it to achieve a range of stylistic effects.

Song for Night, while written in Standard English, is even more emphatic in its rejection of mimetic realism than *Beasts of No Nation*. The book immediately draws readers' attention to its own artificial quality with its powerful opening sentences: 'What you hear is not my voice. I have not spoken in three years' (Abani, 2007a: 19). Readers are asked to believe that the words they are 'hearing' are the narrator's 'thoughts', which they are able to perceive because they 'have gained access to [his] head' (p. 21). These words are further identified as renditions in English of My Luck's mental reflections in his Igbo mother tongue: 'you are in fact hearing my thoughts in Igbo' (p. 21). Addressees are thus immediately requested to suspend their disbelief, and immerse themselves in a parallel reality that does not obey the laws of the 'real' world. The immersion in this alternative universe only reinforces the sense of shock experienced when the reason behind My Luck's muteness is revealed. He reports that, when he was in boot camp, a doctor severed his and his comrades' vocal chords, so that, if one of the young soldiers should be 'blown up by a mine,' the others would not be scared by their friend's 'death screams' (p. 35). But this brutal silencing has not had the intended effect, since the narrator adds that 'in the silence of our heads, the screams of those dying around us were louder than if they still had their voices' (p. 35).

Because Abani does not extensively draw on either Nigerian English or Pidgin in his narrative, his debt to Saro-Wiwa is less overt than Iweala's. Intertextual links between *Song for Night* and *Sozaboy* may be posited (see Tunca, 2013: 140), but the eeriest echo between the two texts is perhaps to be found – somewhat bizarrely and maybe entirely incidentally – in a short passage from Saro-Wiwa's novel ('I don't know how long I die. But I think I die for very very long time': 1994 [1985]: 113), and a quotation by the French playwright Molière used as epigraph to Abani's novella: 'We die only once, and for such a long time' (2007a: 17). The English version of Molière's statement, unlike the French original ('On ne meurt qu'une fois, et c'est pour si longtemps!': Molière, 1656: Act V, Scene 3), is ambiguous, since dying 'for a long time' can mean either that the state of death is eternal (the French playwright's actual suggestion) or that the process of dying is very slow. In *Song for Night*, it is the second, 'erroneous' interpretation that most closely fits My Luck's story, although the reader, and the protagonist himself, remain unaware of this fact until well into the narrative – some might even say until the very last page. In line with this, the argument that I wish to develop is that the strategy of Abani's novella is based on an accumulation of misunderstandings and linguistic ambiguities, to the extent that the text lends itself to two distinct readings: one empathetic with the narrator, the other heavily ironic. It is the uncovering of these two levels of comprehension that prompts the recognition that Abani's book does *not* 'follow the convention of the child soldier narrative that is also found in human rights reports' (Coundouriotis, 2010: 194), but rather challenges it, perhaps even to the point of satirizing it. As Abani's linguistic manipulations are less visible than Iweala's, and maybe bolder in their subtlety, they will be discussed last, after the examination of *Beasts of No Nation*.

Commenting on the 'rotten English' that he devised, Saro-Wiwa states in the Introduction to his novel that his invented idiom 'thrives on lawlessness, and is part of the dislocated and discordant society in which Sozaboy must live' (1994 [1985]: n.p.). This description also appropriately captures the narrator's idiolect in Iweala's book. Without going as far as saying that *Beasts of No Nation* 'openly imitate[s]' the language of Saro-Wiwa's book (Coundouriotis, 2010: 195), Iweala's experimental debt to the disorderly style of *Sozaboy* can hardly be denied. One of the most salient characteristics of Agu's language – second only to its deviation from Standard English, I would say – is its internal 'incoherence', especially on the grammatical level. For example, the Standard English (henceforth SE) structure 'make + direct object + bare infinitive' occurs a few times (e.g. 'making it go away': 2; 'making him live': 54) but, in the majority of cases, it is replaced by the Nigerian English (henceforth NE) variant including 'to' (Jowitt, 1991: 115), which is also found in many other varieties of African English (henceforth AE; see Schmied, 1991: 69). Thus, one finds countless examples such as 'making me to think' (Iweala,

2005a: 2, 4) or 'making me to agitate' (p. 31). These two different constructions are supplemented by a third, where the final infinitive is replaced by an '-ing' form (e.g. 'make me to coughing': p. 3; 'making him to shaking': p. 147). Other instances such as 'making me to happying' (p. 35) or 'making you to sadding' (p. 69) exemplify this pattern too, but with the addition of a category shift (here, an adjective used as a verb) that Jowitt identifies somewhat deprecatorily as a 'vulgar [error]' rather than a widely acceptable variant in NE (1991: 61). These category shifts are not used persistently throughout the novel either, since one finds examples such as 'I am sadding' (Iweala, 2005a: 158), but also 'Part of me is feeling sad' (p. 71). In some cases, these shifts have a semantic function, as they refer to a process rather than a state – for example, 'it is harding to breath' (p. 23) visibly means 'it is becoming hard to breathe'. However, even this device is not used consistently, as illustrated by the clauses 'My belly is tighting and my neck is becoming stiff' (p. 150), where a steady reliance on category shifts would have demanded the presence of 'stiffing' after 'tighting'.

Therefore, on a descriptive level, it can be said that the language of the novel finds inspiration in NE, but does not display any visible constancy or regularity in its use of NE variants, and neither does it show any discernible evolution towards or away from either SE or NE. A similar conclusion can be drawn with regard to Nigerian Pidgin (henceforth NP), whose grammatical traces are generally more discreet than those of NE. The presence of function words seems limited to the occasional use of the NP preposition 'for' (e.g. 'he is putting his hand for ground': p. 23; 'child is not coming for this place': p. 135), and to that of the word 'past', which approximates NP 'pass' and is used to express a comparative relation (e.g. 'green past any colour': p. 4; 'nice past anything': p. 114), a feature already noticed by Lambert (2011: 239). Lexical manifestations of NP are discreet too, and are restricted to a few words such as 'chop' (Iweala, 2005a: 58, 134, used in alternation with the SE equivalent 'eat', e.g. pp. 38, 47) and 'chook' (e.g. pp. 29, 37, 47), which means 'stab' in SE.

At this stage the reader of this chapter is entitled – even encouraged – to ask the following question: apart from demonstrating that Agu's is a disjointed, makeshift language, how does this description add to the comprehension of the book's *stylistic* strategy? The above, in fact, rather constitutes a necessary point of departure. The constant shifts in grammatical standards identified in the previous paragraphs mean that readers of the novel hardly have a firm basis for their linguistic interpretation of the text. This complicates the reading process, and leads to a series of localized stylistic effects. A case in point involves the use of the verb 'stop' and its ensuing patterns. Towards the beginning of the narrative, these structures are used in their conventional SE forms – for instance, 'the second you are stopping to think about it' predictably refers to the act of pausing to think about what is happening in the war (p. 15), while the soldiers' advice to Agu to 'stop worrying' (p. 15) has the same meaning as this phrase usually has in SE. Yet, later in the novel, after Agu's silent friend Strika has collapsed and the narrator believes that 'Strika is saying something' for the first time, Agu recounts: 'I am stopping to move' (p. 163). The context makes it clear that the only possible interpretation of this clause is that Agu actually stops mov*ing* – he had indeed been 'pretending to be walking away' (p. 163) – but these non-standard verb patterns slow down the processing of the narrative action. Like the long syntactic constructions identified by Madelaine Hron, these patterns often bring with them the consequence that readers are 'forced to reread' and 'to revisit and reassemble' the events being described (2008: 41).

This technique – whether intentional or not on the author's part – does not simply slow down the reading process, but it also, more importantly, presents a dislocated picture of events that has a defamiliarizing effect. Two linguistic features present in the novel will suffice to illustrate this point. The first is linked to the narrator's changing use of plural noun forms. Agu has a tendency not to use the plural inflectional '-s' suffix where it is expected in SE – this is particularly noticeable in his multiple references to body parts such as eyes, arms and legs: he often speaks of 'his eye' instead of 'his eyes' (e.g. Iweala, 2005a: 8, 174), and of 'arm and leg' instead of 'arms and legs' (e.g. pp. 75, 89). Conversely, he overgeneralizes the use of the plural marker '-s' in a series of cases, a feature typical of AE (Schmied, 1991: 70). For example, he regularly pluralizes SE mass nouns (e.g. 'grasses'), sometimes resulting in disregard for SE semantic distinctions (e.g. Iweala, 2005a: 'pulling out her hairs': p. 83). He also adds '-s' markers to historical irregular SE forms and, with the single exception of 'the grasses under my feet' (p. 41), he always speaks of 'feets' and 'teeths' instead of 'feet' and 'teeth'. Concord, on the other hand, does not follow any clear pluralizing logic, since Agu says that 'my feets *is* feeling like *they* are belonging to the man standing next to me' (p. 87, my italics). The narrator also often speaks of 'womens', but at other times he uses the forms 'women' and 'woman' to refer to several female individuals. As a result, morphological inflection is no reliable guide to picture situations; in certain cases, it is all but impossible to reach interpretative certainty at once. For instance, when Agu and his fellow soldiers are walking in a city in search of 'food and drink and womens' (p. 124), the following description is provided:

> On each side of us there is building with two or three floor and as we are walking, woman is just looking down at us and I am seeing how they are just holding cloth around their breast like that.
> (p. 127)

The phrase 'woman is', read in SE, initially seems to indicate that the soldiers walk past a single woman looking down from a building, but this lone female figure then multiplies with the occurrence of 'they' and 'their'. This stylistic device produces an effect akin to that of the 'garden path' structures examined in Chapters 2 and 3, for readers are forced to reassess what is likely to have been their original interpretation of the sentence. Here, the initial 'misreading' is not related to the identity of the speaker as it is in *Purple Hibiscus* or *Half of a Yellow Sun*, but more radically to the very situation being depicted. Using a phrase uttered by Agu himself, one might well describe the reader's reaction to such passages in these terms: 'I am confusing' (p. 77).

The use of '-ing' instead of the expected SE '-ed' ending in the above expression may cause stumbling similar to that provoked by the passage just examined, since the form 'confusing' more readily evokes the SE word 'baffling' or the progressive form of the verb 'confuse' than the verbal adjective 'confused', for which it actually stands in the book. Despite the absence of a direct object in the clause 'I am confusing', the present progressive form is all the more likely to suggest itself as the novel is replete with it. The narrative's non-standard use of the progressive aspect occurs not only where one would have expected the simple form of the SE historic present (e.g., 'he is saying' instead of 'he says'), but also with state verbs (e.g. 'I am knowing' instead of 'I know'). In the latter case, the feature can easily be traced back to NE (Jowitt, 1991: 114) and AE (Schmied, 1991: 67), a comment also valid with regard to Agu's general simplification of the tense system and his tendency to avoid 'complex' tenses such as the past perfect (Schmied, 1991: 66). While this data is useful in helping to uncover the writer's possible sources of inspiration, these sociolinguistic details are perhaps less significant than the *effects* potentially achieved by Agu's constant use of the present progressive.

As one of the most noticeable features of the narrator's idiolect, the ubiquitous use of the present progressive in *Beasts of No Nation* has already been the subject of repeated critical attention. Iain Lambert, for example, remarks that the density of progressive forms 'provides an immediacy which is effective in conveying the adrenalin rush that Agu is experiencing' (2011: 289). In another study, Madelaine Hron writes that this linguistic feature conveys the impression that 'all actions seem to be continuously ongoing, interminable' (2008: 41). These analyses are conflicting to say the least, but the contradiction epitomizes the range of semantic nuances that can be assigned to progressive forms, depending on the verbs to which the aspect is applied and the textual environment in which these verbs occur. Indeed, part of the difficulty in circumscribing the effect of the progressive form in the narrative lies in the fact that this aspect simply does not invite a single, uniform interpretation. To highlight but one essential difference, the use of the progressive in SE does not have the same effect when it is used with an 'event verb' or a 'state verb'. The progressive usually '*stretches* the time-span of an "event verb", but *compresses* the time-span of a "state verb"' (Leech, 2004: 19, italics in original). To briefly illustrate this statement, a sentence containing an event verb, such as 'He jumps across the stream', is generally understood to be a live description of a single action, whereas the same sentence in the present progressive, 'He is jumping across the stream', is more likely to refer to a longer series of repeated actions. Conversely, a sentence containing a state verb, such as 'I enjoy reading', is usually taken to denote a permanent inclination, whereas 'I am enjoying reading' is likely to refer to a temporary situation that is currently in progress. Crucially, *Beasts of No Nation* ignores these basic distinctions, prompting questions as to the symbolic significance of this grammatical blurring to the narrator's bewildered state of mind. In the novel, progressive forms are used with state verbs even when SE would have required simple forms – for instance, Agu's question to Strika, 'Are you liking plantain?' (Iweala, 2005a: 16), is meant to be an enquiry about the mute boy's tastes, not about his enjoyment of plantain at that particular moment in time. More interestingly perhaps, progressive forms are also used with event verbs when these obviously refer to single actions. For example, the clause 'one of the men is jumping down from the enemy truck' (p. 24) actually depicts a scene where a man jumps down from a vehicle only once. Such occurrences create confusion especially when the use of the progressive aspect is coupled with the simplification of the tense system mentioned above. When Agu, for instance, reports that '[t]he boy who is hitting me is running' (p. 4), the individual in question, Strika, has in fact stopped hitting the narrator several moments before. Once again, contextual elements will allow attentive readers to decode Agu's statement, but a pattern can nonetheless be said to emerge: events that are consecutive in the 'real time' of the story are presented as both simultaneous and ongoing in what might be termed the narrator's 'psychological time'.

The relevance of this observation should become clearer in what follows. In the novel, the use of progressive forms with event verbs is particularly striking in scenes depicting violence, because these passages contain a lot of 'momentary verbs' – that is, verbs such as 'kick' and 'hit', which 'refer to happenings so momentary that it is difficult to think of them as having duration' (Leech, 2004: 24). The impact of these progressive forms can be assessed with more precision by examining a short extract from the book:

> He [Commandant] is taking my hand and bringing it down so hard on top of the enemy's head and I am feeling like electricity is running through my whole body. The man is screaming, AYEEIII, louder than the sound of bullet whistling and then he is bringing his hand to his head, but it is not helping because his head is cracking and the blood is spilling out like milk from coconut. I am hearing laughing all around me even as I am watching him trying to hold his head together. He is annoying me and I am bringing the machete up and down and up and down hearing KPWUDA KPWUDA every time and seeing just pink while I am hearing the laughing KEHI, KEHI, KEHI all around me.
>
> (Iweala, 2005a: 25–6)

This excerpt exemplifies the 'stretching' effect of event verbs mentioned above: the beginning of the passage, 'He is taking my hand and bringing it down', is suggestive of a slow, deliberate demonstration rather than a sudden movement. The progressive form in 'I am bringing the machete up and down' also evokes duration. Even if this gesture is repeated – as indicated by the iconic repetition 'up and down and up and down' – the progressive form is not the expected grammatical choice in SE, since this aspect is typically used for longer background actions interrupted by briefer, more 'important' ones. In this case as in the one mentioned above ('The boy who is hitting me is running': p. 4), short and consecutive actions (here, the repeated strikes of the machete) are presented as one long, ongoing process in Agu's 'psychological time'. The result could be described as a disturbing slow motion effect, particularly salient in a form such as 'his head is cracking' which, in SE, grammatically suggests that the victim's skull is only progressively coming apart. By elongating the time span of the scene, these accumulated progressive forms embody Agu's impression, reported shortly after this extract, that 'the world is moving … slowly' (p. 26).

The progressive form no doubt contributes to the overwhelming impression left by this passage on the reader, but this grammatical feature evidently does not do so by itself. It is indeed combined with a series of lexical items that reinforce the troubling nature of the scene. Verb choices, for instance, are significant: 'I am bringing the machete up and down', contains a verb of the type identified in Chapter 2 as a 'material' process involving an Actor, i.e. a verb of action (here denoting intention) that does not try to minimize the perpetrator's responsibility in his own act. Agu is thus *not* 'unambiguously a victim in the reader's eyes', contrary to what Coundouriotis has stated (2010: 196), but he nonetheless is, to an extent, 'a channel through which his commander's violence passes' (p. 196). Indeed, Agu rather disturbingly performs the very gesture first executed by his Commandant, who carried out the initial action of 'bringing down' the machete at the beginning of the excerpt.[3] The fact that Agu does not attempt to conceal his active participation in the massacre is also evidenced by the presence of the material processes 'hitting', 'beating', and 'cutting' (p. 26) in the sentences following the quoted extract. Yet, at the same time, the boy's use of verbs such as 'hearing', 'seeing' and 'watching' are indicative of mental and behavioural processes, which tend to situate him as a witness to the action rather than as the person responsible for the crime being committed. He is, disturbingly, presented as *both* at once.

Other stylistic choices add to the troubling effect of the scene. For example, the simile 'like milk from coconut' brings in a reference to an item of food that may enhance the visceral impression left by the description of the victim's bloody skull. According to Hron, such 'similes serve to translate the indescribable horrors of war ... or incommunicable emotions, such as the feeling of killing' (2008: 42). Hron's observation relating to emotions is a comment on another simile found in the excerpt, 'like electricity is running through my whole body' (Iweala, 2005a: 25). Interestingly, the sensations that Agu's mind can only access through the remoteness of simile are later expressed in a most direct way by his body, through uncontrolled physical reactions: 'I am vomiting everywhere. I cannot be stopping myself ... I am growing hard between my leg' (p. 26). The discrepancy between Agu's hesitant language and the extreme nature of his physical and emotional experience during the massacre scene perhaps finds its most striking illustration in his use of the clause 'He is annoying me' to justify his repeated hitting of the man. Since 'annoyance' is hardly an acceptable reason for killing another human being, the word undoubtedly points to the inadequacy of the narrator's language in dealing with the traumatizing situation in which he finds himself. However, even Agu's limited linguistic repertoire contains simple words (such as the adjective 'angry', which he also uses as a verb) that would have been at least slightly more appropriate in these circumstances than the word 'annoying'. This, then, may perhaps suggest a broader interpretation: could it be that Agu's idiolect is not only a reflection of his disjointed experiencing of traumatic events, but also a *symbol* for the poor approximation of 'reality' that is human language as a whole?

This idea may be explored by taking a short detour via one of the book's most noticeable linguistic characteristics: its pervasive recourse to onomatopoeia. This device is exemplified three times in the above extract alone, in the words 'AYEEIII', 'KPWUDA KPWUDA', and 'KEHI, KEHI, KEHI'. In this passage as in many others, onomatopoeic expressions stand out by virtue of being written in capital letters, presumably following the graphological convention whereby capitals convey the loud volume of sounds and utterances. These capitalized onomatopoeias are of the 'nonlexical' type, which means that they use 'the phonetic characteristics of the language to imitate a sound without attempting to produce recognizable verbal structures, even those of traditional [i.e. lexical] "onomatopoeic" words' (Attridge, 2004: 136).[4] Onomatopoeias, relying as they do on an imitative principle, are often associated with expectations of unmediated signification, and this may indeed be the initial impression left by the many instances contained in *Beasts of No Nation*. Symptomatically, Molara Wood states that the novel 'deliver[s] aural punches that are startling in their immediacy' (2008: 147). Many of the nonlexical onomatopoeias contained in the novel are startling indeed but, as Attridge rightly points out, '[o]nomatopoeia does not lead us into the realm of direct and concrete significance' (2004: 138); rather, this device 'requires *interpretation* as much as any other system of signs does' (p. 141, italics in original).

The interpretation of conventional nonlexical onomatopoeias largely works in a manner similar to the decoding of lexical and grammatical words. For instance, the ability to recognize that the onomatopoeia 'WHOOSH' refers to things 'flashing by' in SE (Iweala, 2005a: 114) depends on a speaker's competence in this particular language. A similar comment may be formulated about the recognition of the Igbo throbbing sound 'KWUD KWUD' (p. 24). But Attridge's point above in fact relates to more creative, unconventional onomatopoeias such as those found in the work of James Joyce. To decode the Irish writer's sometimes puzzling combinations of letters, the critic argues, readers must rely on their knowledge of 'the conventions of ... the rhetorical device of onomatopoeia itself', including, for instance, 'the convention that a repeated letter automatically represents a lengthened sound' (2004: 140). Readers of *Beasts of No Nation* rely on precisely such knowledge to establish that the scream 'AYEEIII' (Iweala, 2005a: 25) uttered by Agu's victim is of a certain length. In other words, the supposed effect of 'immediacy' conveyed by onomatopoeias is actually mediated via precise linguistic rules.

Another point raised by Attridge is that, because 'the imitative effects of onomatopoeia ... remain extremely imprecise' (2004: 145), many unconventional onomatopoeias depend 'on their immediate context' for interpretation (p. 143). Such is the case of those found in Iweala's novel when they do not correspond to either SE or Igbo conventional items. For instance, it is highly unlikely that readers, regardless of their linguistic background, would recognize 'KPWISHA' (Iweala, 2005a: 9) as being the sound of splashing water if the onomatopoeia did not occur in the context of an incident where this liquid is poured over Agu. A closer look at the other onomatopoeias present in the novel reveals that they are *all* contextualized or explained in this way, which effectively renders their semantic contribution negligible. As a result, onomatopoeias rather seem to serve the symbolic function of marking the frontier of what Agu's language is (un)able to convey. Words such as 'KPWAP', 'KPWING' (p. 20) or 'KPWOM' (p. 67), in which the Igbo twin letters 'kp' and 'kw' creatively collide, are 'not ... means of gaining knowledge about the world' (Attridge, 2004: 145); they do not *imitate* sounds as much as they *intimate* the inimitability of the reality on which they are based.

As suggested above, this conclusion seems to apply to Agu's language as a whole. The narrative idiolect's constant challenging of grammatical rules imparts the disjointedness of Agu's life by making for a disorienting reading experience, but the unruly language does not imitate the effects of trauma as much as overtly gesture towards the distinctiveness of the protagonist's subjective representation of events. Put differently, the book's unconventional form highlights the role of the linguistic medium as an artificial interface, not a direct and transparent link, between the narrator's ordeal and readers' engagement with it. Even impressions of 'immediacy' created by onomatopoeias are ultimately illusory, as they rely on the unconscious negotiation of precise linguistic conventions. However, the evocative power of these words undoubtedly remains, signalling that the artificiality of the representation offered by the novel may be precisely the gateway through which the remoteness of the original experience may best be appraised. By casting its story in an invented code that constantly demands interpretative adjustments, *Beasts of No Nation* could even be said to embody its own reflection on the 'genre' of the child soldier narrative as one that cannot, and should not, be apprehended without a form of critical distance. In this sense, Iweala's experimental style partakes of the more general tendency displayed by a number of fictional child soldier narratives, which 'exhibit narrative strategies that can challenge complacent readings' (Mackey, 2013: 102). The specificity of *Beasts of No Nation*, as I have tried to show, is that its invented idiom opens up the universe of the child soldier, but also enacts its own failure to escape the limits of linguistic representation.

A similar concern with representation seems to be at the heart of Chris Abani's *Song for Night* (2007a) which, in non-identical twin fashion, approaches this issue in a rather different way, by implausibly casting its reader in the role of a hearer who has access to its narrator's thoughts expressed in Igbo, as already mentioned above. One reviewer, commenting on the opening sentence of the novella ('What you hear is not my voice': p. 19), has stated that this beginning 'both acknowledges the reader and assumes that the reader "hears" a voice as s/he reads the written narrative, while also foreshadowing the revelation that the main character has no voice' (Zott, 2008: 1). This response has been described as 'perhaps ... overly literal' (Krishnan, 2014: 39), an opinion one is inclined to share in view of Zott's later observation that 'This isn't an easy position for a reader to accept' (2008: 1). However, the reviewer's statement that the novella 'assumes that the reader "hears" a voice' (Zott, 2008: 1) is particularly interesting in the context of a stylistic analysis because, linguistically speaking, this is *exactly* what Abani's text does.

In the terminology of linguistics, the type of assumption to which Zott refers is known as a 'presupposition'. Presuppositions are, broadly speaking, 'the shared background assumptions that are taken for granted when we communicate' (Griffiths, 2006: 143). More precisely, they refer to particular types of inferences considered to be on the boundary between the domains of semantics and pragmatics: they rely on the widely accepted meaning of words, but also on the context in which these words occur. To illustrate this with a simple example, a sentence such as 'My brother has stopped smoking' presupposes that I have a brother, and that he had been smoking. These two presuppositions are of different types. The one triggered by the possessive 'my' is known as an 'existential presupposition'. As its name indicates, this kind of inference assumes the existence of certain referents, which are always part of a noun phrase. An existential presupposition is typically triggered by a definite article, a demonstrative or a possessive determiner, a genitive construction, a personal pronoun or a proper noun. The second type of inference contained in my example sentence – the fact that my brother had been smoking – is known as a 'logical presupposition'. This kind of presupposition is notoriously more difficult to spot, as its list of triggers is open-ended, but a few typical categories of words can nonetheless be cited. Among these are change-of-state verbs (such as the verb 'stop' used in my own sentence), factive predicates including 'regret', 'know' or 'discover' (which precede a complement clause that the speaker assumes to be true), or iterative words such as 'again', 'another' and 'return' (which include morphological evidence of repetition).[5]

The opening sentence of *Song for Night* triggers at least two presuppositions: first, the fused relative clause 'What you hear' (which can be paraphrased as 'the thing that you hear') triggers the logical presupposition that 'you hear something'. Relative clauses are indeed among the well-known triggers of presuppositions, and it is this precise linguistic phenomenon that prompted Zott's 'literal' response. Additionally, the opening sentence triggers the existential presupposition that 'I have a voice', which is however cancelled by the ensuing mention that 'I have not spoken in three years' (Abani, 2007a: 19) and by the revelation that My Luck can no longer speak. This 'defeasibility', which is a widely recognized property of presuppositions, is a sign of the pragmatic, rather than purely semantic, nature of these linguistic assumptions.

Inferences which are not pragmatic but are 'derived solely from logical or semantic content' (Levinson, 1983: 103–4) are known as 'entailments'. This term, derived from formal logic, 'refers to a relation between a pair of propositions such that the truth of the second proposition necessarily follows from (is entailed by) the truth of the first, e.g. *I can see a dog – I can see an animal*. One cannot both assert the first and deny the second' (Crystal, 2008: 169–70, italics in original). Entailment is not always easy to distinguish from presupposition, but a simple and generally reliable way to differentiate between them consists in applying the so-called 'negation test': whereas presupposition is not affected by negation, entailment is – either because the entailment disappears, or because it becomes unverifiable. If I negate my example sentence and say that 'my brother has not stopped smoking', the presupposition that he had been smoking remains; if, on the other hand, I negate Crystal's sentence and state that 'I cannot see a dog', it is unclear whether I can still see an animal or not – I may, for instance, still be able to see a cat. As entailment and presupposition pervade all types of discourse, it is only natural that *Song for Night* should contain its fair share of both. The interest resides in the particular artistic use to which some of these inferences are put, a fact I will explore later in this chapter.

The logical presupposition that opens Abani's novella could already be said to fulfil a discreet aesthetic function, as this element confers the narrative a sense of immediacy. In this case, the chosen linguistic structure is hardly manipulative at all, but presupposition (and, to an extent, entailment) will come to play a more misleading role in the book, along with the notion of 'conversational implicature', which I will now briefly introduce. This concept goes back to the work of H. P. Grice (1975), who posited that interlocutors hold some specific assumptions about the collaborative nature of conversational exchanges. He called the general idea underlying these expectations the 'cooperative principle'. This principle states that speakers typically make conversational contributions in such a way as to ensure the success of their communicative act in the particular circumstances in which it takes place. This idea informs Grice's theory of implicature, which postulates that four general rules, known as 'maxims', guide the efficient cooperative use of language. The categories identified by Grice are those of quantity, quality, relation (also known as relevance), and manner. The details of his theory support its scientific relevance, but a schematic summary will suffice for my purposes here:

Maxim of quantity – say as much as is needed (no more, no less).
Maxim of quality – try to make your contribution one that is true.
Maxim of relation – be relevant.
Maxim of manner – be perspicuous.

(Based on Grice, 1975: 45–6)

In conversational situations, participants generally assume that their interlocutor observes the cooperative principle and fulfils its maxims. To give an example cited by Grice, if a statement made by speaker A, *'I am out of petrol'*, receives the reply from speaker B that *'There is a garage round the corner'*, speaker A will assume that this indirect statement obeys the maxim of relevance, and he or she will therefore access the conversational implicature that the garage in question is open and has petrol to sell (Grice, 1975: 51, italics in original). Situations where maxims are blatantly breached will also generate implicatures – for instance, a tautology such as *'War is war'* is entirely uninformative at the level of what is said (it flouts the maxim of quantity), but it is informative at the level of what is implicated (p. 52, italics in original). Grice's theory was originally designed to analyse conversations, and scholars have pointed out the limitations of the model in particular situations (see a few examples in Black, 2006: 24). However, it has also been established that the interaction between characters, and between narrator and reader, in the literary context largely relies on similar communicative principles, and that Grice's theory may therefore be useful in the interpretation of fictional discourse as well (Black, 2006: 27–34).[6]

The argument that I wish to develop in relation to *Song for Night* will be based on the idea that the concepts introduced above – especially presupposition and implicature – play an important role in the novella, and that they do so in two principal ways. At a basic level, they form the backbone of the book's narrative strategy, which relies on readers' perception that My Luck has survived a mine explosion, which, in fact, he has not. In this case, linguistic theory mainly has an explanatory function, as it can show precisely how the book creates and maintains the illusion that My Luck is alive. But the examination of these textual elements rapidly leads to another, more revealing level of analysis. As I will attempt to demonstrate, the novella does not simply fool its readers initially, but it also teases them throughout by repeatedly, unbeknownst to them, poking fun at their empathetic involvement in the narrator's search for his lost comrades.

At first, the deceptive strategy pursued in the novella hardly draws attention to itself. Thus, in contrast to the opening paragraphs of the book, which require a radical suspension of disbelief, the beginning of the actual narrative action is rather straightforward. My Luck simply reports: 'I have become separated from my unit. I don't know for how long since I have only just regained consciousness' (Abani, 2007a: 21). These sentences pose no problems of comprehension – 'I have regained consciousness' simply entails that 'I am conscious', and therefore that 'I am alive'. The unexceptional nature of this initial statement allows the narrative to then slip in a far more questionable logic:

> The rule of thumb is that if you hear the explosion, you survived the blast ... I heard the click and I heard the explosion even though I was lifted into the air. But the aftershock can do

that. Drop you a few feet from where you began. When I came to, everyone was gone. They must have thought I was dead and so set off without me ...

(p. 22)

This excerpt reiterates that My Luck is conscious by mentioning that 'I came to', a fact that is this time (predictably) presupposed by virtue of its inclusion in a time clause (another typical presupposition-trigger). The accuracy of the 'rule of thumb' in this particular situation is implicated (via the maxim of relation), and the power of persuasion of the narrator's argument is then reinforced by syllogistic reasoning. Most readers will assume that, since My Luck has 'hear[d] the explosion', he has really 'survived the blast'. A greater level of attentiveness is required to notice that the premise of this syllogism is fundamentally flawed, for the young soldiers cannot possibly know whether those who died did not hear the explosion too. Following this, still at the scene of the blast, My Luck continues his interior monologue and reflects on the pleasure he finds in the crimes that he has committed during the war:

I enjoy it [the killing], revel in it almost. Not without cause of course: they did kill my mother in front of me, but still, it is for me, not her, this feeling, these acts. The downside of silence is that it makes self-delusion hard. I rub my eyes and spit dirt from my mouth along with a silent curse aimed at my absent comrades. If they'd checked they would have noticed that I wasn't dead.

(pp. 22–3)

The final sentence in this passage takes the form of a 'past unreal conditional', which establishes that the action contained in the 'if-clause' is 'contrary to fact' (Leech, 2004: 125). In other words, My Luck indirectly but unambiguously asserts that his comrades did not check if he was dead whereas, in the 'reality' of the narrative, they most likely did but left the scene without their fellow soldier because he was no longer alive. Unaware of his own passing, the narrator then reasserts that he is alive for the third time in a single paragraph, via the presupposition triggered by the factive verb 'notice'.

The opening pages of the novella contain countless similar examples of entailment and presupposition that refer to My Luck's state of being conscious and alive. These would be unremarkable if it were not for the fact that the situation they set up blocks access to a series of implicatures. For instance, when My Luck asserts that 'silence … makes self-delusion hard' (Abani, 2007a: 22), readers naturally follow the narrator's train of thoughts, and take the clause to be part of My Luck's forthright confession about the pleasure he finds in killing; the maxim of relation being fulfilled, there is no reason for them to search for any additional implicature. Yet there *is* another level of meaning at play, considering that My Luck's entire narrative is based upon the 'self-delusion' that he is still alive. The statement is thus ironic – and this fact, for reasons already explored in Chapter 3, also makes it polyphonic. However, the irony found in *Song for Night* differs from the examples in *Half of a Yellow Sun* in two major ways. First, irony in Abani's novella is not used to express disapproval of the views being stated, but it works in more indirect ways which I will try to elucidate in what follows. Second, in *Song for Night* the ironist is not the narrator or another character, but clearly the implied author. There are many such precedents in fiction. In her book *Pragmatic Stylistics*, Elizabeth Black mentions cases where '[t]he implied author communicates with the reader "over the head", as it were, of the narrator, who may be unaware of the ironies generated by his [the narrator's] discourse' (2006: 116). What makes Abani's novella distinctive, however, is that the implied author not only communicates 'over the head' of the narrator, but also over that of the first-time reader.

One might go as far as saying that the ironic devices used throughout the novella are part of a 'game' of implicature, of which only the implied author knows the exact workings – at least upon one's initial discovery of the book. Upon subsequent readings, one may begin to get a sense of what the rules of this writerly game might be. I will attempt to isolate three of them in the next few paragraphs. The first rule, of which I already gave an illustration above, might be formulated as follows: 'generate entailments and presuppositions so as to block ironic implicatures'. Another example will help to illustrate this further. A little less than halfway through the narrative, My Luck spends some time near a river that carries floating corpses, and he is happy to find 'earthenware pots full of rainwater' (Abani, 2007a: 65–6) that can quench his thirst. The narrator unsuspectingly states: 'Drinking the river water, with all the rotting corpses it holds, will surely kill me' (p. 66). The change-of-state verb 'kill' triggers the presupposition that My Luck is alive, and thus simply supports the entailments and presuppositions already found at the beginning of his narrative. If one considers the sentence from an *authorial* perspective, however, the irony is unmissable. Yet, as My Luck's living state is constantly being presupposed, the ironic meaning of the sentence is highly likely to remain hidden from the first-time reader.

This irony can be regarded as a device that works at the expense of the clueless protagonist as much as the unsuspecting reader. The difference, of course, is that the imaginary character is entirely at the mercy of his creator's ploys, while the deception of the reader occurs as a result of his or her own negotiation of the text. The relevance of this remark will perhaps become clearer by examining examples that follow rule number two in the implied author's game: 'use idiomatic or metaphorical expressions so as to generate implicatures and mask the irony behind the literal meaning of these phrases'. The book contains countless illustrations of this principle. For instance, before finding the earthenware pots mentioned above, My Luck is feeling increasingly thirsty as he cannot drink the water from the river, which is 'poisonous with the dead'. He reports: 'I am dying of thirst' (p. 53). At this point, My Luck is walking along the bank and visibly not dehydrated to the point of collapsing, so competent speakers will automatically interpret his remark in its metaphorical sense. They will do so by accessing an implicature: since the maxim of quality is flouted (My Luck is not literally 'dying' of thirst), the clause can only be understood figuratively. In hindsight, one realizes that the narrator really *is* 'dying', as his search for his lost platoon turns out to be a journey towards the final state of death. In other words, such cases trick readers into retrieving implicatures, and lead them to miss the irony underlying the literal meaning of My Luck's words. In another instance, the narrator observes that he is 'living on the edge of death' (p. 118). Here, one naturally retrieves the metaphorical meaning that My Luck constantly finds himself in dangerous situations, whereas the phrase also ironically refers to the literal location where the protagonist spends his entire tale.

The chances of being duped by the implied author are fairly high, for the trap is set up carefully – the reader does not continue to adhere to My Luck's viewpoint without reason. As the narrator himself is unaware of his ghost-like condition, he constantly provides rational explanations for the odd incidents in which he is involved. At some point in the narrative, he enters the 'Die Hard Motel and Eatery',[7] and pretends not to see an old soldier who speaks to him. When the man complains that 'Even the dead ignore me', the boy attributes his interlocutor's remark to '*Shellshock*' (p. 90, italics in original); he then uses the same explanation to account for the behaviour of another man who enquires whether My Luck is a demon (p. 99). Bewildered by the accumulation of such bizarre occurrences, the narrator fleetingly wonders if he is dead, but then concludes: 'I am pretty sure I would know if I was [a ghost] … When I pinch myself it hurts, so I know am not a ghost' (p. 104). Once again, a presupposition introduced by the factive 'know' in the present tense encourages the interpretation that My Luck is 'not a ghost', and therefore alive.

Yet the events depicted in the story increasingly work *against* the logical presuppositions triggered by the text. This tension lies at the basis of rule number three in the implied author's game: 'see how much irony you can get away with before the naive reader catches on'. At the beginning of the novella, ironic implicatures are indeed most likely to remain undetected because they are particularly discreet. For instance, My Luck's observation that being alone 'radically decreases your chances of survival' (p. 24) will probably fail to be registered as ironic, because it is entirely relevant to the version of events in which the young soldier is alive. The narrative, however, becomes bolder as it progresses. About one third through the story, when a vast majority of readers are still bound to believe that the protagonist is alive and looking for his comrades, My Luck reflects on the different '[p]ros and cons of being [a mine diffuser] at the front of every battle' (p. 49). He draws up a list of advantages, of which the third item is particularly revealing in retrospect:

Pros—

- Prime pillaging opportunities.
- The battle is over quicker.
- If you die, it is quick (*unless you fall victim to a mine, which can be a slow death sometimes*).

(p. 49, my italics)

This parenthesis is actually hidden inside a list of five items, and the irony is almost certain to remain undetected by those still unaware that My Luck is undergoing the 'slow death' mentioned here. The point, however, is that the novella tests its own ironic boundaries in increasingly conspicuous fashion. It teases the reader by multiplying implicatures, featuring odd incidents, and even blatantly stating what the empathetic reader refuses to acknowledge. Thus, after My Luck has embarked in a canoe on the river whose 'current has changed direction' (p. 79), the narrator enters into an imaginary dialogue with the dead bodies:

> The corpses seem to be mocking me. They seem to say, *Don't worry, you'll be one of us soon, you'll join us in this slow dance.*
> My Luck is dead.
> This is what my mother would say if I die in this war.
> (p. 79, italics in original)

The fact that the narrator is no longer alive cannot be asserted more clearly than in the sentence 'My Luck is dead'. The authority of this statement is nonetheless rapidly withdrawn by being reattributed to the boy's deceased mother in the conditional sentence that follows – a sentence which, one might add, contains an umpteenth presupposition that My Luck is alive. This excerpt can be regarded as yet another manifestation of the 'garden path' effect, a phenomenon encountered several times in the present study. However, in Abani's case, the added twist is that the initial, so-called 'erroneous' interpretation turns out to be the one that the reader should in fact have retained.

The implied author's game of irony is exemplified in more passages that can be cited here, but another illustration deserves to be mentioned by virtue of its particular significance. My Luck, finding himself in a field full of mysterious 'phantom soldiers' (p. 108), debates whether 'the apparitions ... are real' (p. 109):

> In this place everything is possible. Here we believe that when a person dies in a sudden and hard way, their spirit wanders confused looking for its body. Confused because they don't realize they are dead. I know this.
> (p. 109)

The protagonist in effect diagnoses his own condition, whose nature also explains his own cluelessness – like the wandering spirits, My Luck spends much of the narrative feeling 'confused' (pp. 37, 58, 84, 147). The irony is heightened by the fact that the protagonist presupposes the veracity of his statement (again using the factive 'I know'), but is unable to relate it to his present state. This paradox seems to be of more than passing importance. Indeed, it appears particularly relevant that the experience which the protagonist is unable to identify as being his own should find its origins in local folklore. In the novella, ancestral tradition is embodied in the figure of the narrator's grandfather, present only in My Luck's distant memories. The old man teaches his grandson Igbo legends and a song that the boy is then unable to recall (p. 74) until well into the narrative, when he approaches his final state of death (p. 123). Since My Luck's inability to remember the song, along with the denial of his ghostly condition, testifies to his incapacity to establish direct connections with his own Igbo heritage, the narrator's state of amnesia and confusion may well be symbolic of his severance from his cultural ties, a rupture precipitated by the war.

No doubt this claim would deserve further investigation, but the above outline suffices to establish that the novella's irony seemingly serves distinguishable purposes, depending on whether it is interpreted as being at the protagonist's expense, or at the reader's. My main interest has been in the latter case, which more visibly relies on the ironic effects produced by the linguistic phenomena of entailment, presupposition and implicature. Crucially, the impact of the ironic instances that I have identified is not limited to isolated passages, but extends to the novella's wider artistic strategy. This can be illustrated with a final example, which deftly exploits rules number two and three of the authorial game. Near the end of the book, My Luck hitches a ride on a train in the hope of finding his comrades more quickly, and he reaches the station where he had arrived after fleeing the North of the country at the beginning of the conflict. He disembarks and then takes a look back, but 'by some trick of the light the train has rusted over' and 'the station fallen into ruin' (p. 149). The narrator dismisses the phenomenon as a figment of his imagination ('Mirages are common here': p. 149), and walks a short distance away from the station. The road then 'suddenly sheers away, ending abruptly in a cliff' (p. 151):

I don't remember there being a cliff here. Not that I am sure I remember where I am, even though the sign at the train station was the same one I saw when I rode the train of death down from the north. Anyway, why would anyone build a road that leads to a dead end at a cliff edge?

(p. 152)

The 'train of death' mentioned by My Luck is metaphorical, as it refers to the series of carriages loaded with dead bodies on which he fled to Igboland after the massacres (p. 98), but the irony of this phrase in the context of the narrator's journey towards death hardly needs to be pointed out. Similarly, the 'dead end' that he mentions describes the cul-de-sac at which he arrives, but it can also be regarded as a veiled reference to the final state of being 'dead' that he is about to reach. It is probably no coincidence either that My Luck literally happens upon the 'edge' of a cliff while at the 'edge of death', an expression he used earlier.

Those who fail to spot these ironic references do not simply miss an occasion to experience the author's dark humour. At this late stage in the narrative, My Luck has been involved in so many surreal incidents that readers cannot but suspect that the hero is either hallucinating (which is his own interpretation of the events above: p. 152), or that he is a spirit trying to find its way towards a final resting place. The more closely readers empathize with My Luck's plight and adhere to his perspective of the situation, the less likely they are to detect the ironic use of idioms and metaphors that I have pointed out. This is a key observation. Critics specializing in trauma narratives, a category to which child soldier stories undeniably belong, typically perceive unchecked identification with traumatized characters and narrators as a sign of readers' uncritical – and unethical – appropriation of other people's trauma (see e.g. LaCapra, 2001). In my view, it is highly significant that the novella's irony is entirely lost precisely on those who put themselves in such an unethical position of vicarious victimhood. The author, in other words, is playing a rather nasty trick on those who fail to observe the necessary critical distance with which child soldier narratives ought to be approached.

This is a bold subterfuge. As Elizabeth Black states, 'irony is a thoroughly dangerous strategy' (2006: 119) because, when it is missed, it becomes a 'face threatening act' that is likely to generate 'embarrassment and a sense of exclusion' (p. 76). But this, I would argue, is exactly what the implied author aims for by playing his game of linguistic hide-and-seek. Indeed, the mild 'embarrassment' experienced by the duped readers upon discovering previously unnoticed instances of irony prompts the realization that they have failed to recognize the boy's tale as an artificial, carefully orchestrated *representation* of a child soldier's story. Thus, one might go as far as stating that the novella satirizes vicarious responses to 'real-life' child soldier testimonies, which ignore the gulf between the 'reality' of the child soldier and its representation. Crucially, the irony in *Song for Night*, once detected, cannot fail but put a constantly renewed sense of distance between the reader and the world represented in the artistic work. A similar role could very well be assigned to the multiple anachronisms contained in the book, which I mentioned in the introduction to this chapter. In light of the author's ironic strategy, debates over the historical inaccuracy of these elements are not merely superfluous, but they become revealingly symptomatic of readers' and critics' unconscious desire to cling to the idea that fiction is, and necessarily must be, aligned with reality, an approach that the novella itself challenges, deconstructs, and even provocatively mocks.

As these comments indicate, Abani's *Song for Night* uses subtle linguistic ploys to set up a narrative strategy that indirectly tackles fraught questions linked to the representation of the child soldier experience and to the reception of such contemporary accounts. In this sense, Abani's book could be said to thematize, or even *theorize*, what Iweala's novel more directly *enacts* through its experimental form. While the above examination certainly refutes any possibility of seeing either of these works as complacent and conventional, the evaluation of the novels' ultimate success will largely depend on the individual reader. *Song for Night* might not be a stylistic curio like *Beasts of No Nation*, but the deceptive straightforwardness of Abani's language may be what eventually confers his artistic venture greater power – provided, of course, that one has a taste for the irony displayed by this scheming, evil twin.

Conclusion

Echoing a quotation by the African-American writer Alice Walker (1983: 84), Chimamanda Ngozi Adichie concludes her famous TED talk, 'The Danger of a Single Story', with the following words: 'when we reject the single story, when we realize that there is never a single story about any place, we regain a kind of paradise' (2009a). This declaration, along with Adichie's speech itself, has been widely praised for its hopeful celebration of the potential of literature to capture the complexity and multifariousness of the human experience. However, at least one commentator has informally described this statement in less flattering terms, characterizing it as 'oddly postlapsarian' – and hence, conventionally Christian and far more conservative than it appears to be at first sight. This critical assessment, made during a conference session in 2010, struck a chord with my atheist self. Despite my admiration for Adichie, it had me convinced for years; it was only recently that I decided to investigate it further. I will briefly present this analysis here – my reasons for doing so will shortly become clear.

Readers of this book should by now have the necessary linguistic knowledge to join me in taking the first analytical step. It can indeed be established that the perception of Adichie's statement as being 'postlapsarian' rests on the presence of the iterative 'regain', which triggers the logical presupposition that we had a kind of paradise in the past, but then lost it. Then again, one might notice, this is not *quite* the mythology of paradise lost, for what we regain is not paradise itself, but '*a kind of* paradise'. In linguistics, 'kind' is known as a 'type noun' – that is, a noun that can be used either to refer to a specific subtype of a category, or to hedge an utterance. In Adichie's statement, 'a kind of' may be said to somewhat ambiguously cover these two meanings – in one reading, we regain 'a type of' paradise of which there are several; in another, we regain an approximation of paradise. In either case, the inclusion of the type noun 'kind' means that 'paradise' can only be interpreted in one of its extended senses, recorded in the *Oxford English Dictionary* as 'a peaceful unspoilt place', or a 'state or condition of supreme bliss or happiness'. These definitions of the word are, of course, originally derived from religious tradition, but they are by no means literal references to the Garden of Eden of Genesis. Thus, while Adichie's statement, like Walker's before her, appeals to the idyllic notion of an unblemished mankind who once lived in an ideal world, the scope of the utterance is undoubtedly more than narrowly Christian. The 'fall' described by Adichie mostly relates to the 'single story' of Africa produced by colonialism, not the one caused by the Biblical Eve; the one recorded by Walker is embodied in African-American communities' alienation from their Southern cultural inheritance in Northern American ghettoes. In short, the writers' arguments can be said to be historical, philosophical, and political; whether postlapsarian and conservative should be added to this list is now debatable.

These are not purposeless musings. In just over five hundred words, the above paragraphs illustrate the methodology followed throughout this book. I started from another scholar's pronouncement about one of Adichie's statements, then provided linguistic evidence in order to ground the impression that I shared with this commentator. Further examination of the Nigerian writer's utterance led me to notice a detail that I had initially missed (namely the presence of a type noun), and to revise my earlier hypothesis accordingly. I have not gone back to an emotional and superficial celebration of Adichie's declaration, but I have allowed this critical process to refine my understanding of the statement's possible ideological basis and, ultimately, to rather drastically reorient the argument that I set out to present. This is the 'philological circle' discussed in Chapter 1: the basic methodology of stylistics.

There is no need to rehearse in detail what I presented as the potential assets of the literary-linguistic approach in the opening section of the book. Suffice it to say that, for every 'hunch' that stylistic techniques have allowed me to substantiate, they have helped me to discount another, and identify the reasons behind my initial misreading. Needless to say, this does not mean that no imprecisions or infelicitous interpretations remain in this study – my claim has never been one to perfection or pure 'objectivity'. Rather, what I have attempted to find, whenever possible, are points of entry into texts, approaches that might constitute the basis for methodologically sound, pedagogically-oriented debates.

I believe that stylistics can achieve much more for Nigerian fiction, as it can easily lend its critical apparatus to the deciphering of unsolved riddles, old and new. A classic among such literary enigmas is the 'elusive indeterminacy of the narrator's identity' (Ogede, 2007: 18) in Chinua Achebe's *Things Fall Apart* (2001 [1958]), a novel where the 'status of the narrator and his or her authority' is regarded to this day as '[o]ne of the problematics of the text' (Gikandi, 1991: 44). I concur with Gikandi that the concern should not be so much with establishing the precise 'identity' of the narrator as though he or she were a real person, but rather with 'how this narrator functions in the text' and how 'his/her shifting focalization' impacts upon the interpretation of the novel (p. 45). Stylistics has something to contribute to this discussion. Specifically, it might help to shed further light on the narrator's possibly ironic attitude towards the protagonist Okonkwo – the details of this hypothesis, however, are best left for another volume.

More recent Nigerian fiction provides many aesthetic riddles too. Here again, one short example will suffice. Chika Unigwe's third novel, *Night Dancer* (2012), is set in Nigeria and tells the story of two women, Mma and her estranged mother Ezi. Stylistically speaking, the book owes much to Achebe and those of his generation in its use of proverbs, relexified items and Igbo words. On the thematic level, the narrative situates itself in the tradition of female novelists such as Flora Nwapa and Buchi Emecheta. Despite these multiple literary echoes, Unigwe's novel is anything but an Achebe imitation or an unimaginative rehash of the women's stories told by first- and second-generation female writers. In my evaluation, the book is stylistically innovative, subtle in the characterization of its protagonists and in the portrayal of their emotional journeys. But what motivates this personal (and as yet unsubstantiated) assessment of Unigwe's novel? This is an intuition that stylistics may help to illuminate. Even more importantly, using linguistic theories in the appraisal of the aesthetic qualities of the book is likely to generate a series of interpretative observations.

Things Fall Apart and *Night Dancer* are but two examples chosen at the expense of countless others in the rich body of Nigerian fiction, which is itself only a single literary tradition among many others on the African continent. The interest of examining linguistic minutiae in a small selection of texts, as I have done in this book, lies not only in uncovering the subtlety and craft of individual narratives, but also in anticipating what the pieces of the puzzle, once put together, may one day yield. At this stage the picture remains incomplete, but some questions can nonetheless be formulated. Beyond the culturally specific aspects of language in Nigerian literature, is there such a thing as a 'poetics' of Nigerian fiction? Or, more broadly, is there a literary-linguistic 'aesthetics' of African literatures? Since, for the past few decades, prose texts in these literary traditions seem to have favoured certain genres (such as the *Bildungsroman* or the child soldier narrative) that have allowed comparative literary research to emerge, is it possible that particular methods of stylistic analysis – focused on, say, the linguistic expression of metaphors persistently found throughout the corpus – might also quasi-systematically yield pertinent results?

That these questions remain unanswered confirms that this study has only been a timid incursion into what might one day become the fully-fledged sub-discipline of 'African stylistics'. Much remains to be done for, even if 'interdisciplinarity' has become a buzzword in many academic circles nowadays, the combination of stylistics and African – or, more generally, postcolonial – literatures continues to provoke as much incomprehension and hostility as it does enthusiasm. Plenty of postcolonial literary scholars seem to have an acute allergy to linguistics, and more than one stylistician I have come across simply did not see the point in studying African texts for their own sake. But still, there is hoping that, one day, scholars will heed Adichie's call, and realize that we all need to reject the 'single story' – or perhaps, more accurately, the 'single methodology' – of our academic disciplines too.

Notes

1 Towards an 'African Stylistics'?

1. These different responses were reprinted, along with an edited version of Wali's original article, in the journal's anniversary issue, in a section entitled 'African Literature: Who Cares?'.
2. This piece, also published in *Transition*, was later reissued under the title 'The African Writer and the English Language' in Achebe's book of essays *Morning Yet on Creation Day* (1975).
3. The nature and merits of these interventions are well documented and do not need to be rehearsed here. See, for example, the special issue of *Research in African Literatures* on 'the language question' (1992, ed. Richard Bjornson); for a more recent evaluation of the debate with a focus on Achebe and Ngũgĩ, see Ashcroft (2009: 103–9).
4. A few examples include Adejare (1992) and Akekue (1992), both inspired by systemic-functional grammar; Adegbija (1998, speech-act theory); Essien (2000, discourse analysis); and Winters (1981, transformational-generative grammar and quantitative stylistics).
5. Provided this remark has any validity at all, the explanation it offers can of course only be partial. Undoubtedly linguists who venture into the domain of literary studies are generally more prone to work on texts from a cultural background similar to theirs.
6. Even if the phrase 'the African critic' refers to 'the critic from Africa' in this particular context, Ngara does not advocate that the study of African literatures should be the prerogative of Africans alone. As he writes a few paragraphs later,

> If a European critic knows Africa well, is honest and unbiased, and is a competent critic using sound critical standards relevant to African art, there is no reason why his pronouncements on African literature should not be as valid as those of informed African critics.
>
> (1982: 8)

7. This major flaw was first pointed out by Short *et al.* (1998) in their heated response to Mackay's article, but it can easily be verified independently. For instance, Mackay spends several pages disputing the 'objectivity' of articles by Ronald Carter and Paul Simpson published in a 1989 collection of essays edited by these two scholars, but he conveniently leaves out some of the nuanced comments made by the editors in their Introduction: 'it is naive to pretend that any application of linguistic knowledge ... can

result in an "objective", value-free laden interpretation of data. The system will inevitably be partial' (Carter and Simpson, 1989: 6).

8. On the reasons why a verb such as 'fail to' can be considered a negation, see Jeffries (2010a: 106–13). For an interesting overview of the link between pragmatic theory and negation, see Nahajec (2009: 111–16).

9. I am particularly thinking of theories of codeswitching (e.g. Myers-Scotton, 1993), which can provide an interesting basis for the analysis of character interaction in novels such as Adichie's *Purple Hibiscus* and *Half of a Yellow Sun*. I have briefly discussed codeswitching in Adichie's first novel elsewhere (Tunca, 2008: 159–65), and have additionally examined the interaction between English and Nigerian Pidgin in the experimental novel *Another Lonely Londoner* by Gbenga Agbenugba (1991; see Tunca, 2009). To readers with a broader interest in culturally-related linguistic approaches to (West) African literatures, I heartily recommend Chantal Zabus' aforementioned *The African Palimpsest* (2007).

2   Of Palm Oil and Wafers

1. This is certainly the case as far as Beatrice Achike is concerned. By way of illustration, the fact that she decides to go back to her husband after an umpteenth beating (Adichie, 2003: 249) is initially interpreted by readers as weakness and submission on her part, but in retrospect it is obvious that she returns to the family home only to finish off what she has started: by then, she has already begun putting poison in Eugene's tea with the intention of killing him.

2. In what follows I will rely directly on Halliday and Matthiessen's book, as their precise explanations serve the particular points that I wish to emphasize. However, it is far more common for stylisticians to work with their own adaptations of Halliday's theory – see, for example, Simpson (1993: 86–95; 2004: 22–6) and Jeffries (2010a: 37–50).

3. For the sake of clarity and consistency across the entire book, I use the traditional terminology 'verb phrase' and 'noun phrase', but Halliday and Matthiessen favour the equivalent expressions 'verbal group' and 'nominal group'. Similarly, I opt for the more common terms 'active' and 'passive' below, but the two linguists use the words 'operative' and 'receptive'.

4. I am aware that the gerunds 'singing' and 'stinging', assonantal and alliterative in my sentence, may not be close enough in the narrative to be technically described as such.

5. Recall that 'Kambili' means 'let me live' in Igbo. The opening of the present chapter indicates that the interpretation I have assigned to the narrator's name here may not have been intended by Adichie. However, as Chantal Zabus has wisely stated, 'the semantic potential of a text always outgrows the author's intention' (2007: 135).

6. The phrase 'speech and thought presentation' is used by Leech and Short (2007: 255–81) to refer to the way characters' speech and thought are represented in fiction. The authors decide to treat speech *and* thought

in the same chapter because 'most of the features involved in differ-
entiating modes of character speech are paralleled by similar modes of
character thought' (p. 255). Considering that this area of study has
received a good deal of attention from stylisticians and literary critics
alike, I do not judge it necessary to provide a definition of terms such
as 'direct speech' or 'free indirect speech'. Useful examples, definitions
and analyses are available in Leech and Short (2007: 255–81), and Short
(1996: 288–325). It is on these works that the terminology used in the
rest of this chapter is based.

7. In traditional examples of 'garden path' sentences, readers initially attribute to a word or phrase a syntactic function that turns out to be the wrong
one. For instance, in a well-known example such as 'the girl told the story
cried', 'told' is initially interpreted as a verb in the simple past tense that
is part of the verb phrase heading the main clause, but it actually turns
out to be a past participle heading a dependent clause (the sentence in fact
means 'the girl who was told the story cried'). In the example from *Purple
Hibiscus*, the 'garden path' effect is a pragmatic one, since readers are not
led to reassess the propositional content of the initial clause, but rather the
identity of its speaker.

8. The passage that has been analysed is not the only one in which this
appears to be the case (see e.g. Adichie, 2003: 67–8 and 104 for similar
examples). This intertwinement of free indirect thought and free indirect
speech occasionally occurs with characters other than Eugene, but the
extracts involving him are by far the most ambiguous cases.

9. In the last third of the novel, only two instances might be viewed as traces
of Kambili's allegiance to her father's dogmatic views. Upon returning
from Nsukka, she says: 'For a moment, I wondered if Papa was right, if
being with Papa-Nnukwu had made Jaja *evil*, had made us *evil*' (p. 192, my
italics). Importantly, the quotation takes the form of an indirect question,
indicating that Kambili no longer accepts the fact that being in contact
with Papa-Nnukwu may have caused her to become 'evil' without careful consideration. Furthermore, she entertains the thought only '[f]or a
moment' before dismissing it. On another occasion, Kambili reports that
'we [Jaja and Kambili] both knew that Papa did not approve of people
speaking in tongues because it was what the *fake* pastors at those *mushroom* Pentecostal churches did' (p. 208, my italics). Here, the disdainful
'fake' and 'mushroom' might be interpreted as reported speech. Even if
this were not the case, none of the quotations reflect contempt for traditional Igbo religion – the view long shared by Kambili and her father, and
which was challenged by Father Amadi.

3 'The Other Half of the Sun'

1. The association between objectivity and journalism is Adichie's own:
'I don't think it's fiction's job to be objective; I'm not a journalist'
(Adichie, 2009b). I invoke the notion as an 'ideal' rather than a concrete

stance for, as the writer adds in the same discussion: 'I don't even believe that there is such a thing as "objective"... everybody has a point of view.'

2. Depending on the context, the term 'schema' is sometimes used interchangeably with the more precise labels 'frame' and 'script'. In Jeffries and McIntyre's words, '*schema* is a general term for an element of background knowledge', but 'some writers prefer alternative terms in order to flag up the varied nature of schemas' (2010: 128, italics in original). Among these words, 'frame', is used 'to describe knowledge related to visual perception', while 'script' refers to 'schematic information about complex sequences of events' (p. 128).

3. For an in-depth analysis of the role of objects and material culture in Adichie's novel, see Cooper (2008: 133–50).

4. What runs implicitly through Jeffries' argument is perhaps best made explicit here: the aim of pointing out the different cultural and temporal standards regarding the status of children is to draw attention to the relative rather than absolute value of these ideologies, and not to pass judgement on the potential superiority of one over the other. If Westerners might be outraged by the idea of child 'servants', many Africans might greet with similar resistance some typically 'Western' ideologies – for instance, the fact that it is considered perfectly acceptable to send elderly family members away to die in institutions where they are nursed by strangers.

5. Interestingly, the narratorial 'flavour' of the term 'Master' was even more clearly marked in earlier versions of the text. When the opening chapter of *Half of a Yellow Sun* was published in short story form in the journal *Granta*, Ugwu's Aunt did not utter the word 'Master' at all (instead referring to Odenigbo as 'him': Adichie, 2005: 19), and the narrator adopted the more descriptive phrase '*the* Master' throughout (my italics), a form which cannot possibly be used by the *characters* to address the lecturer directly.

6. That this is an intertextual link to Conrad is made all the more plausible by the fact that the adjective 'inscrutable' is discussed by Achebe in his famous 1977 essay on *Heart of Darkness* (published in revised version as 'An Image of Africa: Racism in Conrad's *Heart of Darkness*', 1988). Adichie's familiarity with Achebe is no longer to be demonstrated – as is well known, the younger author has often called her elder 'the writer whose work is most important to me' (e.g. Adichie, 2007).

7. Such is also his position during the massacre of Igbo people that he witnesses at Kano airport, leading the character to wonder whether he had been, in that instance, 'nothing more than a voyeur' (Adichie, 2006b: 167). The novel falls short of providing a positive answer to this question, instead choosing more subtly to foreground Richard's perception of these events as 'external, outside of him', 'watched ... through the detached lens of knowing he was safe' (p. 168).

4   Art is a Journey

1. The character is called Ifeyinwa in *The Landscapes Within* and Ifeyiwa in *Dangerous Love*. In both versions of the novel, her name is said to mean 'there's nothing like a child' (1981: 98; 1996: 79). I will refer to her as

'Ifeyi(n)wa' in the text, except in quotations, where I will keep the spellings used in the novels.

2. The theme of slavery was already hinted at in *The Landscapes Within* since, towards the end of the novel, Omovo journeys to the city of Badagry, a former slave port. However, the identification of Badagry as a historical site linked to the slave trade requires a certain degree of familiarity with colonial history. *Dangerous Love* takes a different approach: it explicitly tackles the theme of slavery, but merely refers to the town to which Omovo travels as 'B-'. I have suggested possible interpretations for this namelessness elsewhere (Tunca, 2004: 93).

3. Conceptual metaphors are written in small capitals by convention. In Zoltán Kövecses's words, 'The use of small capital letters indicates that the particular wording does not occur in language as such, but it underlies conceptually ... metaphorical expressions' (2010: 4). This explanation is also helpful in emphasizing the distinction between 'conceptual metaphors' (which, as Kövecses points out, are not usually found in language as such) and 'metaphorical linguistic expressions' (which are the linguistic realizations of these conceptual metaphors). Both 'conceptual metaphors' and 'metaphorical linguistic expressions' are, however, frequently referred to using the shorthand term 'metaphor'.

4. These definitions are borrowed from the online version of the *Oxford English Dictionary*, on which I will rely to define most of the words analysed in this chapter. Linguists (semanticists in particular) may object to such reliance on dictionaries because of these reference works' debatable scholarly authoritativeness, but dictionary definitions serve my purpose here, which is to show how Okri creatively exploits the popular, conventional meanings of terms. As an interdiscipline, stylistics often involves a compromise between theoretical precision and methodological flexibility; I concur with Paul Simpson that 'the need for ... manageability' sometimes 'overrides some of the finer points of linguistic theory' (1993: 117, n1).

5. The 'traffic jam' is yet another expression of the LIFE IS A JOURNEY metaphor. In a phrase such as 'the traffic jam of our lives', the metaphorical mapping is not an unusual one – it may be summarized as '[d]ifficulties in life are impediments to travel' (Lakoff and Turner, 1989: 3).

6. The poem mentioned in this quotation is sent to Omovo by his brother Okur after the latter has left the family home. It reads: 'When I was a little boy / Down the expansive beach I used to roam / Searching for strange corals / And bright pebbles / But I found sketches on the sand / While voices in the wind / Chanted the code of secret ways / Through the boundless seas' (1996: 57). This short text also contains elements reminiscent of the ART IS A JOURNEY metaphor and, to an extent, of the ART IS A CHASE metaphor (see Tunca, 2008: 281–3).

5 'Bi-textual' Poetics

1. In fact, the latter word originally referred to a piece that was meant to be sung (*Oxford English Dictionary*). However, while in contemporary popular

usage the term roughly encompasses the meanings of 'poetic' and 'emotional', in specialized academic discussions it more often than not refers to the feelings expressed by a poet or the I-persona in a poem. Since *Becoming Abigail* features an extradiegetic narrator (i.e. one that is external to the story) who recounts events that are at least partly focalized through the character of Abigail, the term 'lyrical' is perhaps best avoided as an analytical tool. In what follows, I will therefore restrict my discussion to the adjective 'poetic'.

2. These include the main character's ritualistic display of her mother's dishes (1996: 26; 2006b: 47) and the mention of jazz (which plays a greater symbolic role in 'Jazz Petals').

3. Despite much common ground, there are also many differences between the short story and the novella: the protagonist of the short story is called 'Abigail' by her father because she looks like her mother (whose name was Abigail), but the young heroine in fact has a different birth name that is never revealed; the character in the short story is 15, whereas Abigail in the novella is 14; in the short story, the protagonist's father does not commit suicide, whereas he does in the novella; in the 2000 text, the main character is both forced into prostitution and raped by Peter, whereas in the novella she fights off her first client, is chained to a doghouse as punishment and is later raped by Peter; in the short story, the protagonist rips off her rapist's (presumably a client's) penis with her teeth, while in the book this vengeful act is directed at Peter; in the short story, Derek is apparently single, and his relationship with the girl is exposed by her foster mother, whereas in the novella he is married, and he and Abigail are caught in the act by his wife. This list is not exhaustive.

4. Readers familiar with the field of pragmatics will have recognized the underlying principles of H. P. Grice's (1975) 'cooperative principle'. A full account of this theory here would only dilute the argument, but its tenets will be explained in Chapter 6, where the model assumes a more central methodological position.

5. The incident as it is recounted in the short story 'Becoming Abigail' definitely suggests the latter interpretation: 'Its pound-weight of caramel and treacle *promise* the full measure of his guilt' (2000a: 248, my italics). With the inclusion of 'pound-weight', this early version also more clearly underlines the double meaning of the phrase 'full measure', which can be the 'total extent of' something abstract, and the 'specific, standard amount' of something concrete, typically an item that is bought.

6. This transformation can be regarded as a literal incarnation of the common linguistic phenomenon of synaesthesia, wherein different senses are blended. The adjectives 'sharp', 'brittle' and 'deep' used in *Becoming Abigail* (and in conventional language) to describe a sound originally relate to touch and dimension.

7. This short analysis of rhythm relies on the theoretical framework proposed by Geoffrey N. Leech in his book *A Linguistic Guide to English Poetry* (1969: 103–30). In his section on 'metre', he makes the convincing argument that

the 'measure' is a more reliable guide than the 'foot' of traditional prosody as a unit of rhythm in English (pp. 112–13).

8. The textual indicators that refer to these incestuous feelings are faint and likely to be missed upon first reading, but Abani clearly identifies the existence of this subtext in an interview: 'the father commits suicide to prevent himself from enacting any abuse on his own daughter', a fact that Abigail 'recognize[s] … even in the moment of her own grief'. Suicide, according to Abani, can therefore sometimes be regarded as 'an act of courage or an act of love' (2009a).

6   Children at War

1. Francesca Giommi makes a similar observation in relation to what she regards as the narratives' indeterminate settings:

   The book [Abani's *Song for Night*] does not give any direct clue as to which country it takes place in or when, except for some reference to the Igbo ethnic group and tradition, which induces us to suppose it refers to the Biafran war. The location remains intentionally undefined, similarly to the choice of Uzodinma Iweala, … who locates his debut novel, *Beasts of No Nation*, in an unnamed war-torn West African country.

   (2011: 180)

   Giommi's eventual critical assessment, however, is altogether different from that of Coundouriotis, as she sees both narratives as 'focusing on the devastating effects [civil wars] have on humanity at large' (2011: 180). Allison Mackey shares a somewhat similar stance: she speaks of 'the ambiguity of location in Iweala's and Abani's narratives', and adds that 'these texts implicate a larger web of responsibility in the face of human rights horrors that span vast global networks' (2013: 108).

2. Dalley further notes a reference to 'satellite phones' (2013: 451; see Abani, 2007a: 48). To this, one might add My Luck's reflection, 'I shot the sheriff' (2007a: 39), after killing the platoon leader nicknamed John Wayne. This is not an anachronism as such, but the character's use of these particularly distinctive words from a 1973 Bob Marley song certainly stretches the boundaries of plausibility.

3. Considered in isolation, this linguistic remark may not carry much weight. However, it is striking that a similar association is established between Agu and the Commandant in at least one other case. In the first part of his narrative, Agu uses the SE word 'attention' (Iweala, 2005a: pp. 4, 43), until the term is shouted by the Commandant and reported as follows: 'TENSHUN!' (p. 53). Subsequently, Agu uses 'tenshun' in his narrative on at least six occasions (e.g. pp. 119, 137, 172), while 'attention' is used in the sense 'standing at attention' only once (p. 103). This might indicate

that the Commandant exerts an influence on Agu that the boy cannot resist, and perhaps that the narrator unconsciously takes on some of his Commandant's linguistic mannerisms, or indeed personality traits. In any case, if such elements are to be given interpretative significance, it is above all in symbolic rather than literal terms, since Agu does not use direct speech in his narrative – the first occurrence of 'tenshun' clearly remains his own interpretation of the Commandant's use of the word 'attention'.

4. Lexical onomatopoeias include nouns or verbs such as '*thud, crack, slurp* and *buzz*' (Simpson, 2004: 67, italics in original).

5. There are many more triggers of logical presupposition. One of them, comparative constructions, was cited in passing in Chapter 5 ('as real as this one': Abani, 2006b: 17), and a few more examples will be mentioned later in this chapter. However, readers wishing to access a longer list of presupposition-triggers are encouraged to consult Levinson (1983: 181–5); useful selections of examples, approached from stylistic or critical discourse analytical perspectives, can also be found in Jeffries (2010a: 95–8), and Simpson and Mayr (2010: 82).

6 . Needless to say, to be relevant to literary analysis, Grice's theory needs to be understood within the framework set up by the literary genre itself. For instance, the maxim of manner, under which fall several sub-maxims, including 'avoid ambiguity' and 'be orderly' (Grice, 1975: 46), is almost systematically breached in contemporary fiction, but Grice's model still applies, for such flouting generates implicatures: readers respond to any lack of clarity (caused, say, by the insertion of seemingly digressive flashbacks) by assigning it interpretative significance. Despite the commonplace flouting of maxims, fiction still operates along certain communicative expectations, such as the 'default' assumption of narratorial reliability. In this light, the violation of maxims by an unreliable narrator (that is, his or her deliberate breaching of these maxims in order to deceive) may come to play an interesting role in literary analysis.

7. Notice the pun and irony in the term 'die hard'. If interpreted literally, this phrase can be viewed as a reference to My Luck's violent death. This seems to be confirmed by the narrator's later mention of 'a person [who] *dies* in a sudden and *hard* way' (Abani, 2007a: 109, my italics – I examine this quotation in more detail below). Additionally, the compound 'die hard', when understood in its accepted idiomatic meaning, may be perceived as a reference to both My Luck's and the reader's stubborn adherence to the belief that the protagonist is alive.

References

Abani, Chris (1996) 'Jazz Petals', in Kadija Sesay (ed.) *Burning Words, Flaming Images: Poems and Short Stories by Writers of African Descent*, London: SAKS, pp. 22–7.

Abani, Chris (2000a) 'Becoming Abigail', in Courttia Newland and Kadija Sesay (eds) *IC3: The Penguin Book of New Black Writing in Britain*, London: Hamish Hamilton, pp. 247–53.

Abani, Chris (2000b) *Kalakuta Republic*, London: Saqi.

Abani, Chris (2005) Interview by Carlye Archibeque, *Poetix*, http://poetix.net/abani.htm (accessed 31 October 2011).

Abani, Chris (2006a) 'Abigail and My Becoming', *Truthdig*, http://www.truthdig.com/report/item/20060419_chris_abani_unintended_worship (accessed 21 January 2014).

Abani, Chris (2006b) *Becoming Abigail*, New York: Akashic.

Abani, Chris (2006c) 'An Interview with Poet and Fiction Writer Chris Abani', by Ron Singer, *Poets & Writers*, http://www.pw.org/content/interview_poet_and_fiction_writer_chris_abani (accessed 21 January 2014).

Abani, Chris (2006d) 'Of Ancestors and Progeny: Moments in Nigerian Literature', *Black Issues Book Review*, 8(6): 24–5.

Abani, Chris (2007a) *Song for Night*, New York: Akashic.

Abani, Chris (2007b) 'Writer Chris Abani Taps Geopolitics, Emotion', interview by Farai Chideya, NPR, http://www.npr.org/templates/story/story.php?storyId=16078964 (accessed 21 January 2014).

Abani, Chris (2008) Reading in the 'Incroci di Civiltà' series, Libreria Mondadori, Venice, Italy, 29 March.

Abani, Chris (2009a) 'A Conversation with Chris Abani', interview by Patty Paine, *Blackbird*, 8(1), http://www.blackbird.vcu.edu/v8n1/features/abani_c/conversation_page.shtml (accessed 21 January 2014).

Abani, Chris (2009b) 'Foreword', in Council of Literary Magazine and Presses, *CLMP Literary Press and Magazine Directory 2009/2010*, Los Angeles: Red Hen, n.p.

Abani, Chris (2013) 'Painting a Body of Loss and Love in the Proximity of an Aesthetic', *The Millions*, http://www.themillions.com/2013/11/painting-a-body-of-loss-and-love-in-the-proximity-of-an-aesthetic.html (accessed 21 January 2014).

Achebe, Chinua (2001 [1958]) *Things Fall Apart*, London: Penguin.

Achebe, Chinua (1974 [1964]) *Arrow of God*, 2nd edn, Oxford: Heinemann.

Achebe, Chinua (1965) 'English and the African Writer', *Transition*, 18: 27–30.

Achebe, Chinua (1975) 'The African Writer and the English Language', in *Morning Yet on Creation Day: Essays*, London: Heinemann, pp. 55–62.

Achebe, Chinua (1988) 'An Image of Africa: Racism in Conrad's *Heart of Darkness*' (1977), in *Hopes and Impediments: Selected Essays 1965–1987*, Oxford: Heinemann, pp. 1–13.

Adamson, Sylvia (2003) 'Text, Context and the Interpretative Community', unpublished paper presented at the Modern Language Association conference, San Diego, USA.

Adeeko, Adeleke (1998) *Proverbs, Textuality and Nativism in African Literature*, Gainsville: University Press of Florida.

Adegbija, Efurosibina (1998) 'Toward a Speech-Act Approach to Nigerian Literature in English', in Edmund L. Epstein and Robert Kole (eds) *The Language of African Literature*, Trenton, NJ: Africa World Press, pp. 41–56.

Adejare, Oluwole (1992) *Language and Style in Soyinka: A Systemic Textlinguistic Study of a Literary Idiolect*, Ibadan: Heinemann.

Adejunmobi, Moradewun (1999) 'Routes: Language and the Identity of African Literature', *Journal of Modern African Studies*, 37(4): 581–96.

Adesanmi, Pius and Chris Dunton (2005) 'Nigeria's Third Generation Writing: Historiography and Preliminary Theoretical Considerations', *English in Africa*, 32(1): 7–19.

Adichie, Chimamanda Ngozi (2002) 'Half of a Yellow Sun', *Literary Potpourri*, 12, http://www.literarypotpourri.com/12_Nov/Mid_Month.html (accessed 20 October 2007).

Adichie, Chimamanda Ngozi (2003) *Purple Hibiscus*, Chapel Hill, NC: Algonquin Books of Chapel Hill.

Adichie, Chimamanda Ngozi (2004a) 'Author, Chimamanda Ngozi Adichie', interview by Jenni Murray, *Woman's Hour*, BBC Radio 4, 17 March, http://www.bbc.co.uk/radio4/womanshour/2004_11_wed_02.shtml (accessed 20 October 2007).

Adichie, Chimamanda Ngozi (2004b) 'Nigerian Identity is Burdensome', interview by Wale Adebanwi, *Nigerian Village Square*, http://www.nigeriavillagesquare.com/bookshelf/nigerian-identity-is-burdensome-the-chimamanda-ngozi-adichie-interview.html (accessed 21 January 2014).

Adichie, Chimamanda Ngozi (2005) 'The Master', *Granta*, 92: 17–41.

Adichie, Chimamanda Ngozi (2006a) 'Buildings Fall Down, Pensions Aren't Paid, Politicians Are Murdered, Riots Are in the Air... and Yet I Love Nigeria', *Guardian*, 8 August, http://www.guardian.co.uk/commentisfree/2006/aug/08/comment.features11 (accessed 30 July 2008).

Adichie, Chimamanda Ngozi (2006b) *Half of a Yellow Sun*, London: Fourth Estate.

Adichie, Chimamanda Ngozi (2006c) 'Half of a Yellow Sun', *Leonard Lopate Show*, WNYC, 13 September, http://www.wnyc.org/story/52648-half-of-a-yellow-sun (accessed 21 January 2014).

Adichie, Chimamanda Ngozi (2007) 'The Writing Life', *Washington Post*, 17 June, http://www.washingtonpost.com/wp-dyn/content/article/2007/06/14/AR2007061401730.html (accessed 21 January 2014).

Adichie, Chimamanda Ngozi (2009a) 'The Danger of a Single Story', *TED*, http://www.ted.com/talks/chimamanda_adichie_the_danger_of_a_single_story.html (accessed 21 January 2014).

Adichie, Chimamanda Ngozi (2009b) Interview by Harriett Gilbert, *World Book Club*, BBC World Service, 6 June, http://www.bbc.co.uk/programmes/p01b9nqd (accessed 21 January 2014).

Adichie, Chimamanda Ngozi (2012) 'To Instruct and Delight: A Case for Realist Literature', *Commonwealth Foundation*, http://www.commonwealth-foundation.com/sites/cwf/files/downloads/Commonwealth_Lecture_2012_Chimamanda_Ngozi_Adichie.pdf (accessed 21 January 2014).

Adichie, Chimamanda Ngozi and Binyavanga Wainaina (2011) 'Conversation', *Lannan Foundation*, 28 September, http://www.lannan.org/events/chimamanda-ngozi-adichie-with-binyavanga-wainaina1 (accessed 21 January 2014).

'African Literature: Who Cares?' (1993) *Transition*, 75–6: 328–41.

Agbenugba, Gbenga (1991) *Another Lonely Londoner*, London: Ronu.

Akekue, Doris (1992) 'Mind-Style in *Sozaboy*: A Functional Approach to Language', in Charles Nnolim (ed.) *Critical Essays on Ken Saro-Wiwa's Sozaboy: A Novel in Rotten English*, London: Saros, pp. 16–29.

Anyokwu, Christopher (2011) 'Igbo Rhetoric and the New Nigerian Novel: Chimamanda Ngozi Adichie's *Purple Hibiscus*', *African Symposium*, 11(1): 80–90.

Arana, R. Victoria (2010) 'Fresh "Cultural Critiques": The Ethnographic Fabulations of Adichie and Oyeyemi', in Walter P. Collins III (ed.) *Emerging African Voices: A Study of Contemporary African Literature*, Amherst, MA: Cambria Press, pp. 269–313.

Armah, Ayi Kwei (1976) 'Larsony or Fiction as Criticism of Fiction', *Asemka*, 4: 1–14.

Arndt, Susan (1998) *African Women's Literature: Orature and Intertextuality*, Bayreuth: Bayreuth African Studies.

Ashcroft, Bill (2009) *Caliban's Voice: The Transformation of English in Post-Colonial Literatures*, London: Routledge.

Attridge, Derek (2004) *Peculiar Language: Literature as Difference from the Renaissance to James Joyce*, 2nd edn, London: Routledge.

Bakhtin, M. M. (1981) *The Dialogic Imagination: Four Essays*, trans. Caryl Emerson and Michael Holquist, Austin: University of Texas Press.

Bamiro, Edmund (2006) 'Nativization Strategies: Nigerianisms at the Intersection of Ideology and Gender in Achebe's Fiction', *World Englishes*, 25(3&4): 315–28.

Bandele, Biyi (1999) *The Street*, London: Picador.

Bandele-Thomas, 'Biyi (1991) *The Sympathetic Undertaker and Other Dreams*, Oxford: Heinemann.

Beilke, Debra (2006) '"Blue Tongues of Fire": Suppressing the Mother('s) Tongue in Chimamanda Ngozi Adichie's *Purple Hibiscus*', unpublished paper presented at the African Literature Association conference, Accra, Ghana.

Bjornson, Richard (ed.) (1992) *Research in African Literatures*, 23(1), special issue on 'the language question'.

Black, Elizabeth (2006) *Pragmatic Stylistics*, Edinburgh: Edinburgh University Press.

Boehmer, Elleke (2009) 'Achebe and His Influence in Some Contemporary African Writing', *Interventions*, 11(2): 141–53.

Bruce, Karen (n.d.) 'Listening to the Silences: Women's Silence as a Form of Oppression and a Mode of Resistance in Chinamanda [sic] Ngozi Adichie's *Purple Hibiscus*', unpublished essay.

Carter, Ronald and Paul Simpson (1989) 'Introduction', in Ronald Carter and Paul Simpson (eds) *Language, Discourse and Literature: An Introductory Reader in Discourse Stylistics*, London: Routledge, pp. 1–20.

Casey, Maud (2007) 'Broken Boy Soldier', *New York Times*, 16 September, http://www.nytimes.com/2007/09/16/books/review/Casey-t.html (accessed 21 January 2014).

Chinweizu, Onwuchekwa Jemie and Ihechukwu Madubuike (1975) 'Toward the Decolonization of African Literature', *Transition*, 48: 29–37, 54, 56–7.

Chinweizu, Onwuchekwa Jemie and Ihechukwu Madubuike (1983) *Toward the Decolonization of African Literature*, Vol. 1: *African Fiction and Poetry and Their Critics*, Washington, DC: Howard University Press.

Cook, Guy (1994) *Discourse and Literature: The Interplay of Form and Mind*, Oxford: Oxford University Press.

Cooper, Brenda (2008) *A New Generation of African Writers: Migration, Material Culture and Language*, Woodbridge and Scottsville: James Currey and University of KwaZulu-Natal Press.

Costantini, Mariaconcetta (2002) *Behind the Mask: A Study of Ben Okri's Fiction*, Rome: Carocci.

Costantini, Mariaconcetta (2005) '"The Fruit of Much Restlessness": Literary Creation and Revision According to Ben Okri', in Sabine Coelsch-Foisner and Wolfgang Görtschacher (eds) *The Author as Reader: Textual Visions and Revisions*, Frankfurt am Main: Peter Lang, pp. 245–59.

Coundouriotis, Eleni (2010) 'The Child Soldier Narrative and the Problem of Arrested Historicization', *Journal of Human Rights*, 9(2): 191–206.

Crystal, David (2008) *A Dictionary of Linguistics and Phonetics*, 6th edn, Malden, MA: Blackwell.

Dalley, Hamish (2013) 'Trauma Theory and Nigerian Civil War Literature: Speaking "something that was never in words" in Chris Abani's *Song for Night*', *Journal of Postcolonial Writing*, 49(4): 445–57.

Dawson, Ashley (2010) 'Cargo Culture: Literature in an Age of Mass Displacement', *WSQ: Women's Studies Quarterly*, 38(1&2): 178–93.

Deandrea, Pietro (2009) 'Unravelling Unpersons: Inscribing the Voice of Contemporary Slavery in the UK', *Textus: English Studies in Italy*, 22(3): 665–80.

Deuber, Dagmar (2005) *Nigerian Pidgin in Lagos: Language Contact, Variation and Change in an African Urban Setting*, London: Battlebridge.

Dubois, Sylvie and David Sankoff (2001) 'The Variationist Approach toward Discourse Structural Effects and Socio-interactal Dynamics', in Deborah Schiffrin, Deborah Tannen and Heidi E. Hamilton (eds) *The Handbook of Discourse Analysis*, Malden, MA: Blackwell, pp. 282–303.

Ehrenreich, Ben (2006) 'Persistence of Memory', *Los Angeles Times*, 14 May, http://articles.latimes.com/2006/may/14/books/bk-ehrenreich14 (accessed 21 January 2014).

Ekwe-Ekwe, Herbert (2005) 'Chimamanda Ngozi Adichie', in *Literary Encyclopedia*, http://www.litencyc.com/php/speople.php?rec=true&UID=6014 (accessed 30 July 2008).

Epstein, Edmund L. and Robert Kole (eds) (1998) *The Language of African Literature*, Trenton, NJ: Africa World Press.

Essien, Ako (2000) 'Discourse Analysis and Characterization in the Novel', in Ernest N. Emenyonu (ed.) *Goatskin Bags and Wisdom: New Critical Perspectives on African Literature*, Trenton, NJ: Africa World Press, pp. 51–63.

Faraclas, Nicholas G. (1996) *Nigerian Pidgin*, London: Routledge.

Fish, Stanley (1980) 'What Is Stylistics and Why Are They Saying Such Terrible Things about It?' (1973), in *Is There a Text in This Class? The Authority of Interpretive Communities*, Cambridge MA: Harvard University Press, pp. 68–96.

Fowler, Roger (1977) *Linguistics and the Novel*, London: Methuen.

Fowler, Roger (1986) *Linguistic Criticism*, Oxford: Oxford University Press.

Fowler, Roger (1996) *Linguistic Criticism*, 2nd edn, Oxford: Oxford University Press.

Fraser, Robert (2002) *Ben Okri: Towards the Invisible City*, Horndon: Northcote.

Gates, Henry Louis, Jr (1984) 'Criticism in the Jungle', in Henry Louis Gates Jr (ed.) *Black Literature and Literary Theory*, New York: Methuen, pp. 1–24.

Gikandi, Simon (1991) *Reading Chinua Achebe: Language and Ideology in Fiction*, Oxford: James Currey.

Giommi, Francesca (2011) 'Negotiating Freedom on Scarred Bodies: Chris Abani's Novellas', in Annalisa Oboe and Shaul Bassi (eds) *Experiences of Freedom in Postcolonial Literatures and Cultures*, London: Routledge, pp. 176–84.

Gone with the Wind (1939) Directed by Victor Fleming, Selznick International Pictures.

Grice, H. P. (1975) 'Logic and Conversation', in Peter Cole and Jerry L. Morgan (eds) *Syntax and Semantics 3: Speech Acts*, New York: Academic Press, pp. 41–58.

Griffiths, Gareth (1971) 'Language and Action in the Novels of Chinua Achebe', *African Literature Today*, 5: 88–105.

Griffiths, Patrick (2006) *An Introduction to English Semantics and Pragmatics*, Edinburgh: Edinburgh University Press.

Halliday, M. A. K. (1971) 'Linguistic Function and Literary Style: An Inquiry into the Language of William Golding's *The Inheritors*', in Seymour Chatman (ed.) *Literary Style: A Symposium*, London: Oxford University Press, pp. 330–65.

Halliday, M. A. K. (1985) *An Introduction to Functional Grammar*, London: Edward Arnold.

Halliday, M. A. K. and Christian M. I. M. Matthiessen (2014) *Halliday's Introduction to Functional Grammar*, 4th edn, London: Routledge.

Harrow, Kenneth W. (2013) 'The Amalek Factor: Child Soldiers and the Impossibility of Representation', *Postcolonial Text*, 8(2): 1–20.

Hawley, John C. (2008) 'Biafra as Heritage and Symbol: Adichie, Mbachu, and Iweala', *Research in African Literatures*, 39(2): 15–26.

Herman, Luc and Bart Vervaeck (2007) 'Ideology', in David Herman (ed.) *The Cambridge Companion to Narrative*, Cambridge: Cambridge University Press, pp. 217–30.

Hewett, Heather (2005) 'Coming of Age: Chimamanda Ngozi Adichie and the Voice of the Third Generation', *English in Africa*, 32(1): 73–97.

Hodges, Hugh (2009) 'Writing Biafra: Adichie, Emecheta and the Dilemmas of Biafran War Fiction', *Postcolonial Text*, 5(1): 1–13.

Hron, Madelaine (2008) 'Ora na-azu nwa: The Figure of the Child in Third-Generation Nigerian Novels', *Research in African Literatures*, 39(2): 27–48.

Igboanusi, Herbert (2001) 'Varieties of Nigerian English: Igbo English in Nigerian Literature', *Multilingua*, 20(4): 361–78.

Iweala, Uzodinma (2005a) *Beasts of No Nation*, London: John Murray.

Iweala, Uzodinma (2005b) 'Galley Girl Catches up with Uzodinma Iweala', interview by Andrea Sachs, *Time*, 29 November, http://content.time.com/time/nation/article/0,8599,1135918,00.html (accessed 21 January 2014).

Iweala, Uzodinma (2006) 'Uzodinma Iweala', interview by Robert Birnbaum, *Morning News*, 9 March, http://www.themorningnews.org/article/uzodinma-iweala (accessed 21 January 2014).

Jakobson, Roman (1960) 'Closing Statement: Linguistics and Poetics', in Thomas A. Sebeok (ed.) *Style in Language*, Cambridge, MA and New York: Technology Press of Massachusetts Institute of Technology and Wiley, pp. 350–77.

Jeffries, Lesley (2001) 'Schema Affirmation and White Asparagus: Cultural Multilingualism among Readers of Texts', *Language and Literature*, 10(4): 325–43.

Jeffries, Lesley (2010a) *Critical Stylistics: The Power of English*, Basingstoke: Palgrave Macmillan.

Jeffries, Lesley (2010b) *Opposition in Discourse*, London: Continuum.

Jeffries, Lesley and Dan McIntyre (2010) *Stylistics*, Cambridge: Cambridge University Press.

Jowitt, David (1991) *Nigerian English Usage: An Introduction*, Ikeja: Longman Nigeria.

Jowitt, David (1996) Review of *Dangerous Love*, by Ben Okri, *Wasafiri*, 24: 62–3.

Kanneh, Kadiatu (1997) 'What is African Literature? Ethnography and Criticism', in Mpalive-Hangson Msiska and Paul Hyland (eds) *Writing and Africa*, London: Longman, pp. 69–86.

Kerrigan, Michael (1996) 'A Landscape of Losses', review of *Dangerous Love*, by Ben Okri, *Times Literary Supplement*, 5 April, p. 26.

Kövecses, Zoltán (2010) *Metaphor: A Practical Introduction*, 2nd edn, Oxford: Oxford University Press.

Krishnan, Madhu (2012) 'Abjection and the Fetish: Reconsidering the Construction of the Postcolonial Exotic in Chimamanda Ngozi Adichie's *Half of a Yellow Sun*', *Journal of Postcolonial Writing*, 48(1): 26–38.

Krishnan, Madhu (2013) 'On National Culture and the Projective Past: Mythology, Nationalism, and the Heritage of Biafra in Contemporary Nigerian Narrative', *Clio*, 42(2): 187–208.

Krishan, Madhu (2014) 'The Storyteller Function in Contemporary Nigerian Narrative', *Journal of Commonwealth Literature*, 49(1): 29–45.

LaCapra, Dominick (2001) *Writing History, Writing Trauma*, Baltimore, MD: Johns Hopkins University Press.

Lakoff, George (1987) *Women, Fire, and Dangerous Things: What Categories Reveal about the Mind*, Chicago: University of Chicago Press.

Lakoff, George and Mark Johnson (1980) *Metaphors We Live By*, Chicago: University of Chicago Press.

Lakoff, George and Mark Turner (1989) *More Than Cool Reason: A Field Guide to Poetic Metaphor*, Chicago: University of Chicago Press.

Lambert, Iain (2011) 'Chris Abani's *Graceland* and Uzodinma Iweala's *Beasts of No Nation*: Nonstandard English, Intertextuality and Ken Saro-Wiwa's *Sozaboy*', *Language and Literature*, 20(4): 283–94.

Lanham, Richard (1991) *A Handlist of Rhetorical Terms*, 2nd edn, Berkeley: University of California Press.

Leech, Geoffrey N. (1969) *A Linguistic Guide to English Poetry*, London: Longman.

Leech, Geoffrey (2004) *Meaning and the English Verb*, 3rd edn, London: Routledge.

Leech, Geoffrey (2008) *Language in Literature: Style and Foregrounding*, Harlow: Longman.

Leech, Geoffrey and Mick Short (1981) *Style in Fiction: A Linguistic Introduction to English Fictional Prose*, Harlow: Pearson.

Leech, Geoffrey and Mick Short (2007) *Style in Fiction: A Linguistic Introduction to English Fictional Prose*, 2nd edn, Harlow: Pearson.

Levin, Samuel R. (1965) 'Internal and External Deviation in Poetry', *Word*, 21: 225–37.

Levinson, Stephen C. (1983) *Pragmatics*, Cambridge: Cambridge University Press.

Lindfors, Bernth (1973) *Folklore in Nigerian Literature*, New York: Africana.

Mackay, Ray (1996) 'Mything the Point: A Critique of Objective Stylistics', *Language and Communication*, 16(1): 81–93.

Mackey, Alison (2013) 'Troubling Humanitarian Consumption: Reframing Relationality in African Child Soldier Narratives', *Research in African Literatures*, 44(4): 99–122.

Mantel, Hilary (2004) 'I Have Washed My Feet Out of It', review of *Purple Hibiscus*, by Chimamanda Ngozi Adichie, *London Review of Books*, 26(20), 21 October, http://www.lrb.co.uk/v26/n20/mant01_.html (accessed 30 July 2008).

Marx, John (2008) 'Failed-State Fiction', *Contemporary Literature*, 49(4): 597–633.

Masterson, John (2009) 'Posing, Exposing, Opposing: Accounting for Contested (Corpo)Realities in Chimamanda Ngozi Adichie's *Half of a Yellow Sun*', in Charlotte Baker (ed.) *Expressions of the Body: Representations in African Text and Image*, Oxford: Peter Lang, pp. 137–60.

Mengestu, Dinaw (2007) 'Children of War', *New Statesman*, 17 June, http://www.newstatesman.com/books/2007/06/africa-war-burma-beah-sudan (accessed 21 January 2014).

Mills, Sara (1995) *Feminist Stylistics*, London: Routledge.

Mitchell, Margaret (1936) *Gone with the Wind*, New York: Macmillan.

Molière (1656) *Le Dépit amoureux* in Eugène Despois (ed.) *Œuvres de Molière*, vol. 1 (1873), Paris: Hachette, pp. 400–520.

Myers-Scotton, Carol (1993) *Social Motivations for Codeswitching: Evidence from Africa*, Oxford: Oxford University Press.

Nahajec, Lisa (2009) 'Negation and the Creation of Implicit Meaning in Poetry', *Language and Literature*, 18(2): 109–27.

Ngara, Emmanuel (1982) *Stylistic Criticism and the African Novel: A Study of the Language, Art and Content of African Fiction*, London: Heinemann.

Ngũgĩ wa Thiong'o (1986) *Decolonising the Mind: The Politics of Language in African Literature*, London and Nairobi: James Currey and Heinemann.

Ngwira, Emmanuel Mzomera (2012) '"He Writes about the World That Remained Silent": Witnessing Authorship in Chimamanda Ngozi Adichie's *Half of a Yellow Sun*', *English Studies in Africa*, 55(2): 43–53.

Nnaemeka, Obioma (2003) 'Nego-Feminism: Theorizing, Practicing, and Pruning Africa's Way', *Signs*, 29(2): 357–85.

Nnolim, Charles E. (2000) 'Trends in the Criticism of African Literature', in Ernest N. Emenyonu (ed.) *Goatskin Bags and Wisdom: New Critical Perspectives on African Literature*, Trenton, NJ: Africa World Press, pp. 3–15.

Nørgaard, Nina, Beatrix Busse and Rocío Montoro (2010) *Key Terms in Stylistics*, London: Continuum.

Novak, Amy (2008) 'Who Speaks? Who Listens? The Problem of Address in Two Nigerian Trauma Novels', *Studies in the Novel*, 40(1&2): 31–51.

Nwoga, Donatus Ibe (1975) 'Appraisal of Igbo Proverbs and Idioms', in F. Chidozie Ogbalu and E. Nolue Emenanjo (eds) *Igbo Language and Culture*, Ibadan: Oxford University Press, pp. 186–204.

Nwoye, Onuigbo (1991) 'Igbo Proverb as Politeness Strategy', *Africana Marburgensia*, 24(2): 19–31.

Obiechina, Emmanuel (1993) 'Narrative Proverbs in the African Novel', *Research in African Literatures*, 24(4): 123–40.

O'Connor, Maurice (2008) *The Writings of Ben Okri: Transcending the Local and the National*, New Delhi: Prestige.

Ogede, Ode (2007) *Achebe's Things Fall Apart*, London: Continuum.

Ogwude, Sophia O. (2011) 'History and Ideology in Chimamanda Adichie's Fiction', *Tydskrif vir Letterkunde*, 48(1): 110–23.

Oha, Obododimma (1998) 'The Semantics of Female Devaluation in Igbo Proverbs', *African Study Monographs*, 19(2): 87–102.

Ojukwu, Emeka (1969) *The Ahiara Declaration (The Principles of the Biafran Revolution)*, Geneva: Markpress.

Okorafor-Mbachu, Nnedi (2004) Review of *Purple Hibiscus*, by Chimamanda Ngozi Adichie, *Other Voices*, 40, http://www.webdelsol.com/Other_Voices/Reviews40.htm (accessed 30 July 2008).

Okri, Ben (1981) *The Landscapes Within*, Harlow: Longman.

Okri, Ben (1996) *Dangerous Love*, London: Phoenix.

Okri, Ben (1997) 'Whisperings of the Gods: An Interview with Ben Okri', by Delia Falconer, *Island Magazine*, 71: 43–51.

Okri, Ben (2002) *In Arcadia*, London: Weidenfeld & Nicholson.

Okri, Ben (2011a) 'Magical Ben Okri Casts a Spell on His Readers', interview by Nima Elbagir, *African Voices*, CNN, 28 June, http://edition.cnn.com/2011/WORLD/africa/06/28/ben.okri.nigeria (accessed 21 January 2014).

Okri, Ben (2011b) *A Time for New Dreams*, London: Rider.

Okri, Ben (2012a) 'Painter of Secrets', interview by Anupama Raju, *Frontline*, 30 November, 105–8.

Okri, Ben (2012b) *Wild*, London: Rider.

Okri, Ben (2013) 'Diallo's Testament', London: National Portrait Gallery.

Ouma, Christopher (2012) 'Chronotopicity in Chimamanda Ngozi Adichie's *Half of a Yellow Sun*', in Samson Opondo and Michael J. Shapiro (eds) *The New Violent Cartography: Geo-Analysis after the Aesthetic Turn*, London: Routledge, pp. 33-48.

'Out of Nigeria' (2009) *South Bank Show*, ITV, 10 and 17 May.

Owomoyela, Oyekan (2008) 'Iweala, Uzodinma', in *The Columbia Guide to West African Literature in English Since 1945*, New York: Columbia University Press, pp. 119–20.

Oxford English Dictionary, http://www.oed.com (accessed 20 October 2007 and 21 January 2014).

Pachocinski, Ryszard (1996) *Proverbs of Africa: Human Nature in the Nigerian Oral Tradition. An Exposition and Analysis of 2,600 Proverbs from 64 Peoples*, St. Paul, MN: Professors World Peace Academy.

Palmberg, Mai and Kirsten Holst Petersen (2011) 'Whose Biafra? Chimamanda Ngozi Adichie's *Half of a Yellow Sun*', in Annalisa Oboe and Shaul Bassi (eds) *Experiences of Freedom in Postcolonial Literatures and Cultures*, London: Routledge, pp. 191–201.

Ranzenberger, Katherine (2014) 'Chris Abani Talks Art, Loss and Experience', *Central Michigan Life*, 20 February, http://www.cm-life.com/2014/02/20/chris-abani-talks-art-loss-and-experience (accessed 23 April 2014).

Richard and Judy (2007) Channel 4, 14 March.

Rimmon-Kenan, Shlomith (2002) *Narrative Fiction: Contemporary Poetics*, 2nd edn, London: Routledge.

Saro-Wiwa, Ken (1994 [1985]) *Sozaboy: A Novel in Rotten English*, Harlow: Longman.

Saro-Wiwa, Ken (1992) 'The Language of African Literature: A Writer's Testimony', *Research in African Literatures*, 23(1): 153–7.

Schmied, Josef J. (1991) *English in Africa: An Introduction*, London: Longman.

Schultheis, Alexandra (2008) 'African Child Soldiers and Humanitarian Consumption', *Peace Review: A Journal of Social Justice*, 20: 31–40.

Semino, Elena (2002) 'A Cognitive Stylistic Approach to Mind Style in Narrative Fiction', in Elena Semino and Jonathan Culpeper (eds) *Cognitive Stylistics: Language and Cognition in Text Analysis*, Amsterdam: John Benjamins, pp. 95–122.

Shelton, Austin (1969) '"The "Palm-Oil" of Language: Proverbs in Chinua Achebe's Novels', *Modern Language Quarterly*, 30(1): 86–111.

Short, Mick (1996) *Exploring the Language of Poems, Plays and Prose*, Harlow: Pearson.

Short, Mick, Donald C. Freeman, Willie van Peer and Paul Simpson (1998) 'Stylistics, Criticism and Myth Representation Again: Squaring the Circle with Ray Mackay's Subjective Solution for All Problems', *Language and Literature*, 7(1): 39–50.

Simoes da Silva, Tony (2012) 'Embodied Genealogies and Gendered Violence in Chimamanda Ngozi Adichie's Writing', *African Identities*, 10(4): 455–70.

Simpson, Paul (1993) *Language, Ideology and Point of View*, London: Routledge.

Simpson, Paul (2004) *Stylistics: A Resource Book for Students*, London: Routledge.

Simpson, Paul and Andrea Mayr (2010) *Language and Power: A Resource Book for Students*, London: Routledge.

Soyinka, Wole (1975) 'Neo-Tarzanism: The Poetics of Pseudo-Tradition', *Transition*, 48: 38–44.

Strehle, Susan (2011) 'Producing Exile: Diasporic Vision in Adichie's *Half of a Yellow Sun*', *Modern Fiction Studies*, 57(4): 650–72.

Talib, Ismail S. (2002) *The Language of Postcolonial Literatures: An Introduction*, London: Routledge.

Tepper, Anderson (2005) 'Suffer the Children', *Washington Post*, 20 November, http://www.washingtonpost.com/wp-dyn/content/article/2005/11/17/AR2005111701379.html (accessed 21 January 2014).

Todd, Loreto (1982) 'The English Language in West Africa', in R.W. Bailey and Manfred Görlach (eds) *English as a World Language*, Ann Arbor: University of Michigan Press, pp. 281–305.

Toolan, Michael (1990) *The Stylistics of Fiction: A Literary-Linguistic Approach*, London: Routledge.

Tunca, Daria (2004) 'Ben Okri's *The Landscapes Within* and *Dangerous Love*: Vision and Revision', *BELL New Series 2: The Language/Literature Interface*, 85–101.

Tunca, Daria (2008) 'Style Beyond Borders: Language in Recent Nigerian Fiction', unpublished PhD thesis, University of Liège, Belgium.

Tunca, Daria (2009) 'Linguistic Counterpoint in Gbenga Agbenugba's *Another Lonely Londoner*', *Matatu*, 36: 195–211.

Tunca, Daria (2012) 'Appropriating Achebe: Chimamanda Ngozi Adichie's *Purple Hibiscus* and "The Headstrong Historian"', in Pascal Nicklas and Oliver Lindner (eds) *Adaptation and Cultural Appropriation: Literature, Film, and the Arts*, Berlin: De Gruyter, pp. 230–50.

Tunca, Daria (2013) '"We die only once, and for such a long time": Approaching Trauma through Translocation in Chris Abani's *Song for Night*', in Marga Munkelt, Markus Schmitz, Mark Stein and Silke Stroh (eds) *Postcolonial Translocations: Cultural Representation and Critical Spatial Thinking*, Amsterdam: Rodopi, pp. 127–43.

Tutuola, Amos (1952) *The Palm-Wine Drinkard*, London: Faber & Faber.

Unigwe, Chika Nina (2004) 'In the Shadow of Ala: Igbo Women's Writing as an Act of Righting', unpublished PhD thesis, University of Leiden, The Netherlands.

Unigwe, Chika Nina (2012) *Night Dancer*, London: Jonathan Cape.

Uspensky, Boris (1973) *A Poetics of Composition: The Structure of the Artistic Text and Typology of a Compositional Form*, trans. Valentina Zavarin and Susan Wittig, Berkeley: University of California Press.

Walder, Dennis (2010) *Postcolonial Nostalgias: Writing, Representation, and Memory*, London: Routledge.

Wales, Katie (2006) 'Stylistics', in Keith Brown (ed.) *Encyclopedia of Language and Linguistics*, 2nd edn, vol. 12, Oxford: Elsevier, pp. 213–17.

Wales, Katie (2011) *A Dictionary of Stylistics*, 3rd edn, Harlow: Pearson.

Wali, Obiajunwa (1963) 'The Dead End of African Literature', *Transition*, 10: 13–15.

Walker, Alice (1983) 'Zora Neale Hurston: A Cautionary Tale and a Partisan View' (1979), in *In Search of Our Mothers' Gardens: Womanist Prose*, San Diego: Harcourt, pp. 83–92.

Washburn, Lindy (2004) 'Out of Africa, a Coming-of-Age Story', *Record*, 31 October, http://www.highbeam.com (accessed 30 July 2008).

Weaver, Jason (2008) 'Chris Abani – *Becoming Abigail*', *Spike Magazine*, http://www.spikemagazine.com/chris-abani-becoming-abigail.php (accessed 21 January 2014).

Whittaker, David (2011) 'The Novelist as Teacher: *Things Fall Apart* and the Hauntology of Chimamanda Ngozi Adichie's *Half of a Yellow Sun*', in David Whittaker (ed.) *Chinua Achebe's Things Fall Apart: 1958–2008*, Amsterdam: Rodopi, pp. 107–17.

Widdowson, H. G. (1975) *Stylistics and the Teaching of Literature*, London: Longman.

Winters, Marjorie (1981) 'An Objective Approach to Achebe's Style', *Research in African Literatures*, 12(1): 55–68.

Wood, Molara (2008) 'Uzodinma Iweala: *Beasts of No Nation*', *African Literature Today*, 26: 145–8.

Zabus, Chantal (1991) *The African Palimpsest: Indigenization of Language in the West African Europhone Novel*, Amsterdam: Rodopi.

Zabus, Chantal (2007) *The African Palimpsest: Indigenization of Language in the West African Europhone Novel*, 2nd edn, Amsterdam: Rodopi.

Zott, Debra (2008) Review of *Song for Night*, by Chris Abani, *Transnational Literature*, 1.1, http://dspace.flinders.edu.au/dspace/bitstream/2328/3247/1/Song%20for%20night%20review.pdf (accessed 21 January 2014).

Index

Abani, Chris, 3,
  4, 21, 25
  'Becoming Abigail' (short story),
    123–4, 126, 128, 184
  Becoming Abigail (novella), 24–5,
    122–45, 183–5
  'Jazz Petals', 123, 184
  Song for Night, 25, 146–50, 152–3,
    163–74, 185–6
Achebe, Chinua
  influence on Nigerian writing, 3,
    4, 28, 146, 177
  and Joseph Conrad's *Heart of
    Darkness*, 182
  and the language debate, 7, 8, 179
  language in the work of, 27, 28,
    29, 32
  Things Fall Apart, 80, 177
Actor, *see* participants, in model of
  transitivity
Adichie, Chimamanda Ngozi, 1, 3,
    17, 21, 146, 175–6, 178
  Half of a Yellow Sun, 23–4, 64–99,
    125, 148, 156, 168, 180, 181–2
  Purple Hibiscus, 17, 22, 23, 26–63,
    69, 91, 125, 156, 180–1
aesthetics
  and literary evaluation, 9, 11, 13,
    14, 16, 37, 165, 177, 178
  and politics, 23, 65, 70
  of violence, 126
African literatures
  and the language debate, 2,
    6–8, 179
  the linguistic analysis of, 8–14, 16,
    17, 22–3, 27–8, 178
agency
  linguistic, 38, 43
  meronymic, 38

as power, 58, 116, 140, 143,
    144, 145
Agent, *see* participants, in model of
  transitivity
alliteration, 52, 139, 140, 180
anachronism, 149, 174, 185
anadiplosis, 140–1, 142
anthropological fallacy, 9–10, 65
anticipatory constituents, 19
antonymy, 130
apposition, 19, 83, 84, 129
arbitrariness, 15, 16
Armah, Ayi Kwei, 11, 12
assonance, 52, 139, 140, 180
authenticity, 7, 9, 11, 26, 30, 151

Bakhtin, Mikhail, 55, 69, 70, 81, 82,
    85, 87, 92, 97
Bandele, Biyi, 18–20, 22
Beasts of No Nation, 25, 146–52,
    153–63, 174, 185–6
Becoming Abigail, 24–5, 122–45,
    183–5
Behaver, *see* participants, in model
  of transitivity
behavioural process, *see* process
  types, in model of transitivity

Carrier, *see* participants, in model of
  transitivity
Chinweizu *et al.*, 11, 12
circularity, 15, 16, 17
class, social, 70, 77, 78, 79, 80,
    81, 97
codeswitching, 2, 78, 180
cognitive stylistics, *see* stylistics,
  cognitive
conceptual metaphor, 24, 101,
    105–16, 118, 120, 183

Printed and bound by CPI Group (UK) Ltd, Croydon, CR0 4YY